Crowned

Check out Julie Linker's charming novel

Disenchanted Princess

Crowned

Julie Linker

Simon Pulse

New York   London   Toronto   Sydney

SIMON PULSE

An imprint of Simon & Schuster Children's Publishing Division

1230 Avenue of the Americas, New York, NY 10020

Copyright © 2008 by Julie Linker

All rights reserved, including the right of reproduction
in whole or in part in any form.

SIMON PULSE and colophon are registered
trademarks of Simon & Schuster, Inc.

Designed by Tom Daly

The text of this book was set in Arrus.

Manufactured in the United States of America

First Simon Pulse paperback edition November 2008

2 4 6 8 10 9 7 5 3 1

Library of Congress Control Number 2008932599

ISBN-13: 978-1-4169-6052-2

ISBN-10: 1-4169-6052-X

To Daddy—I love you.
And to my sweet farm boy from Oklahoma—
what would I do without you?
—J. L.

In a major beauty pageant,
the daggers are sharpened daily.

—Pamela Lamont

Chapter One

In preparing for this pageant, how much did you spend on wardrobe?

To-Do List:
1. Study for algebra final
2. Paint nails
3. Rob bank

"Can I borrow two thousand dollars?" I look hopefully across the lunch table at my best friend, Justine Renault, who, unlike me, is incredibly rich.

Yeah, while my grandfather spent the sixties selling "love beads" out of a beat-up version of the Mystery Machine, Justine's grandfather was busy going to Harvard medical school and inventing some sort of super-important surgical thingy that "revolutionized twenty-first-century medicine" and made a bajillion trillion dollars. Can you say, "Life is so not fair"?

"For what?" she replies absently, turning a page of the (yawn) *Newsweek* magazine spread out beside her lunch.

In addition to being incredibly rich, Justine is also incredibly smart, which means she reads the most boring magazines ever. Seriously. I can't even read the covers of her magazines without going to sleep.

And for the record, I know this looks bad. But I swear I don't normally go around asking my friends for large sums of money. Or any sums of money, for that matter. This is a special situation. The special part being that I'm desperate.

Plus, I'm totally going to pay her back—with interest, even. I had Riley Pilkington, the school's resident math whiz, figure out a repayment plan and everything.

"Oh, you know," I say casually. "College application fees, cheerleading camp, stuff like that."

Justine looks up, frowning. "But the PTA is paying for us to go to camp this year. And you already mailed all your college applications. We went to the post office last week after practice. Remember?"

Rats. I totally forgot about going to the post office together last week. And that the PTA is paying for cheer camp.

Sigh. Why do I even try to lie? I totally stink at it.

Sure enough, Justine's expression has gone from confused to suspicious. "What are you up to?" she asks, narrowing her eyes.

"Nothing," I say innocently.

"You're lying."

"No, I'm not."

"Yes, you are. You're twirling your hair. You always twirl your hair when you're lying."

I start to shoot back that *she's* the one who is lying, because everyone knows I would never, ever engage in behavior that could cause split ends, but then I notice the clump of blond hair wound around my index finger. "Er, that doesn't mean anything," I say, yanking it loose. "And I wasn't twirling. I was . . . finger-combing."

Justine ignores me. "Just tell me what's going on," she says impatiently. "You know you will eventually, so you may as well get it over with."

"Nothing! I already told you."

"Presley," she says threateningly.

I blow out a breath. "Oh, all right. I need it to buy a new evening gown."

"You want me to loan you two thousand dollars for an *evening gown*?" She looks at me as if I'm deranged. Not because she's appalled I would pay that much for a dress but because she knows what the dress is for.

And what is that, you ask? Well, Justine would call it a "cattle market," or if she was really worked up, a "misogynist tool of patriarchy," but to non-insane people, the Miss Teen State contest is generally what's known as a beauty pageant.

(Shhh. Don't tell anybody I used the b-word, okay? You're supposed to say "scholarship pageant." All the major pageants did away with the b-word back in the eighties because it's not politically correct. Which is great and everything, but seriously—who wants to be called a "scholarship queen"?)

Yep, that's right. My name is Presley Ashbury, and I'm a beauty queen. Big hair, fake tan, sparkly rhinestones—these are the things that make my heart go pitter-patter. So if you cringe at the sight of a tiara or have a bunch of freaky feminist issues, you should probably make a break for it now, while you still can. Otherwise, you're going to end up quizzing me on current events and helping me practice my talent routine, because Miss Teen State is only *two weeks* away.

Aaack! Why did I have to think about that? Now I feel all nervous. Although, that could be because of the scary way Justine is scowling at me. I'm not sure.

"It's not just any evening gown," I say lightly, trying to ignore her I-can't-believe-you expression. "It's a fully liquid-beaded Mark Taylor original." I reach into my messenger bag and pull out the picture I printed off the Queen's Closet web-site. "See?" I push the picture toward her, my face hopeful.

Maybe she'll forget about her pesky little moral standards once she sees how *unbelievably gorgeous* this dress is. I'm not kidding; on a scale of one to ten, this gown is, like, a twenty-five. The girl who is selling it must be crazy. Or broke. Just a basic Mark Taylor gown starts at around six thousand, so I can only imagine how much she paid for it originally.

And she's only asking two thousand dollars for it! You have no idea what an awesome deal that is. I mean, Justine and I could probably sell it after Miss Teen State and *make* money. It would be an investment. You know, like mutual funds. Except way better because mutual funds don't "mold to your curves and sparkle outrageously under stage lights."

Unfortunately, Justine isn't interested in admiring Mark Taylor's genius.

"I don't care if it's made out of diamonds sewn on by

magical fairies," she scoffs, shoving the picture back at me. "You know how I feel about those contests."

Sigh. So much for her being seduced by brilliant evening gown couture. Ever since the public library had Feminist Literature Month last fall, Justine has been on this whole Gloria Steinem, women's rights, blow-up-the-glass-ceiling-with-dynamite craze. Which means she now thinks beauty pageants are evil and degrading and blah, blah, blah. The list goes on and on. Let's just say that allowing someone to give you a numerical score based on how your butt looks in a swimsuit isn't exactly a feminist's idea of a rockin' good time.

I tried to point out to Justine that maybe it's a teeny-tiny bit hypocritical of her to have that kind of attitude about pageants, considering she's a CHEERLEADER (hello—surely, jumping around in a little skirt cheering on a bunch of guys isn't exactly proper feminist behavior either, right?), but she says it's not the same thing because "cheerleading is a legitimate athletic sport."

Plus, she's on this whole quest to get our state education system to pass a law that says schools have to provide cheerleaders for girls' sports teams just like for boys. So, you know, she's like an inside agent, working for gender equality or whatever. I don't know. We used to argue about it a lot, but now we've basically agreed to disagree. Not about girls' teams having cheerleaders—I think that's a great idea too—I mean about pageants being degrading and pointless. (And just to clarify—I *totally* support women's rights; I just don't see what my wanting to be Miss Teen State has to do with them.)

Justine and I have agreed to disagree about a lot of things in the ten years that have passed since we first met in Mrs. Dixon's second-grade class. Or rather, in the ten years that have passed since Mrs. Dixon tricked Justine into becoming my personal tutor by telling her she was a "classroom assistant" and giving her a red teacher's pencil.

Poor Justine. She thought she was going to get to grade papers and decorate the special bulletin board outside in the hall, and instead, she ended up teaching me how to read. And write. And whatever else you learn in second grade. Basically, if it hadn't been for Justine, I'd be totally illiterate.

I know. It sounds sort of mean of Mrs. Dixon, but I can see why she did it. I mean, there were, like, a gajillion kids in that class, and we didn't have an aide or anything. I can just picture the moment when Mrs. Dixon, probably on the brink of a nervous breakdown, realized that the teeny-tiny girl with the red braids and purple glasses was a child prodigy who was already reading Harry Potter by herself and could multiply decimals in her head. And *then*, when she realized all it took to sucker said child prodigy was a meaningless title and a fifteen-cent pencil . . . well, it must have been like winning the teacher's lottery. Lucky for her, Justine's parents don't believe in private education or children skipping grades; otherwise, Justine would have been either off at some school for geniuses or in, like, tenth grade.

Lucky for me, too. Because Justine and I have been inseparable ever since then, despite our million or so differences. I guess there's just something about bonding over "The cat sat on the mat" that you never get over.

"Well, what if it wasn't for a pageant?" I say quickly, before she can launch into a lecture about how I'm setting the women's movement back fifty years. "What if I was going to wear it for something else?"

Her eyebrow lifts. "Such as?"

"Prom," I say automatically.

"Prom was three weeks ago."

"Oh. Right."

Rats! Does she have to remember *everything*? It's okay, though. I still have the mutual fund angle. I'll tell her to think of it as an investment, not a dress.

But before I can open my mouth, the bell rings.

"Ohmigod, we're going to be late!" Immediately panicked, Justine leaps out of her chair and starts frantically gathering up her stuff. FYI: Justine is *obsessed* with being on time. She's always convinced she's about to be late for class or cheer practice or wherever, even though she's never been late for anything in her life. Seriously. Even her period is freakishly punctual. Every twenty-eight days, between the hours of five and seven in the evening, no exceptions. And that's natural. She's not on the Pill or anything. But that's Justine for you. She's even got her ovaries whipped into shape.

I close my mouth. Oh, well. Maybe I can grovel after school.

I normally spend the two-minute walk from the caf to the main hall complaining about how much I hate my next class (chemistry—ugh), but as we spill out into the hall with the rest of the crowd, I'm greeted by a sight that makes me forget all about Mr. Crowley and his stupid periodic table.

In fact, it makes me forget about pretty much everything.

Because directly in front of me, right next to the handicapped water fountain, is Gabe Phillips, a.k.a. MY BOYFRIEND, sucking face with a girl who is clearly NOT ME.

Chapter Two

What does the word "loyalty" mean to you?

As a strong, self-confident woman of the new millennium, I've always assumed that if I ever caught one of my boyfriends *in flagrante* (which is the Italian term for when you walk out of the cafeteria and see your boyfriend with his tongue down some other girl's throat), I would handle the situation like a mature adult. No screaming. No crying. No taking a bat to his car like that Carrie Underwood song. I would just calmly inform him that we were over, delete his number from my cell phone, and never think about him again.

The Italians have a name for this, too. It translates to "ideas that sound good in your head but totally suck in real life."

But we'll get to that part in a sec.

"Oh. My. God." Justine's voice (a mixture of equal parts shock/revulsion/indignation) is what clues me in that the unpleasant vision I'm having isn't some sort of weird hallucination brought on by my prepageant diet of low-fat rice cakes and sugar-free gum. (Don't judge. You try "eating sensibly" when you're two weeks out from parading around in front of five hundred people in nothing but a bathing suit and a pair of five-inch Lucite heels.)

The spectacle across the hall is actually happening. My boyfriend is kissing another girl. No, not just kissing—*making out* with her. Passionately. In public.

Before I say anything else, let me give you the CliffsNotes on Gabe.

1. He's a senior.
2. He's H-O-T. Broad shoulders, muscular arms, washboard stomach, sun-streaked hair, adorable dimple. Think young David Beckham.
3. He's nice. Not geeky, use-me-for-a-doormat nice or annoying your-hair-looks-lovely-today-Miss-Teacher nice, just regular nice.
4. He's an *awesome* baseball player. And I don't just mean he's the star of the school baseball team (although, of course, he is). I'm talking serious talent. As in, he's going into the MAJOR LEAGUE DRAFT.
5. He's crazy popular. Normally, baseball players aren't a big deal (it's all about football, baby), but Gabe is an exception due to aforementioned Major League potential.
6. He's totally devoted to me even though skanky freshman and sophomore girls are always showing up at baseball practice in cleavage-showing tops and making goo-goo eyes at him. Oh, wait. That was the old Gabe. The one who didn't go around KISSING OTHER GIRLS IN FRONT OF THE WHOLE SCHOOL.

Justine turns to look at me, her eyes bulging. This is the part where I'm supposed to say or do something, but I seem to have lost the ability to speak. Or move. I think I'm in shock.

Luckily, one of the good things about pageants is that they teach you how to handle stress gracefully, so it only takes me a moment to recover my composure and take charge of the situation.

"WHAT DO YOU THINK YOU'RE DOING?" My graceful shriek reverberates around the hall at roughly fifty trillion decibels.

"Presley, no," Justine hisses, snatching frantically at my elbow. Like a good best friend, she's trying to keep me from making a Big Scene Everyone Will Talk About, but it's too late. Thanks to my super-human screech, everyone in the hall has now turned around to stare at me.

Well, *almost* everyone. Gabe is still preoccupied with the ~~slut~~ girl hanging off his neck. At least, I assume it's a girl. It's sort of hard to make a positive ID due to the way Gabe has her pressed up against the wall. It could be a guy, for all I know.

Actually, you know what would be awesome? (Well, not awesome, but fractionally less mortifying?) If it really *was* a guy!

No, I'm serious. I mean, think about it. That way, I wouldn't be the poor girl whose boyfriend cheated on her (hello—can you say "cliché"?); I'd just be the girl whose boyfriend went crazy and turned into a pervert. (Not that *I* think gay people are perverts, of course. But sadly, not very many of my classmates are as progressive as me. This is the Bible Belt, after all.)

And just think about all the time and misery it would save me when the inevitable comparison game reared its ugly head! I wouldn't have to lie awake at night obsessing about whether this new chick is smarter/prettier/thinner/funnier [insert assorted other desirable qualities here] than me.

I could just say, *Oh, well. He was struggling with his identity*, and go on with my life, secure in the knowledge that his decision to stray had nothing to do with me.

Seriously, I think I'm onto something here. This is, like, a *Cosmo* article waiting for somebody to write it. Not me, of course; publishing an article in *Cosmopolitan* is hardly appropriate beauty queen behavior. Plus, that's the sort of thing that really needs a personal touch, and as much as I've just warmed up to the idea, the odds that Gabe has suddenly switched teams are basically nil.

Yes, I'm sure. Sigh. The boy doesn't own a single hair care product (unless you count Suave shampoo, which I don't) and thinks ESPN is the only television channel. Need I say more?

Which brings us back to where we left off. Now, what was I doing? Oh, that's right. Freaking out.

"WHAT ARE YOU DOING?" I scream at him again, sealing my fate as the number one topic of gossip for the next week.

"Shush!" Justine almost yanks my arm out of its socket. I think she's not-so-subtly trying to get me to stop yelling and go back into the cafeteria, but I can't. I'm committed now.

You'd assume the sound of my (extremely loud and angry) voice (twice!) would make Gabe jump guiltily away from the ~~tramp~~ girl and start stammering out a bunch of pitiful excuses, or at the very least make him turn around, but no.

HE GOES RIGHT ON KISSING HER.

Clearly, I'm going to have to change tactics here. Hysterical screaming just isn't cutting it. So I fly across the hall and jump on his back.

"What the—" Gabe stumbles backward, thrown off balance by the sudden hundred and ten pounds wrapped around his torso. (Okay, okay. A hundred and fifteen pounds. Geesh.) (All right! A hundred and twenty, but that's all I'm going to cop to.)

"Presley! Stop it!" Justine shrieks. She rushes over and grabs on to my waist, trying to pull me down. Which is admirable and everything, but seriously. Can't she see that we're a teeny-tiny bit past worrying about appearances? I mean, I just tackled my boyfriend in the middle of the hall. The gossip train has *so* already left the station.

"Presley?" Gabe echoes, sounding bewildered, like he's never heard the name before. Apparently, all the kissing has damaged his memory.

"Presley, your girlfriend?" I jab my heel into his stomach to jog his memory.

He grunts in pain and I smile.

See why I don't want to get down? Kicking him is so much easier from up here. I only wish I'd worn actual heels today instead of my wedges. I also wish I'd worn my new peasant blouse from Charlotte Russe instead of this old Gap T-shirt. If you're going to cause a scene in front of the whole school, you want to look as fashionable as possible, you know?

"I mean it," Justine pants, locking her arms around me like a vise. "Let. Go."

Okay. Now she's just being annoying. If she wants to help me, why doesn't she do something useful? Like go around to the front and kick Gabe in the kneecaps?

Note: I'm really not a violent person, I swear. I feel like I'm not making a very good first impression, what with the money thing at lunch and now this little altercation. Which is disturbing, because according to *Pageant Girl* magazine ("Dress to Impress: How Frosted Lipstick Can Kill Your Interview" March 2008), it can take *five whole years* to change somebody's initial opinion of you. Five years! That's crazy. So maybe you could, like, try to withhold judgment for a little bit? At least until tomorrow? That's when I go to the nursing home and read to old people.

"No, *you* let go." I push at her hands, trying to get her to release me, but for somebody whose digital talking bathroom scale has never announced any number over ninety-nine, she has a surprisingly strong grip.

"No, *you.*" She lets her legs go limp so that she's hanging off me like a dead weight.

"Mother . . ." Gabe lets loose a string of unprintable curses as he is once again forced to do fancy footwork to stay upright. Poor baby. Now he has not one but *two* angry females dangling off his back. Well, technically Justine is dangling off *my* back, but you know what I mean.

"Fight, fight, fight." The crowd edges forward eagerly, clearly thrilled by this turn of events. They look creepily similar to the people in this video about Roman gladiators my history teacher, Mr. Sims, made us watch last semester (not the one with Russell Crowe, unfortunately). You know, where people, like, had a picnic and partied while they watched these poor schmucks get ripped to shreds by lions and stuff? Gross.

Although, I have to admit, I wouldn't mind having a lion or maybe a small bear to set loose on Gabe right about now. Too bad the closest thing I have to a man-eating deadly predator is my Hello Kitty keychain.

"Baby, please." Gabe cranes his head over his shoulder, trying to see my face. "I can explain. Get down and let's talk about this rationally."

Ha. I can't wait to hear his expl—Wait a minute. Did he just refer to me as "baby"?

I kick him with my other foot. How dare he use a term of endearment after what he was just doing? And where is the ~~whore~~ girl he was doing it with? My eyes dart toward the spot by the water fountain where they were standing, but all I see is . . . well, the water fountain. I frown. Where did she go? The water fountain is right in front of the girl's bathroom. . . . Did she run in there while I was preoccupied with attacking Gabe?

I sweep the area with my gaze again. Crap. She must have. What a chicken. But it doesn't matter. Because there's only one way out, and she can't stay in there forever. Plus, you know, I'm a girl too, so I can totally go in there after her.

"Fight, fight, fight." Behind me, the chanting is getting even louder.

Sigh. Why do people always do that? Don't they realize that a crowd of teenagers intoning "fight, fight, fight" is like flashing the Bat-Signal over Gotham? Except instead of super-hot Christian Bale, a ticked-off teacher is going to show up with a handful of detention slips.

Annoyed, I unlock my legs from around Gabe's waist. As much as I'd like to give him another kick (or ten), I have no interest in spending my free time sitting in the detention room with Coach Tackett and half of Lincoln High's juvenile delinquent population.

"Okay, you can release your death grip now," I tell Justine. "I'm getting down."

"Thank God."

The crowd groans in disappointment as we drop to the ground. This isn't the development they were hoping for.

"Presley, baby." Gabe whirls around to face me.

Finally. This is the part where he gets on his knees and begs me to forgive me. First he'll say something about being a stupid idiot who doesn't deserve my love, and then he'll cling to my—

"I want to date other people."

My fantasy is interrupted by Gabe's sudden outburst of gibberish. Did he just, like, speak in Latin or something?

I blink at him. "Excuse me?"

"I want to date other people. You know, break up." He slides his hands into the pockets of his Diesels and regards me casually, like he's just announced he'd rather go to Burger King than McDonald's.

Okay, time out. This is *so* not in the script. He's supposed to grovel and act pitiful, and then *I'm* supposed to break up with *him*. He's throwing out completely unauthorized dialogue here. I look at him stupidly. "What are you talking about?"

"I . . . want . . . to . . . break . . . up," he repeats, enunciating each word reeeeeallly slowly and clearly, like the way my mom used to talk to me when I was a little kid and she was trying to tell me something important. *Look both ways before you cross the street. Don't play with matches. Take those earrings off the cat.* Except what he's saying is, *I never want to see you again.*

He tilts his head, obviously waiting for a response, so I draw myself up to my full height, cross my arms over my chest, and say haughtily, "Fabulous. Have a nice life. Don't let the door hit you on the way out."

At least, that's what I mean to say.

What comes out is, "You want to break up?" in a little, squeaky, you-just-drove-a-stake-through-my-heart voice.

Great.

I must look as pathetic as I sound, because Gabe suddenly looks like he'd rather be giving up hits on the pitching mound than having this conversation. "Look, why don't we talk about this later? After school—"

"No," I say forcefully. "I want to talk about it now." Is he insane? Does he think I can sit through *three whole periods* with this hanging over my head?"

Above me, the bell signaling the start of fifth period starts jangling. Great. Now I'm dumped *and* tardy.

"Pres, I have to go," Justine says miserably.

I immediately feel like a piece of gum on the bottom of somebody's shoe. Poor Justine. Her worst fear has finally come true, and it's all my fault.

"It's okay," I say reassuringly. "We'll talk after school."

She looks relieved. "Okay." She flicks Gabe a you're-a-total-slime look and disappears down the hall. The crowd has already drifted away, bored by the absence of blood and/or broken bones.

I turn back to Gabe. "What the hell do you mean, you want to break up?"

Oh, wow. That sounded *so* much better. Much more *I am woman hear me roar*, you know?

My sudden attitude change flusters Gabe even more. Confrontation makes him super-nervous. Not that I care.

He runs a hand agitatedly through his hair. "It's just that, well . . . um, you see . . ."

"It's just that he's met someone else," a female voice cuts in smoothly. A girl with glossy black hair and mile-long legs steps up and presses herself against Gabe's side. She wriggles her fingers at me. "Hi, Presley."

I look back and forth between them, dumbstruck. This. Is. Not. Happening. *Please* tell me this is not happening. Being cheated on and dumped is bad enough, but this takes it to a whole new level of misery.

Because Gabe's new "someone else" happens to be someone I know very, very well. Not because we're friends—just the opposite.

You see, last summer she tried to kill me.

Chapter Three

How do you handle people not liking you?

Okay, so maybe "kill" is a little strong. I suspect she was actually trying to break my leg when she put the hair gel on my pointe shoes last year at Miss Teen State, but still. If I'd plunged off the stage into the orchestra pit and broken my neck (which totally could have happened), I doubt she would have shed any tears.

I'm just saying.

And now my boyfriend is dumping me for her. I swallow the bile rising in my throat. "Megan Leighton? You're screwing around with Megan Leighton?"

"I—er—you see—," he stammers stupidly. His face is flushed, like he's just pitched nine innings.

"No, I don't see," I spit out.

Megan steps in front of Gabe and fixes me with her contact-enhanced green eyes. "It's not rocket science, sweetie. You and Gabe are O-V-E-R. He's with me now."

I'm sorry, did she just SPELL at me? What is this, the first grade? Next she'll tell me that she and Gabe have been K-I-S-S-I-N-G in a tree.

I'm about to spell her a four-letter word of my own when a new voice joins the conversation.

"Well, isn't this a nice little party?" Mr. Smooter, the vice principal, comes to a halt beside me and surveys the three of us with a smirk. "I assume all three of you have a hall pass?" It's clear from the tone of his voice and the mwah-ha-ha expression on his face that he assumes no such thing, but he's one of those people who likes to draw out the torture. It's part of his charm.

Fast-forward ten minutes and I'm huddled in a bathroom stall with no boyfriend, the beginnings of what promises to be a bitch of a headache, and a personally autographed slip from Mr. Smooter inviting me to come to school tomorrow at seven a.m. to "contemplate the value of the hall pass" in morning detention. But don't worry, I won't have to do all the contemplating alone—because, of course, Gabe and Megan will be there too! Isn't that fabulous news?! I'll get to spend a *whole hour* with them! Really, the only way this day could get any better would be if a giant meteor crashed through the roof of the school and fell directly on my head!

Cursing Mr. Smooter, I wad the slip into a ball and shove it into the "feminine hygiene receptacle" above the toilet paper holder. At least Justine was gone when he came up. Whew. Talk about a dodged bullet. The tardy is going to be bad enough, but if she'd gotten detention, she'd probably need, like, professional therapy or something.

Once the evil slip is safely out of sight, I dip my hand into the zippered pocket of my messenger bag and take out my emergency 3 Musketeers bar. I suppose hiding in a bathroom stall and cramming chocolate into my mouth isn't exactly the scenario Mr. Smooter had in mind when he told me to go to wherever I was supposed to be, but hello—I can't just go to chemistry and act like everything is normal. Because in case you didn't notice, MY BOYFRIEND JUST DUMPED ME.

FOR MY ARCHENEMY.

Fighting the tears stinging my eyes, I rip the silver paper off the 3 Musketeers and shove practically the whole bar in my mouth. It's stale because it's been in my bag for probably six months, but I don't care. I'm what the magazines call an "emotional eater." Which basically means that whenever something bad happens, I gain ten pounds, but whatever. I'll worry about that later.

I chew furiously as questions stab my brain like knives. How long has Gabe been seeing her? How did it start? Did everybody in the whole school already know about it except me (and Justine)? How could I be so clueless that I didn't even suspect? Is it serious? Does he [shudder] love her? When did he fall out of love with me? *Why* did he fall out of love with me? And, the most burning question of all . . . HOW COULD HE DO THIS TO ME??

I mean, even if he didn't want to be with me anymore, you'd think he'd have enough basic decency not to be so cruel.

Although, you haven't really met Megan yet, so you can't appreciate the enormity of the situation. Here, I'll try to tell you about her, although she's really just one of those people you have to be around to get the full effect. Let's see . . . where to start? This is what she looks like in a pageant program book:

Miss Diamond Hills

(Totally Photoshopped picture of Megan here)

Megan Rachelle Leighton

AGE: 17

PARENTS: William and Annabeth Leighton

TALENT: Piano—"Rhapsody in Blue"

PLATFORM: Give the Gift of Life: Organ and Tissue Donation

Which is all true, but if *I* was doing a program book, her bio would look more like this:

Miss Diamond Hills

(Picture of giant skull and crossbones here)

Megan "Megabitch" Leighton

AGE: 17

PARENTS: She is the spawn of Satan

TALENT: Vicious Cruelty to Others/Destroying Lives

PLATFORM: I will be Miss America someday. Oh, yes.

Okay, what else? She's a junior like me, which is the beginning and end of our similarities. When it comes to everything else, we may as well be different species.

Actually, as far as high school goes, we *are* a different species. Megan being a dazzling example of Homo super-rich sapiens and me being a prime specimen of the more common Homo poor-white-trash sapiens.

I know, I know. Now you're going, *Oh, great. Another tired*

Mean Rich Girl vs. Nice Poor Girl story. Let's just skip to the end where Nice Poor Girl gets a makeover and surprises everyone at the big dance. But that's not what this is about, I swear. First of all, I *so* don't need a makeover, and second, I'm actually more popular than Megan.

At least, I'm more popular in the sense that I have a better chance of, like, being elected homecoming queen, or named Cutest Girl in the yearbook, etc. I'm not saying I'm necessarily going to *get* any of those things, mind you—just that I have a better chance of it than she does.

Of course, if Megan ever lowered herself to actually speak to anyone, she'd probably be elected everything, but she prefers not to "intermix with the lower classes," as I overheard her put it to Randi Kaye Blythe backstage at the Miss Diamond Hills pageant last year.

And really, why would she? Thanks to her aloof and above-it-all attitude, the whole school thinks she's this mysterious, untouchable goddess. (Okay, so the hundred-thousand-dollar Audi R8 she drives probably has something to do with it too.) Why would she want to ruin her image by doing something as uncouth as having a conversation with a regular person?

Anyway, Megan and I *do* have one other thing in common besides being in the same grade, as I'm sure all you Nancy Drew types have already figured out. Namely, that we both compete in pageants. Frequently at the same time. Against each other.

And sometimes she beats me. But then, sometimes I beat her. We sort of flip-flop. She wins the crown; I get first runner-up.

At the next pageant, I win the crown, and she gets first runner-up. And so on.

If I wanted to sugarcoat it, I'd tell you that we have a "healthy rivalry," but I can't even *think* the word "sugar" for the next two weeks (the emergency 3 Musketeers doesn't count), so I'll just tell you straight out: We hate each other's guts.

Like, if a magical genie poofed out of a lamp and offered me three wishes, I'd use one of them to send Megan to Antarctica. Forever.

Which is a horrible thing to say, I know. But *Megan* is horrible. I mean, hello—the girl tried to maim and/or kill me last year.

And before you ask: Yes. Sabotage really does go on. Stolen swimsuits, ripped dresses, broken heels, a dash of baby oil or red Jell-O powder added to somebody's sunless tanner—there are *so* many ways somebody can screw with you. And a lot of them aren't the obvious pour-nail-polish-on-an-evening-gown kind of stuff you'd normally expect.

For instance, if somebody really, really wanted to mess with your head, she might, oh, I don't know—USE HER VOODOO WITCH POWERS TO SEDUCE YOUR BOYFRIEND TWO WEEKS BEFORE THE COMPETITION SO THAT INSTEAD OF GETTING READY YOU SPEND ALL YOUR TIME IMAGINING THEM TOGETHER.

Right now you're thinking either (a) *Poor girl, she's inhaled too much Aqua Net,* or (b) *Poor girl, she can't deal with the fact that her boyfriend just dumped her, so she made up this story that sounds like the plot of a bad soap opera.* And I don't blame you. But if you stick around long enough, you'll see that my whole *life* is like a bad soap opera.

Except wait—that's not exactly true. Because if this was a soap opera, I'd be in a tastefully elegant bedroom, shaking my fist and making vows like "I WILL get my boyfriend back from Megan Leighton," or "Megan Leighton will rue the day she ever set foot in this town."

But instead, I'm perched on a closed toilet lid in a mildew-smelling school bathroom trying not to cry. So instead of a character in a bad soap opera, I guess I'm just . . . pathetic.

I force myself to leave the sanctuary of the bathroom and go to my last two classes, algebra and Spanish (ugh and *muy* ugh), and then mercifully the day from hell is over. At least, the academic part, anyway. I still have a squad meeting to get through.

Rah-rah-ugh.

In case you're picturing me as the clichéd super-popular blond cheerleader who everybody envies, let me rid you of that delusion right now. I know that's the way it is at a lot of schools, but here at good ol' Lincoln High, the only thing a cheerleading uniform gets you is free admission to football games. Don't ask me why. We adhere to all the other stereotypes of teenage social hierarchy. Jocks are treated like minor deities, nerds are shunned unless needed for difficult homework assignments, slutty girls are whispered about on Mondays, guys suspected of playing for the other team are cruelly teased by aforementioned deity-jocks, etc., etc. You might say we like to "keep tradition alive."

Because, you know, that sounds better than "we're narrow-minded, insensitive rednecks."

Justine is waiting for me outside the gym with Hunter and Lilly Reeves, our other two best friends. You haven't met Hunter and Lilly yet. Normally, we all eat lunch together, but today the twins (yep, they're twins!) had to go on an all-day field trip for choir. Some kind of performance to raise money for charity, I think? I'm sure one of them told me, but I always have trouble remembering little details like that.

Okay, so technically I have trouble remembering *every-thing*, but that's not exactly the kind of thing a person wants to admit. I'd like to say it's because my brain is so full of complicated smart-people stuff like Justine's, but that would be . . . what's the word? Oh yeah. Lying.

"Ohmigosh, are you okay?" Justine rushes toward me. Her forehead is super-creased, like she's been worrying about me all afternoon. Which she probably has. Worrying is Justine's favorite hobby. About me, herself, her family, global warming, getting into a good college, the plight of the American burying beetle (don't ask) . . . You name it, and she worries about it.

Uh-oh. An evil thought just popped into my head. If I asked her about the Mark Taylor dress right now, I bet she'd totally go for it. You know, because of my life being in scattered ashes at my feet and all. (Can you say "pity loan"?)

No, no, no. Bad Presley. Must not take advantage of best

friend's sympathetic nature. Feelings of guilt and bad karma will result.

"Well, I haven't attacked anyone in the past three hours," I say wryly.

"Jussy told us what happened," Hunter and Lilly say in perfect unison, simultaneously tucking their identical Katie Holmes brown bobs behind their ears.

Hunter and Lilly aren't just regular twins, they're mirror-image twins, which is sort of cool and sort of freaky at the same time. I didn't even know such a thing existed until they moved here from Michigan last year.

Basically, they look exactly alike, except some things are reversed (i.e., "mirrored"). Like, they both have this really dark freckle under their eye, except Hunter's is under her left eye and Lilly's is under her right. And they both have this sort of long, rectangle-shaped birthmark on their arm, but it's the same thing—Hunter's is on her left arm and Lilly's is on her right. Plus, Hunter is left-handed and Lilly is right-handed.

But the absolute freakiest thing about them (in my opinion) is the way they talk at the same time like they share a brain or something. I mean, sometimes I forget that they're two separate people.

"Yeah, you missed an exciting lunch," I tell them. I'm trying to act nonchalant because if Hunter and Lilly go all sympathetic and compassionate on me, I'll lose the careful composure I built during algebra and Spanish and start crying. And I'd prefer to save my tears for the privacy of my bedroom, if you know what I mean. I have a strict no-crying-at-school policy.

Hunter thrusts out her lip at Lilly. "Well, if *somebody* would get over her obsession with going on *American Idol* and let us quit choir, then maybe we'd be around more."

"I'm not obsessed with *American Idol*," Lilly retorts. "I just think it'd be cool for twins to be on there, that's all."

Hunter rolls her eyes. "Oh, come on. You know neither one of us can carry a tune in a bucket, and—"

"You guys, we have to go in." Justine cuts off their argument before it can get started. She taps the dial of her solar-powered wristwatch. (Don't look at me! If she took my advice, she'd be tapping a twenty-thousand-dollar-plus Girard-Perregaux Cat's Eye watch right now.) "The meeting is about to start."

Justine and I head toward the double doors, and the twins trail behind us, bickering in the weird "twin language" they use whenever they think nobody's paying attention. Actually, you know what? I was wrong. The secret twin language is the freakiest thing about them, not the talking in unison. It's like a combination of pig latin and baby talk with a dash of Spanish.

Inside the gym some random guys are playing basketball, and the rest of the cheerleading squad is strewn haphazardly across the first two rows of bleachers chatting, putting on lip gloss, and, yes—Rachel is even braiding Brianna's hair. Normally, we'd all be out on the floor stretching and warming up, but this is a meeting-meeting, not a practice. We have to work out the details of the graduation gala that's coming up this Saturday because—for reasons that escape me and pretty much everyone else—the cheerleading squad is in charge of it.

I know. You're probably picturing some sort of fancy reception with little sandwiches and colored streamers and a big sheet cake that says "Congratulations Seniors!" in big cursive icing letters, aren't you? Ha. If only.

No, "graduation gala" is the name some sarcastic seniors from way back in the eighties bestowed on the annual drunken bash held in a field in the middle of nowhere the weekend before graduation. So instead of sandwiches, streamers, and cake, think beer, bugs, and a bunch of drunk guys acting like idiots.

I'm sure the gala started out as an informal thing, but now it's, like, a mandatory event. Homecoming, prom, and the graduation gala. Those are the Big Three social events. Not that the graduation gala is a school-sanctioned event like prom and homecoming. No way! The gala is strictly off the grid, off the record, on the DL, whatever you want to call it. Now, all the adults *know* about it, of course. Because hello—most of them graduated from Lincoln too. But everyone operates under the "Don't ask, don't tell" policy, so it all works out fine.

As for how the gala turned into the cheerleading squad's responsibility . . . well, I'm just going to chalk that up to one of those strange things that defy logical explanation. Like UFOs or Donald Trump's hair or why my butt gets bigger instead of smaller whenever I run up and down the football stadium bleachers, even though *Shape* magazine says that it's supposed to tone all your—

What were we talking about?

Right. The gala being the cheerleaders' responsibility.

I mean, promote school spirit, unite and motivate spectators at athletic events, provide gallons of alcohol to student body at end of year so everyone can get wasted . . . which one of these doesn't belong in the cheerleading mission statement?

But hey, I didn't make the rules, you know? I'm just trying to get by. And it's not like we just buy a bunch of beer and turn everybody loose. We take everyone's car keys and have designated drivers and everything. Which is good because otherwise I'd have to quit the squad because hello—I'm not having a drunk driving accident on *my* conscience.

I follow Justine into the second row and we all plop down to await the arrival of the grand pooh-bah, Romy Silvers. Also known as our squad captain. Or Captain Evil. Whichever you prefer. Most of the squad leans toward the latter.

She strides in at exactly three thirty on the dot, wearing her usual scowl and a Nike tennis dress. Her tennis racket is looped around her wrist. When she's not torturing innocent cheerleaders, she's apparently some kind of regionally ranked tennis player. Which, if she was anybody else, would be really cool and I'd totally go watch her play, but since she recently told me I had "back fat," I'd just as soon shove her tennis racket down her throat.

I know. That's not a very charitable attitude. But what can I say? I lost my What Would Jesus Do? bracelet.

"Listen up, people!" she barks, pulling out a hot pink clipboard from under her arm. "I have a match in thirty minutes, so I want to knock this out quick."

Right. Because, you know, the rest of us were hoping to stay here all night.

She flips a page on the clipboard. "I've made out everybody's assignments, so I'm going to call them out and then we can discuss any questions."

"Oh, please. What's there to discuss?" Nicole says condescendingly. "All we have to do is get a bunch of beer and plastic cups. It's not like we're putting on the prom here."

Nicole is the only underclassman on the squad, and I'm pretty sure her mom dropped her on her head or something when she was little, because she is a complete *idiot*. It's like she totally missed the part of childhood where you learn not to give attitude to people who can make your life a living hell just for the fun of it, i.e., the captain of the cheerleading squad.

Romy gives her a saccharine smile. "Well, since you're so on top of things, then you won't mind helping me get the alcohol, will you, Nicole?" she says sweetly. "You can get half."

"How am I supposed to do that?" Nicole scoffs. "I'm fifteen. I don't have a driver's license."

Romy shrugs. "Not my problem." Translation: Learn to keep your big mouth shut.

"But I—"

"It's already decided," Romy says loudly, cutting her off. "You can either do it or consider yourself an alternate."

There's a whooshing sound as everybody gasps at the same time. Being demoted to alternate is the *worst* punishment *ever*. It's better to just get kicked off the squad altogether. At least if you're kicked off, that's it—you're done. You can go on with your life.

But if you're an alternate, you still have to go to all the practices and learn all the routines, and you even have to *dress out* at the games. Hello—can you say "humiliating"? Sitting on the bench in your cheerleading uniform in front of everyone?

And it's not like you can say, *Oh, yeah? If you demote me to alternate, I'll just quit.* Not if you're an underclassman and have thoughts of trying out another year. If you resign from the squad (unless it's for a really good reason, like you're in a full body cast or your dad suddenly gets transferred to Argentina), you forfeit your right to ever try out again.

I know. It's so medieval.

And don't bother suggesting something like reporting it to the proper school officials. The buck starts and stops with Romy. We have a cheerleading sponsor, Mrs. Kieklak, the biology teacher, but she's totally lu-lu because she has a gajillion kids. Not kids like students in her classes, I mean kids that came out of her *body*. And they're all really little, so she sort of has other stuff to worry about besides our little cheerleading dramas.

Romy goes down the rest of her list. "Adrian—trash bags. The big lawn-and-leaf kind. Rachel—plastic cups, the cheapest ones they have. Hunter and Lilly—designated drivers. Brianna—ditto. Justine—you're in charge of coffee. Two or three big thermoses in case we need to sober anybody up. Presley"—she runs her finger down the list, looking for my name—"you're designated driver too. We need at least four."

My heart drops. Being a designated driver is pretty much an all-night affair, and this coming weekend is the last one before the pageant. Which means I have a *ton* of stuff to do. And if I stay up all night Saturday playing chauffeur, I'll be too tired to do any of it on Sunday. Rats. Why couldn't I have gotten trash bags like Adrian?

"Er, is there any way I could maybe, possibly, um, if it's not too much trouble . . . I mean, only if it's okay with you, um . . . please switch with somebody else?" I say meekly. Maybe if I act all humble and deferential, she won't annihilate me like Nicole.

She flings the clipboard into the bleachers. "What, so you think you're too good to be a designated driver? Is that the problem?"

Or . . . she could totally freak out and act like a psycho.

"No! I *love* being a designated driver!" I lean forward earnestly, trying to look like driving drunk, puking people around is my absolute favorite activity in the whole world. "It's just that I, um, sort of have a lot of pageant stuff to do this weekend, so I was kind of hoping to, um, you know . . . not stay out too late Saturday night. I could get trash bags," I add helpfully. "Or the plastic cups. Or both. Or, my mom has a really good coffeemaker because, you know, she works at night. . . ." My voice trails off. Romy is caressing the strings of her tennis racket, and she has this weird look on her face, like maybe she's considering beating me with it.

Her tennis racket, I mean. Not her face.

She puts her foot on the bottom bleacher as if she's going

to climb up to the second row, but then she just leaves it there. "Some pageant stuff?" she says mockingly. "Did you say you have some pageant stuff to do?"

I nod fearfully. I would say something like *The air is so quiet you could hear a pin drop*, but the janitor just turned on the giant fan that the school board insists is "just as good as air-conditioning," so actually the air is pretty loud. And windy.

Romy leans forward, one arm resting on the leg that's propped up on the bleacher. "Let me ask you something, Ashbury," she says softly. "Are you a cheerleader, or are you a beauty queen?" The tone of her voice indicates that the difference between these two things is comparable to, say, being a nursery school teacher as opposed to a convicted felon.

"B-both," I stutter. "I mean, um, they're both hobbies I enjoy."

She laughs condescendingly. "That's your problem. Cheerleading isn't a hobby. It's a way of life. A calling. One you're obviously not dedicated to."

OMG, she really is a psycho, isn't she? *A way of life?* Seriously, when did I leave reality and step into Bizarro World? It's like God was sitting around bored, so He said, *Hey, I know something that would be fun—let's ruin a teenager's life.* And then He picked me.

Justine decides it's time to step in. "Romy, c'mon," she cajoles. "Give her a break. Pres can do the coffee, and I'll be a designated driver."

Romy drops her foot back down on the floor. "No. She

can either do the job I've assigned her or sit on the bench with Nicole. And since you're so eager to help, you can get coffee *and* drive." She crosses her arms over her chest and looks defiantly at Justine, waiting for her to challenge her.

Romy *hates* Justine. Like, really, really hates her. Which is kind of ironic, considering Justine is the best person on the squad. (I know, it's so unfair. She's good at *everything*.) But then again, maybe it's not ironic, because I think that's the reason Romy hates her in the first place. She's jealous.

Justine's eyes narrow. "Listen, you—"

"It's no problem," I say loudly, elbowing her in the ribs. I've already caused her to get a tardy today; I'm not going to be the reason she gets demoted to alternate too. "Really. I'm fine with being a designated driver."

"You better be." Romy shoots one last dagger at me with her eyes, then turns on her heel and stalks toward the door. Apparently, the meeting is over.

Whatever. I have bigger problems to worry about than the stupid graduation gala and Romy's anger management problem. You know, like the fact that my life basically exploded into flames a mere three hours ago. And although I'd like to say I can handle the heat, I'm not sure that's true.

But I guess I'm about to find out.

Chapter Four

Can you recall the best advice a family member ever gave you?

No matter how screwed up my life is, I can always count on my mom to give me strong moral guidance.

"I think you should kick her ass," she informs me when I tell her about Megan and Gabe later that night. She picks up her coffee cup, sloshing Folger's Choice all over the front of the Victoria's Secret catalog that just came in the mail. "That's the only thing a girl like Megan understands."

Everyone, meet my mother, the freak.

I know all teenagers think their parents are weird, but in my case it's really true. My parents are freaks with a capital *F*.

Oh, you think I'm exaggerating, do you? Or maybe you're sitting there going, *Whatever. No way are your parents weirder than* my *parents.*

And maybe you're right. Maybe your parents are so bizarre they make mine look like the mom and dad from one of those fifties sitcoms where the mom cooks dinner in high heels and pearls and the dad plays catch in the front yard.

But I doubt it.

Exhibit A: My dad, Eddie, is the lead singer of a punk rock band called Cracked. He has tattoos covering almost every inch of his body. One of his tats is my name. It's on his right bicep, encircled with a heart, right above the names of the three other illegitimate kids he's fathered out of wedlock. (Some dads pass out cigars when they have a baby; my dad gets a tattoo. And FYI, Angelina Jolie, he was doing that before you even *thought* about adopting a Cambodian orphan.)

In addition to his tats, he also has multiple piercings. Tongue, eyebrow, ears, chin—and I suspect some others I don't want to think about. Eeeeew.

He used to be heavy into drugs, but now he's clean. I'd introduce you to him, but he's currently touring the sleazy bar circuit in New Mexico, or Nevada, or some state with a desert—I forget.

Exhibit B: My mother, Holly, is a DJ for the local rock station (on-air name: Hot Holly). Like my dad, she's inked, although (thank God), not near as much. She has a tramp stamp on her lower back, a Chinese symbol on her ankle, and my name on her right shoulder blade. The only things she has pierced are her belly button and earlobes.

She's infatuated with Chad Kroeger, otherwise known as the lead singer of Nickelback, otherwise known as NEVER GOING TO HAPPEN. That doesn't stop her from dreaming, though. She has an on-again off-again relationship with my dad, depending on whether he has any other women knocked up at the time. When she's not with my dad, she is inevitably hooked up with some loser. She has a particular affinity for good-looking guys with large motorcycles and no job.

Exhibit C: Do you really need an Exhibit C? My dad is a *punk rock singer*, people. I think I've made my point.

Needless to say, I was switched at birth.

Seriously. It was an unfortunate incident involving an elderly nurse and mixed-up baby bracelets. Somewhere out there a nice suburban couple with a minivan and a 401(k) is trying to figure out why their seventeen-year-old daughter is brandishing a tongue ring instead of a set of pom-poms. Eventually somebody will figure out what happened and *People* magazine will do a story on it.

Yeah, I totally just made that up. But back to the conversation with my mom.

"Somehow I don't think beating Megan up would help."

"Why not?" she retorts.

Gee, let me count the ways. I can just picture what would happen if I knocked on the door of Megan's fancy-schmancy house and, like, punched her in the face. Not only would I probably get arrested, her mom would make sure I never got within fifty feet of another pageant, much less competed in one.

Did I mention that Megan's mother and aunt were Miss America 1982 and Miss America 1986? Or that her older sister, Caitlyn, is a frontrunner for this year's Miss America pageant?

That's right. Megan comes from a beauty queen dynasty. They're the Kennedys of the pageant world. I know this girl who used to take piano lessons from Megan's mom, and she said that they have a *humongous* display case right in the foyer of their house that has all their crowns lined up in rows on little white satin pillows. She said there must be, like, two or three hundred tiaras in there. Can you imagine?

My mom's idea of displaying my crowns is lining three or four of them up on top of the fish tank. Which, by the way, hasn't had a living fish in it since . . . well, ever. Now that I think about it, I'm not even sure it's *our* fish tank. It probably belongs to one of my mom's ex-boyfriends.

"Because it just wouldn't," I tell her.

"Whatever. It's your life." She crushes out the cancer stick cradled between her fingers and gets up from the table. I keep trying to convince her that smoking is so old school, but she says she can't quit because a DJ's voice is her trademark. And Hot Holly is known for her gravelly, Demi Moore–esque smoker's voice. I told her I'm pretty sure her vocal cords are permanently damaged by this point so it won't make any difference if she quits, but she doesn't believe me.

She opens her mouth in a giant yawn. As she stretches her arms above her head, the hem of her Metallica T-shirt rides up above the waistband of her plaid pajama pants, exposing the silver hoop in her navel. "I was thinking about making macaroni and cheese. Do you want some?" She drops her arms and looks at me expectantly.

"I'd love some. Except I have this little allergy called 'about to wear a bathing suit onstage in front of five hundred people.'"

"Smartass." She snags a dishrag off the counter and tosses it playfully in my direction.

As I duck, my eye catches on the pair of gold strappy sandals sitting neatly on the floor next to the laundry room. The sight causes a big lump to form in my throat. The sandals are my most recent eBay purchase, bought to go with the teal sundress I'm wearing on the first day of the pageant.

I must make some sort of noise because my mom suddenly looks over her shoulder.

"What is it?" she asks quizzically, pulling a blue box of Kraft down from the cabinet.

I gesture wanly toward the sandals. "Now that Gabe and I are broken up, I don't have anybody to walk me at Arrival." My voice is so hoarse I could almost pass for Hot Holly myself.

"So?" She rips open the top of the box and dumps the noodles into a saucepan.

"So . . . I don't have anybody to walk me at Arrival." Geesh. Is she trying to torture me or something? How many times does she want me to say it?

Except wait. I'm sorry, you probably have no idea what I'm talking about. Let me explain.

On the first day of Miss Teen State, the pageant has what's called the Arrival ceremony to present all the contestants to the public and the media. It goes like this: All the contestants stand at the top of this big staircase in the lobby of the convention center where the pageant is held. The attire is "church dress," which means everybody is wearing completely fancy sundresses and party dresses that are totally inappropriate for church. This is normal. Pageant girls follow a dress code different from regular people. Like, "casual wear" doesn't mean jeans and tennis shoes. It means show up in your tightest designer jeans, a sequined top, and spike heels. FYI.

A bunch of men are also at the top of the staircase. These are the contestants' dads. Unlike the contestants, the dads are actually wearing clothing appropriate for church, normally a suit.

One by one, each contestant is announced, at which time her dad escorts her down the staircase. At the bottom are the reigning Miss Teen State, a photographer, and all the people who have come to watch. When the contestant gets to the bottom, the reigning Miss Teen State gives her a rose and a hug and generally acts ecstatic, even though you know she's secretly dying because by that time the next week, one of the girls she's hugging will be wearing her crown.

And then the photographer takes a picture, blah, blah, blah. That's basically it.

If a contestant's dad is sick or dead, or has a tattooed appearance that frequently causes small children to scream and run away in fear, then somebody like a brother or boyfriend can fill in as the escort.

Which is why I suddenly feel like somebody drop-kicked me in the stomach. Gabe is *always* my escort. Not just to Miss Teen State, but to any sort of pageant activity that requires you to be accompanied by a guy in a suit or tuxedo. It's our thing, you know?

At least, it was our thing. I guess now it's his and Megan's thing.

My body tenses as a horrible thought suddenly occurs

to me. Oh, God—what if he walks *Megan* at Arrival? I don't think I could stand it.

My mom's nonchalant voice cuts through the panic swirling around in my head. "Don't stress. I'll get Jed to walk you. He'll love it."

Huh? I mentally run through the list of people we know, trying to figure out who she's talking about. It doesn't take long. "Jed as in your *ex-boyfriend* Jed? As in the guy whose clothes you dumped in the yard and set on *fire*?"

I stare at her incredulously. Jed is a guy she dated a few months ago, and their relationship ended on what my mom called "a bad note" and the police called "willful destruction of property."

She sets the saucepan on the stove and twists the dial to the burner. "That was a long time ago," she says breezily. "We're over it."

Translation: She's totally going out with him again, even though he cheated on her with an intern from the radio station and she made a bonfire out of his clothes in the backyard.

Normally, this would be my cue to give her a "why can't you go out with a nice, normal guy like an accountant" lecture, but tonight I just can't muster up the energy. I've got my own problems. Besides, the last time I lectured her on how she should date somebody with a normal office job, she came home with a guy who ran a "supernatural detection agency."

"I'm going to do my homework," I announce, getting up from the table. (I'm not even going to dignify the Jed suggestion with a response.)

"Okay," she says absently. A stain on the counter has caught her attention, and she's rubbing at it with the rough side of a kitchen sponge.

My mom totally has ADD; she can't concentrate on anything for longer than, like, two minutes. Especially if it's something she thinks is boring, like pageants.

Actually, I have ADD too (hence the fact that I can't remember anything). At least, according to the guidance counselor I do. I've never had, like, a professional evaluation or anything. I mean, unless the guidance counselor counts as a professional, and she probably does because she has a lot of diplomas hanging up in her office. Which means I definitely have ADD. Which means I should probably be on some sort of medication. Too bad I'll never remember to make an appointment, huh? (Oh, come on—that was funny! Sort of.)

Anyway, I have to give my mom credit. She's always been supportive of my pageant career, albeit in a completely bewildered my-child-is-totally-insane sort of way. But really, you can't blame her. Sometimes (usually in situations involving a large roll of electrical tape and the underside of my boobs) I think I'm insane too.

Chapter Five

Do you think there should be more policing of the Internet?

I leave my mom to her carb-loaded dinner and go into my bedroom to study for my upcoming chemistry final. Good study habits are very important, especially when you're . . . Oh, who am I kidding? I'm totally going to my room to call Gabe.

What, you didn't think I was just going to slink off into a cave and lick my wounds in stoic silence, did you? No way. I'm totally calling him and giving him a piece of my mind.

At least, I'd give him a piece of my mind if he didn't have his cell turned off, which he apparently does, as I realize thirty seconds later when his voice mail picks up on the first ring. I consider leaving a message, but what I want to tell him isn't exactly the kind of thing you want digitally recorded.

I snap my phone shut and toss it on my dresser. Fine. I'll just IM him.

Toeing off my pink Crocs (I *only* wear them around the house, I swear), I grab Justine's hand-me-down laptop and clamber onto my daybed. Which is harder than it sounds because I have, like, a thousand stuffed animals on my bed.

You know, a mangled Winnie the Pooh I used to carry around when I was little, a green dog my dad won for me at a carnival when I was in kindergarten, a Beanie Baby somebody gave me for my eighth birthday—that kind of stuff.

I know. I'm a total dork.

My mom says if I can't bear to get rid of them, I could at least put them away in a box, but . . . well, like I said—I'm a dork.

When I'm finally wriggled in satisfactorily among the menagerie, I flip open my laptop and quickly send him an IM.

I stare at the message that immediately pops up on my screen in disbelief. ARE YOU FREAKING KIDDING ME?? Not only does Gabe have his cell phone turned off, he has apparently blocked me from his Buddy List. Unbelievable. What, so yesterday I was his girlfriend and now I'm, like, a stalker or something?

The same thing happens when I try to send him an e-mail. Blocked.

I resist the urge to fling my laptop across the room. Okay, so apparently he *does* think I'm a stalker. Or, more likely, Megan is worried I might be able to convince him that she's only using him to get to me, and she's taking every possible step to prevent that from happening. I mean, it's kind of hard to persuade a guy if you can't even talk to him, right?

I tap my fingers on a Care Bear. *Think, Presley. There must be another way to communicate with Gabe.*

Except there's not. I mean, not unless I want to barge into his house in front of his parents, anyway. Seriously—his mom made him take down his Facebook and MySpace pages after that awful MySpace boyfriend hoax where the poor girl committed suicide, I'm not going to try to trick him by setting up a new screen name or e-mail because that smacks of desperation, and I doubt if any of his friends want to put me on three-way calling. So what form of communication does that leave? Smoke signals? Morse code?

Aaaargh! I shove the laptop off my legs and spend a few minutes pacing the length of the fuchsia rug in front of my bed until I calm down.

Whatever. If this is the way Gabe wants it, fine. I hope he and Megan get married and live happily ever after.

Well, okay. No, I don't. I hope this whole thing blows up in their faces and they spend the rest of their lives tortured by horrible, bone-crushing regret. But that doesn't sound very nice.

My brief surge of anger starts to fade, and I can feel the moisture gathering behind my eyelids. I swallow hard, willing the tears not to fall. Even though I'm alone in my bedroom now, I still don't want to cry.

Well, I *want* to, but I'm not going to let myself. Justine would say I'm repressing my feelings, but it's more like a matter of pride, you know? I'm not going to let this get me down. And, okay, maybe I am repressing my feelings just a teeny-tiny bit, but who says that's a bad thing?

In order to properly repress my emotions I need something to distract myself, so I return to my stuffed-animal throne and pull the laptop back onto my thighs.

Pay attention. You're about to see the way pageant girls drown their sorrows when life isn't working out so well. At least, the way they drown their sorrows when the state competition is coming up and they can't eat two gallons of Ben & Jerry's Chunky Monkey while watching *The Holiday* at two in the morning.

I put my hands on the keyboard and start to type. A few seconds later the pageant world's dirty little secret appears on the screen.

Officially, the Pageant Forum is for exchanging information about mundane stuff—pageant dates, locations, application info, hairdressers who do good extensions, which tanning places have the best beds, stores having sales on gowns, etc.

Unofficially, it's for exchanging anonymous opinions on who has an eating disorder, who needs to look into getting liposuction (or at the very least a good cellulite cream), who was seen puking her guts out on the sidewalk in front of a popular bar, who came back from a "missionary" trip to Brazil looking suspiciously larger in the chest area, who got her nose done, who *needs* to get her nose done, whose mom was seen lunching with a well-known judge, and on and on and on.

It's tacky, it's horrible, it's disgraceful, it's . . . totally and completely addictive.

Watch. I'll show you.

Shifting the laptop to a more comfortable position on my legs, I guide the cursor down the list of sections (Miss, Mrs., Princess, Fair Queen) until I reach the teen forum. A quick double click and twelve pages of threads appear, with titles like "Good Seamstress, Anyone?" "Results of Rose City," "Last Photo Shoot of Season."

Sounds perfectly harmless, right? Ha.

Here's a sampling of the posts in "Results of Rose City":

Sparklebabe: I can't BELIEVE the judges picked Haylee. She looks like a catfish. And her talent dress is HIDEOUS. What happened??

Guest: Sounds like somebody has a bad case of sour grapes. Go spew your venom somewhere else, sparklebabe.

Sparklebabe: Why don't YOU go somewhere else, "Guest"? Or should I say "HAYLEE'S MOM"? BTW, I hope you have a plastic surgery fund for your daughter, because she definitely needs it.

Felicity12: I thought all the girls in the contest looked beautiful and did a great job. Congratulations, girls!

PrissyMissy: Felicity, you're too nice. "All" the girls looked beautiful? Did you see the major fat roll Kassidy R. had in her swimsuit?

See what I mean? The message boards are *horrible*. I try to tell myself that reading them is okay because I just lurk—I never post anything myself—but deep down, I can't help but feel a little guilty. Pageants are supposed to be about growing as a person, helping the community, making friends—not ripping people apart over a little extra cellulite.

If I was a better, stronger, more Christian person, I would shut my laptop right now and never so much as glance at the boards again.

But I can't. I'm like a crack addict.

I exit "Rose City" and go to the board's current hot topic, "Predictions for Miss Teen State." Predicting winners and runners-up is another popular pastime on the boards, mainly because it's the perfect opportunity to discuss the strengths and weaknesses of different contestants. And by "discuss strengths and weaknesses," I mean "totally trash all the girls in the pageant except the one you want to win."

As of last night, eleven people thought I had Miss Teen State in the bag, seven said Megan was the shoo-in, four people were excited to see my new talent routine, two people said I was the worst dancer they'd ever seen, two *other* people said I was an excellent dancer with lots of personality, and one person said my hair was suffering from "peroxide mania."

Oh, and apparently my nose has a prominent bump if you look at me from the side. Which is *so* untrue. I mean, I admit there's a little raised-up spot on the bridge, but I'd hardly call it "prominent." I'm not going to tell everybody I have a deviated septum and go in for a nose job like all the stars do.

And the peroxide thing—that's *totally* unfair. The only thing I've ever put on my hair is lemon juice. And maybe a little Sun-In. And sometimes, in the winter, a teeny-tiny bit of L'Oreal Preference in Champagne Blonde, just so I don't get too dark. But that's it, I swear. There is definitely no peroxide mania going on.

But whatever. You can't let that stuff get to you, or else you'll wind up a total neurotic mess.

I click on "Predictions for Miss Teen State" and am

immediately bummed when I see that there are only two new posts. Rats. I was hoping for a little more action than that. Oh, well.

I go to the new posts.

Guest: I saw Megan L. at the gym a few days ago and she is RIPPED. She was wearing a sports bra and I could see her 6-pack. She's going to blow everybody away in swimsuit.

Tiarachick: Carys W. has the best SS body, IMO.

A laugh bursts out of my mouth. "Guest" is obviously Megan or her mom taking a stab at fiction writing. Because Megan has one of those tall, skinny, fashion model–esque bodies. She couldn't get "ripped" if she hooked herself up to a steroid IV and lived in the gym.

And please, the only six-pack that's ever been on her stomach is the one she paints on with bronzer. The only reason she does well in swimsuit is because her legs are so long.

As for Carys W., I don't even know who that is. Some newbie? It doesn't matter. If I haven't heard of her, she's obviously not a threat.

My eyes flick back up to the Guest post. After a moment's hesitation, my fingers are flying across the keyboard as if they have a will of their own.

Guest123: A little birdie told me that Megan L. and a baseball player put on quite the show in the hallway of her school today. I don't think sloppy PDA is very becoming behavior for a potential Miss Teen State.

The horror hits me before the "Message Successfully Posted" notification even pops up on the screen. OMG, am I *insane*? Megan and I are the only pageant girls who go to our school. She's totally going to know I'm the one who wrote that.

I click frantically on random icons, even though I know it's too late. The message has gone into cyberspace, and now there's no getting it back.

Finally I give up and do what I always do when I've done something colossally stupid. I call Justine.

"I don't get what the big deal is," she says five minutes later when I finish confessing. "You didn't write anything that isn't true. She *did* put on a show in the hall, and that *isn't* good beauty queen behavior. It's not like you put that she ripped off her clothes and did a stripper dance on the lunch table. She can't accuse you of slander or anything."

"But she's going to know I'm the one who posted it."

"Who cares? She deserves it."

The approval in her voice makes my chest puff out. *She's right*, I think silently. *It is time I stood up to Megan.*

I look back at the screen, my confidence spiraling upward. Two anonymous sentences on a message board may not seem like much of an achievement, but it's *huge* for me.

Besides, Megan has already tried to kill me and stolen my boyfriend—what else could she possibly do?

Chapter Six

When you get up in the morning, what do you see when you look in the mirror?

Beep! Beep! Beep!

Aaaaargh. I fling my arm out and fumble around for the evil alarm clock on my nightstand.

Beep! Beep! Beep!

I whack indiscriminately at every object I encounter, but the hideous sound keeps going. Ugh. I drag my head up from my soft pillow and peer around blearily.

The red illuminated numbers are on the other side of the room, instead of at their usual spot next to my bed. And they spell out a horrible message: 5:00 a.m.

Nooooooooo. I flop back down and pull the pillow over my head. *I'm not getting out of bed, I'm not getting out of bed, I'm not getting out of bed . . .*

Beep! Beep! Beep!

Aaaaargh. I fling off the covers and stagger over to the dresser. It's like being hit with a bucket of cold water, which is why I moved the stupid clock last night before I went to bed.

Beep! Beep! Beep!

I click the switch to off just as the display changes to 5:01.

Whimper. For a second I consider just lying down on the floor and going back to sleep, but I manage to shake it off. If I'm going to face Gabe and Megan in morning detention, I need plenty of time to prepare.

In other words, I need plenty of time to do my hair.

Forty-five minutes later, I'm wearing a full set of hot rollers, a Queen Helene Mint Julep Masque (*so* good for your pores—I highly recommend it), and a towel, surveying the contents of my closet.

Okay, *obsessing* over the contents of my closet.

I flip anxiously through the hangers, my brow furrowed. Normally, I don't stress (too much) about what I wear to school, but today isn't a normal day. I have to look fabulous, but I can't look like I'm *trying* to look fabulous. Which sounds easy, but it's so totally not.

It's like the whole "natural" makeup thing. You know, where you have to spend five hours applying taupe eye shadow and highlighter and nude lipstick so you can look like you're not wearing any makeup at all?

CRA-ZY. And who wants to look like they're not wearing makeup, anyway? Duh, that's the whole point.

I cruise through the hangers one more time. Finally I pull out three possibilities and lay them on the bed.

Okay, I can wear (a) my frayed jean skirt with the A&F polo Justine got me for my birthday, or (b) my dark-wash jeans and new peasant blouse from Charlotte Russe (the one I wished I was wearing yesterday), or (c) the hot pink tunic dress and leggings I got on clearance at Express.

Hmmmmn. I survey my selections. Then I reach down and take the tunic/legging combo out of the lineup. It's totally adorable, but the dress is one of those blousy deals, and I don't want to look like I'm pregnant.

Another moment of study and I nix the Charlotte Russe top and jeans too. They're also adorable, but the jeans are super-long, which means I'd have to wear my super-high-heeled sandals. And five-inch heels pretty much scream "I totally got up two hours early to pick out this outfit!"

That means the winner of Presley's a.m. fashion contest is [drum roll] . . . the jean skirt and polo! Ta-da!

Forty-five *more* minutes later: I'm dressed, powdered, curled, perfumed, and bronzed. I look perfect. Nothing could be improved upon.

Forty-seven minutes later: I decide my hair would look better in a headband and take down my carefully arranged high ponytail.

Forty-eight minutes later: I realize that the headband makes my nose look big and that I should have kept the ponytail.

Fifty-three minutes later: Why won't my hair go back up into the #$!% ponytail?

Fifty-five minutes later: I think I've used too much hair spray. My hair looks like it's been attacked by angry birds.

Fifty-six minutes later: I'm *so* not going to school.

Still fifty-six minutes later: I have to go to school or else people will think I'm so distraught over Gabe and Megan that I had to stay home.

Fifty-seven minutes later: Maybe if I change into the peasant top and wear a big pair of dangly earrings, nobody will notice that my hair looks like it's been attacked by angry birds.

Fifty-nine minutes later: Oh, God. If I don't leave in the next thirty seconds, I'm going to be late. Why, oh *why*, did I have to put on that stupid headband?

Sixty minutes later: *#%!

One good thing about my neighborhood is that it's really close to my school. So thanks to a little luck and light traffic, I dash into the detention room just as the round clock on the back wall says straight up seven o'clock.

"Everybody sit down and shut up," Coach Tackett growls. It's obvious from the murderous look on his face that he's not a morning person. And also that he hates our guts. "Any of you make a peep before the eight-fifteen bell, and all of you get d-hall again tomorrow. Are we clear?"

There's an assenting murmur from the people already sitting down as the rest of us scurry to find a seat in the packed room. Under normal circumstances, I would look around to see if any of my friends/semi-friends are here and try to sit near them, but *no way* am I doing that today. Megan and Gabe would totally think I was looking for them.

I beeline for the first empty seat that enters my line of vision, a desk about halfway down the third row, my heels clicking loudly on the white linoleum. (Yeah. I went with the peasant top and heels. Which means I'm going to be totally crippled by the end of the day.)

"Psssst."

The sound comes from my left just as I'm taking out the *CosmoGIRL!* I've brought to keep me occupied. (Okay, the *CosmoGIRL!* I've brought to hide behind.)

I glance over. Sebastian Laffoon is in the row across from me, one seat back, grinning at me like a moron.

Ugh. I cut my eyes back to the front. Maybe he was trying to get somebody else's attention and I just happened to look over.

"Pssst. Presley."

So much for that theory.

I open up the mag and peer intently at a Maybelline ad. Maybe if I pretend like I'm deaf, he'll give up.

Sebastian was perfectly normal and nice in elementary and middle school, but as soon as we hit high school, he turned into a total *perv*. Like, he's one of those guys who will come up to you at your locker and ask you what color panties you're wearing. And other, unprintable things we won't talk about. Eeeeew.

"Pres-ley." His third attempt is so loud I can't believe Coach Tackett doesn't start screaming and give us all another detention.

I whip my head around. *What?* I mouth.

He leans out of his seat and tosses a folded-up square of paper toward me. It makes a perfect landing on the center of my desk.

Great. He's probably, like, drawn a picture of my boobs or something. Exhaling wearily, I set the magazine aside and pick up the note.

Sure enough, when I unfold it, I'm greeted by a stick figure with long hair and two enormous circles in the center of
its chest. The barely legible scrawl underneath the figure says
This would be more realistic if I had a live model.

Ugh. Disgusting. I crumple the paper into a ball and turn
to give him a death glare. Not that it does any good; he's
doubled over in his seat laughing at his cleverness.

Lovely. I would draw a caricature of a tiny penis and give
it back to him, but (a) he'd probably like it, and (b) Coach
Tackett would probably catch me and show it to the whole
class.

I start to turn back around when the corner of my eye
snags on a familiar figure. Actually, *two* familiar figures.

Yep. You guessed it. It's HIM. And HER. They're sitting
across from me too, one row over from Sebastian. But while
Sebastian is one seat behind me, Megan is one seat up, with
Gabe sitting in front of her. You know, so I have a PERFECT
view of them.

And judging from the glossy black curls cascading over her
shoulders and down her back like a Pantene ad, unlike me,
Megan didn't have any hair issues this morning.

I move my eyes over to Gabe. Which is a huge mistake
because he looks adorable. He's slumped down in his seat,
arms crossed, eyes shut, fitted gray T-shirt showing off his
arm muscles even while he's asleep. His hair is obviously
still damp from the shower. I can tell by the way the ends
are curling up in the back. If I was still his girlfriend and

sitting behind him like Megan, I'd be fiddling with it right now.

Moisture starts accumulating at the corners of my eyes. No, no, no. Crying in detention not good. Bad. Very bad.

I hastily turn my attention back to Megan. Why, I have no idea. Apparently, I enjoy making myself feel like crap. Because now I notice that not only does her hair look like she just stepped out of a shampoo ad, she's wearing a cute little pink top with a cute little pink skirt and a pair of cute little pink-and-green-plaid espadrilles.

In other words, she looks totally, completely, impossibly perfect.

OMG, the Dooney & Bourke hooked over the back of her chair just *smirked* at my hobo bag. No, really. It did. I swear. It can tell that I got it on clearance at Target.

As if she can hear my internal paranoid chatter, suddenly Megan turns her head and zeroes in on me with her freakishly green eyes.

Uh-oh. Busted.

I force myself not to look away, even though I'd like to, oh, say—get under my desk.

Great, Presley. Way to show her she can't intimidate you. Let her catch you staring at her like some insecure wimp.

I hold her gaze. She holds my gaze.

After twenty seconds it's official: We're locked in a stare-down.

I lift my chin. I'm *so* going to outlast her.

I hope. My neck sort of has a crick in it.

An eternity passes. I shift awkwardly in my seat. This is stupid. I should just turn around and go back to my magazine. We're not dogs. If I look away first, it doesn't mean I'm acknowledging her as the alpha. It just means that I don't want to spend the whole hour locking eyes with a psycho when I could be doing something productive, like taking the *CosmoGIRL!* quiz to see if I'm "karma crazy."

Right. So I'm just going to calmly turn back to the front.

[mental elevator music]

Any second now. I'm working up to it.

[more mental elevator music]

Is Megan a freaking robot, or what? I don't think she's even blinked.

[mental elevator music replaced by mental cricket chirping]

I think my neck is permanently frozen in this position. Great. I'm going to have to spend the rest of my life with my head turned sideways so everybody can get a good profile view of the bump on my nose.

I'm dangerously close to screaming and running out of the room (sideways) when Megan's face suddenly unfreezes—specifically, her mouth, which curves upward into what can only be described as a malicious smile.

Actually, that's not true. It could also be described as "the way Cruella De Vil smiled when she was about to make fur coats out of adorable helpless puppies." But that's kind of long and my English teacher is always ranting on about how you're supposed to "omit needless words." (See? I'm not totally stupid. I pay attention in class.)

As I watch, Megan slowly extends one of her long, tanned legs and lifts it until it's straight out, parallel to the side of Gabe's desk.

What is she up to? I wonder, bewildered. Is she, like, trying to make sure I see how cute her shoes are or something? Why is she sticking her leg out like that?

My question is answered half a second later when she moves her leg in closer to the desk and starts rubbing her calf sensuously against Gabe's side. She cocks her head and gives me an exaggerated wink, reveling in what has to be my obvious misery.

I jerk my eyes away. Okay, game over. She wins. I may have posted a few sentences on a message board, but my new-found confidence does *not* extend to watching her rub herself all over Gabe.

Fumbling, I pick up *CosmoGIRL!* (why does it have that exclamation point in its name? Every time I see it, I feel like I should do a high kick or something) and start furiously flipping pages. Where is that stupid quiz? I so need a distraction right now.

I keep ripping through the pages, trying to ignore the tears burning my eyes. You know how people who survive, like, awful car accidents say stuff about how their whole life flashed before their eyes? Well, now all these images from my life with Gabe are flashing through my mind like some sort of cheesy movie montage.

The adorable way he kept stumbling over his words the

first time he asked me out, the time at the county fair when the ride we were on got stuck and the guy hanging upside down above us started throwing up and Gabe tilted his body so that the chunks hit him instead of me, the Valentine's Day he made me a card that looked like it had been put together by a blind monkey with a glue stick and a packet of construction paper, the look on his face when he opened the Derek Jeter jersey I got him for his birthday last year.

A big fat tear rolls over my bottom lashes and lands on the mag, right in the middle of a glossy ad for Tampax. Great. So much for trying not to cry. And none of my eye makeup is waterproof. I'm going to look like you-know-what before I even get to first period.

I brush carefully at my eyes, trying to minimize the damage. Except somehow I end up darting another glance over *there*.

Megan is still playing footsie (calfsie?) with Gabe, but now he's awake and sitting up straight. He's also rubbing his hand up and down her lower leg with this sort of glazed, I-can't-believe-I'm-so-lucky look on his face.

By all rights, it's the kind of expression that should make me want to kill him (like yesterday), but instead, I feel this weird, protective thing toward him. Megan has done a total number on him and he doesn't even realize it. And when she doesn't need him anymore . . . well, let's just say it won't be pretty.

Sigh. That's the thing about Gabe. He's *so* gullible. He

always sees the best in people, even if they have little devil horns sprouting right out of their heads.

Take his best friend, Donovan, for example. The guy is a complete drug dealer. He works as a delivery guy for Chevalier's Pharmacy, and he totally steals all kinds of drugs and sells them around school. OxyContin, Xanax, Viocdin—he even offered Justine some Ritalin to "enhance concentration" before the SATs. I mean, the guy is like a walking pharmacy. *Everybody* knows he's a drug dealer. I bet even the teachers know. But does Gabe believe it? No.

When I tried to tell him he needed to stop hanging out with Donovan because he's totally going to get caught and go to jail, and that I wouldn't put it past him to try to implicate Gabe somehow (Donovan is sleazy like that), you want to know what he said? "Donovan can't be a drug dealer. We played Little League together."

We played Little League together? What kind of logic is that? If you played youth sports, you can't be a criminal?

Here's another example: Gabe totally believes in that whole innocent-until-proven-guilty thing. Like, we'll be watching TV and there'll be some story about, say, a man suspected of shooting his wife and trying to make it look like a burglary gone wrong. And they'll flash his picture up and I'm all like, "Ohmigosh, he has a unibrow. He *so* did it."

But Gabe's all, "You don't know that. Until he's found guilty by a court, he's just as innocent as you and me."

Hello? As innocent as me? You don't see *my* picture on CNN, do you? Seriously.

Anyway, you can see how easy it probably was for Megan to draw him into her web of evil. But this is what I don't get: If he's so loyal to people like Donovan and to random strangers on TV, how could he have just ditched me without a backward glance?

Chapter Seven

How do you handle peer pressure when it goes against your values?

ex?" I stare weakly at the back of Justine's head as she slides her AP Calculus folder onto the top shelf of our locker. I should be stowing some of my stuff too, but I'm pretty sure my heart just fell out of my chest and splattered on the floor. At least, it feels like it did.

"You think Gabe and Megan are having s-s-s . . ." I try to make my mouth form the three-letter word, but it refuses to emerge from my lips. " . . . intimate relations?" I finish finally.

"No, I think they're having *sex*," she repeats, because she either (a) enjoys being difficult, or (b) enjoys making me feel like I'm going to throw up.

"Hot, kinky, wild sex." She bangs the locker door shut and wheels around to face me. "Frequently."

Right. It's good she clarified that. I might have been upset if they were having lukewarm, boring, awkward sex. Now I can relax.

"If this is your idea of trying to make me feel better, you're doing a really crappy job."

"You didn't ask me to make you feel better. You asked me

what I thought," she replies calmly, nudging me in the direction of the cafeteria. "So I'm telling you."

I mentally replay the previous thirty seconds. What was it I said to her exactly? Something like . . . Oh. Right. I said, "Why do you think Gabe dumped me like that?" Rats.

Note to self: Never, ever again ask Justine what she thinks about anything.

"Well—well, it doesn't matter what I said," I stammer. "You're my best friend. You have a moral obligation to make me feel better."

"You mean you want me to lie."

"If the truth involves Gabe and Megan being naked together, yes."

"You don't have to be naked to have sex. In Victorian England—"

"La, la, la, la, la . . ." I jam my fingers in my ears and sing loudly to drown out her voice. I don't want to think about Gabe and Megan having *any* kind of sex. Naked. Not naked. Halfway naked. Not in the rain. Not in the dark. Not on a train. Not in a tree. I do not like it, Sam you see.

"Okay, okay. I'm sorry." She drags my hands down. "I'll shut up."

Hunter and Lilly intercept us at the entrance to the cafeteria. "Let's eat outside today," Lilly says brightly.

"So we can work on our tans," Hunter adds.

Without waiting for a response, they bustle Justine and me out the door and into the courtyard.

"Oooh, doesn't it feel good out here?" Lilly plops her lunch sack down on a picnic bench and tilts her face up to the sun. "I'm so glad school is almost out."

"I know. We should start eating out here every day," Hunter declares, sitting down beside her.

"How bad is it?" I ask flatly.

They blink at me, feigning innocence. "What do you mean?" they ask in unison.

I ignore their dumb-and-dumber routine. "Is he sitting at her table or is she at his?"

"Who?" This time they not only speak in stereo, their eyebrows arch in perfect synchronization. If I wasn't so freaked out, I'd be cracking up right now.

"C'mon, you guys. I'm not stupid. Megan and Gabe are sitting together, aren't they? That's why you want to sit out here. So I won't see them." I cross my arms and wait for them to confess, even though I already know I'm right. I mean, please. It doesn't exactly take a genius to figure out that something's up when Hunter and Lilly are claiming they want to sit outside to get a tan. They have that super-white porcelain skin that fries after, like, five minutes.

Hunter looks like she might continue the charade, but Lilly knows the jig is up. "Oh, all right." She sighs, relaxing her face into a normal expression. "You're right. They're sitting together. We were trying to spare you."

"Yeah, we were trying to spare you," Hunter echoes. The twin function in their brains must be switched to off because it's the first time I've ever heard one of them repeat something after the other instead of saying it at the same time.

Justine shakes her head. "You guys, that's sweet and all, but Presley can't slink around school hiding from them. She has to act like it doesn't bother her. Right?" She turns to me for confirmation.

Which is comical because it just so happens that slinking around school hiding from them is *exactly* what I'm planning on doing.

I know. But it's not as wimpy as it sounds. I mean, next week is finals and then we're out for the summer, so it's not like I'd be skulking around for a whole year or anything.

"But it does bother me," I protest. "Especially since *somebody*"—I goggle my eyes exaggeratedly at Justine—"so sensitively said that they're having hot, kinky s-s-s . . ." Great. I'll probably never be able to say that word again. " . . . fun," I finish.

Hunter and Lilly's eyes widen like somebody doused them with those dilating drops from the eye doctor's office. "Ohmigosh, you think they're—," Lilly starts, but I fling up my hand to stop her.

"Can we not talk about that, please?" I ask curtly. Justine saying it out loud was bad enough, but if Hunter and Lilly start talking about it, I really will lose it.

They exchange glances, then nod dutifully, although it's clear from their expressions that they're bummed out. By tacit agreement, the conversation turns to superficial stuff: whether Hunter and Lilly should put blond streaks in their hair (no), whether Justine should tint the windows on her new hybrid car (yes). I try to join in and act like a normal person, but my mind keeps going back to Gabe and Megan (shudder) *together*.

By the time Hunter and Lilly get to the merits of having a Fourth of July barbecue at their house versus going to the lake, I can't take it anymore.

I slam my bottled water down on the table. "I have to do something," I blurt out.

They all stop talking and turn to stare at me. "About . . . ," Hunter prompts.

"About world hunger," I shoot back sarcastically. "About Megan and Gabe. What else would I be talking about?"

Hunter gives me a wounded look. "You don't have to be a bitch."

I immediately feel terrible. "I'm sorry. I'm just in a bad mood. I shouldn't be taking it out on you."

"You *are* doing something about Gabe and Megan," Justine tells me calmly. "You're going on with your life. Haven't you ever heard that saying, 'Living well is the best revenge'?"

Hunter frowns. "I thought it was 'Revenge is a dish best served cold.'"

"No, it's 'Don't get mad, get even,'" Lilly corrects.

"Shut-up-you're-not-helping-anything," Justine says out of the side of her mouth, but it's too late.

"Exactly!" I beam at the twins. "I want to get even. Revenge."

"Thanks a lot. You guys are a big help," Justine tells Hunter and Lilly wryly. She turns to me. "Look, I can see why you want to get back at Megan, but you're better off leaving it alone."

"Why?" The question comes out of my mouth in unison with Hunter and Lilly. Oh, man. I wonder if the freaky twin stuff is contagious or something?

Justine shrugs. "Because it's really not that big of a deal when you think about it."

"Not that big of a deal?" I echo incredulously. "She stole my boyfriend! How is that not a big deal?"

"I know, but it's not, like, a tragedy or anything," she replies logically. She pops a Dorito into her mouth. "I mean, you weren't exactly into him anymore."

"What are you talking about? We went out for *three years*."

"Exactly. You went out for three years." She gestures with a piece of broken Dorito as if I've just proved her point. "C'mon, Pres. You've been thinking about breaking up with Gabe for months now. Megan sort of did you a favor."

I stare at her in disbelief. A favor? Is she INSANE?

"Are you insane?" I say out loud. "A favor is, like, when somebody lets you copy their homework, or gives you a ride, or lets you borrow their earrings. A favor is *not* stealing somebody's boyfriend."

Justine rolls her eyes. "Okay, okay, so it's not a favor," she says, exasperated. "It's a fortuitous coincidence. A *fortunate* coincidence," she amends when she sees my look. We have an agreement about her not using her SAT vocabulary words in normal conversation.

"You didn't tell us you were thinking about breaking up with Gabe," Hunter and Lilly cut in. They give me identical accusing looks. Clearly, their twin switch is back on.

"That's because I wasn't thinking about it," I say point-edly, looking at Justine.

She gives me one of those I-can't-believe-you head shake things, but surprisingly, she doesn't try to argue. Probably because she knows there's nothing to argue about. I mean, yes, I might have made a few teeny-tiny comments about Gabe getting on my nerves. And, okay, *maybe* I said something about wondering what it would be like to kiss certain other cute guys. But that doesn't mean I was planning on breaking up with him.

I decide to drop the subject and get back to the task at hand. "Look, will you guys just help me think of a way to get back at her?"

"Why don't you just go to her house and kick her butt?" Hunter suggests.

My head whips around. "Have you been talking to my mother?"

She gives me a strange look. "Why would I be talking to your mother?"

"Never mind." I brush off my psycho moment and turn back to the rest of the table. "Can't you guys think of any-thing? That doesn't involve getting arrested for physical assault," I add as Hunter starts to speak.

"Oh." She closes her mouth, looking disappointed.

"Anybody?" I persist.

Silence falls over the picnic bench as everybody concen-trates. Well, as Hunter, Lilly, and I concentrate. I can tell by the way Justine is methodically peeling the crust off her turkey sandwich and putting it in her mouth that she's not thinking about Megan and me at all.

Lilly is the first to speak. "Well, there is one thing. . . ." Her voice trails off. "Oh, never mind. It's stupid."

"No, say it," I urge.

"I don't know." She looks uncertainly at Hunter and whispers something unintelligible in freaky twin-speak. Hunter whispers something back at her equally impossible to understand, and then they proceed to have a whole conversation while Justine and I look on in amazement.

"Do you think they do that in front of their boyfriends?" I murmur. Unbelievably, Hunter and Lilly are still "dating" their old boyfriends from Michigan. Personally, I think it's kind of silly to stay with somebody who lives thousands of miles away and you only see twice a year, but whatever. If it makes them happy, I guess I don't have any right to judge.

"Probably," Justine answers, not taking her eyes off the twins. "But I think they all grew up together, so it probably doesn't weird them out."

Finally they break apart and resume speaking normal English.

"Lilly has a good idea," Hunter announces.

"Great. Let's hear it." I gesture at Lilly, indicating that she should get on with it.

She clears her throat. "Okay. You know that guy, Robbie Sweet?"

The mere mention of Robbie Sweet's name makes all of us turn instinctively to look at him.

He's sprawled negligently on top of the faux-stone wall that encloses the courtyard, his chiseled face turned up to the sun, his smoldering eyes hidden by a pair of wraparound Diesel sunglasses. Robbie Sweet is a legend. A god. A myth. The star quarterback who quit the football team for no apparent reason other than that he wanted to; the rich boy who drives an old Corvette instead of the pimped-out SUV that seems to be de rigueur for guys with money; the super-gorgeous guy who seems to exist in his own little bubble of hotness, untouched by the banal trivialities of high school.

As we watch, he reaches down and casually lifts up the bottom of his T-shirt to wipe his face, revealing a set of abs that literally makes my mouth water. Gulp. "What about him?" I breathe, unable to take my eyes off him.

"Well, you know he and Megan used to go out?"

My moment of bliss screeches to a halt. *"What?"* I whip my head back toward Lilly.

"You know he and Megan used to go out," she repeats, apparently mistaking my look of shock and incredulity for a hearing problem.

I shake my head. "Megan and Robbie have never gone out. You must have them mixed up with somebody else."

"Yes, they did," Lilly insists.

"When?" I counter skeptically. I don't claim to be privy to everything that goes on in school, but I'm pretty sure I'd have heard if Megan and Robbie had hooked up. "And pretending to get married at recess in third grade doesn't count," I add.

"We didn't live here in third grade."

I throw up my hands. "Will you just tell me? Lunch is going to be over in, like, five minutes."

Hunter takes over. "They went out last summer," she informs me. "We saw them at the club together all the time."

I quickly process this information. The "club" she's referring to is the country club, a name that I assume is self-explanatory. You know, golf course, swimming pool, fancy restaurant, only people with a gross income of at least a hundred thousand dollars allowed. Hunter and Lilly's dad is a "cosmetic dentist," and their parents hang out there a lot because their mom thinks it's a good way to drum up business. And I guess she's right because they just bought land to build a "dental spa." They're going to offer people manicures, pedicures, massages, and teeth cleanings all at the same time. Which is a weird, yet strangely good idea.

But whatever. I'm totally veering off point here. "Are you sure it was Megan and Robbie?" I press. "I mean, that was back when you guys first moved here. You didn't know anybody yet."

For the record, I'm not trying to accuse Hunter and Lilly of lying or anything. They're totally not like that. I just think they have Robbie or Megan—or both of them—mixed up with somebody else. You know, because they haven't lived here very long and everything. Although, granted, it *is* kind of hard to imagine mistaking some other guy for Robbie Sweet.

Justine finally speaks up. "It must have been a pretty short romance," she comments. "They weren't together by the time school started."

"That's the best part." Hunter leans forward and lowers her voice conspiratorially. "Apparently, Megan was, like, totally infatuated with him and he dumped her."

"She was totally devastated," Lilly puts in.

"Yeah, devastated," Hunter echoes.

Justine and I stare at them. Okay, maybe they *are* the kind of people who lie.

"How could you possibly know that?" Justine demands.

Hunter shrugs. "Lexi told us."

"How would Lexi know?" Justine persists. Alexis—Lexi—is the twin's older sister. I've only met her a couple of times, so I don't know that much about her. Apparently she's still ticked that her parents made her move here right before her senior year of high school. Which, I can understand the trauma and everything, but geesh . . . get over yourself already.

"Because Lexi is friends with Jessica Tate's big sister, Sarabeth, and Sarabeth is friends with Megan's big sister, Caitlyn, and Caitlyn told Sarabeth who told Lexi who told us." Hunter looks at us as if this should be perfectly obvious.

"You forgot your dog's uncle's cousin's grandmother," Justine tells her.

"Shut up," Hunter and Lilly say simultaneously, but they're both grinning.

Despite the convoluted chain of communication, I'm starting to think Hunter and Lilly are right, and Megan and Robbie really did go out. And if that's true, then . . .

"Ohmigosh, that's a totally scandalous piece of gossip, and you kept it to yourselves for a *year*? What kind of people are you?" I stare at them incredulously.

Justine nods. "She's right. That's withholding information."

They drop their heads, ashamed. "We didn't know," Lilly says earnestly. "Like you said, we haven't lived here very long."

"It's okay. We forgive you," Justine says graciously, patting her on the back.

"This time," I add. "Anyway"—I pause to shove at a clump of hair the wind has swirled into my lip gloss—"what does Robbie Sweet have to do with me getting even with Megan?"

"Well, Megan stole your boyfriend, right?" Lilly asks. "So what better way to get back at her than hooking up with the guy she wants but can't have?"

"Huh?" I blink at her, not following.

"If you go out with Robbie, Megan will be jealous," Hunter says, drawing each word out as if I'm mentally challenged.

I look back and forth between Hunter and Lilly, marveling at their identical innocent expressions. Did they just, like, drop in from outer space or something? I mean, I know they've only lived here a year, but shouldn't they recognize basic social hierarchy by now?

"Are you insane? I can't go out with Robbie Sweet," I say incredulously.

"Why can't you?"

"Because he's the kind of guy who dates fashion models

named Yasmin, that's why. I couldn't *pay* him to go out with me."

"That's so not true!" Lilly cries. "He would totally go out with you. Any guy would."

"Totally," Hunter echoes. Her face suddenly lights up with excitement. "Ooooh, I know!" she exclaims. "You should ask him to go to the graduation gala with you. That would be so perfect. Everybody would see you."

I glance over at Justine, who—you'll notice—hasn't made one peep. That's because she knows Hunter and Lilly are insane too. "Will you tell them they're totally crazy?" I plead.

She continues scraping the paper label off her Diet Snapple with her fingernail. "No comment."

Great.

I look back at Hunter and Lilly. "Look, y'all, I appreciate the vote of confidence and everything, but there is no way that's ever going to happen. Robbie Sweet doesn't even know I'm alive."

"So clue him in," Hunter replies, still unfazed.

"What do you want me to do, just walk up and say, 'Hi, I'm Presley. Would you like to go to the graduation gala with me?'"

Hunter and Lilly are either oblivious to my sarcasm or determined to ignore it. "Yes, exactly!" Lilly exclaims. She and Hunter beam at each other triumphantly, thrilled they've finally gotten through to me.

My eyes travel back to Robbie on the stone wall. Now he's sitting up, his elbow propped on his knee, talking on a sleek silver cell phone. He looks like a male model in a cologne ad.

I turn away, shaking my head. Hunter and Lilly are sweet in a totally delusional way, but that doesn't change reality. And reality is that Robbie Sweet wouldn't give me the time of day if I was the last girl on earth.

"Forget it, you guys. That's not going to work." I'm referring to the Robbie idea in general, but Hunter and Lilly are once again oblivious.

"Okay, what about asking him to go have a coffee?" Hunter proposes. "That's low-key."

Lilly quickly jumps on the bandwagon. "And there's always somebody from school hanging out at the coffee shop," she adds excitedly. "Megan would definitely hear about it."

"Or maybe I could just ask him home for dinner. My mom could make her famous macaroni and cheese." This suggestion (which is clearly a joke) causes Justine to spew Diet Snapple out her nostrils, but Hunter and Lilly are *still* clueless.

Lilly frowns. "But if you have him over to your house, nobody will see you guys together."

"Yeah, and how do you know he likes macaroni and cheese?" Hunter asks.

I'm trying to decide whether to run away screaming or just give up and go along with them, but luckily the bell rings, saving me from doing either.

"We'll call you later," Hunter and Lilly promise in unison as they get up from the table.

I look beseechingly at Justine as we follow them, but she just laughs. "You asked for help," she reminds me. "Haven't you ever heard that saying 'Be careful what you wish for because you might get it'?"

"Yeah, yeah, yeah. We've talked enough about sayings for one day. And now I have a new appreciation for that one about silence being golden."

Chapter Eight

How do you give
back to the community?

fter school I switch my killer heels for some grungy flip-flops I scrounge out of Justine's gym bag and drive to Willow Oaks Retirement Center. Remember how I said I was going to read to old people? Well, today is the day.

Actually, I don't really *read* to them. I mean, I will if they want me to, but mostly they just like for somebody to sit and listen to them tell stories about their kids or grandkids or the old days or whatever. Sometimes they show me photo albums, which is cool—especially when they have those old-timey black-and-white pictures from like, a hundred years ago. You know, where the women are wearing those really long dresses and look all serious and stuff? I like looking at those, even though I know that's kind of a nerdy thing to admit.

Do you want to know something that's even *more* nerdy? I like looking at the old people's regular pictures too. I know. I need to get a life. But it's cool to see what they looked like when they were young. Plus, my mom and dad aren't exactly into the whole preserving your family memories with Kodak thing, so it's fun to sort of live vicariously through other people.

Earlene, the receptionist, glances up from her computer as I come through the front door. "Well, if it isn't our little Miss America." She grins, her teeth startlingly white against the gleaming ebony of her skin. "Where's your crown, baby girl?"

My cheeks color automatically, even though we go through this same routine every week. I frown at her. "Some things do get less funny with time, you know."

She gives a deep belly laugh. "Not that one, baby girl. Not that one." She shakes her head, chuckling at the memory of my first visit to Willow Oaks. Which, like I said, you'd think would have lost some of its humor, but yeah—apparently not.

And now I guess I'm going to have to relive my shame for you, aren't I?

Sigh. Okay, but you have to *promise* not to laugh. At least not as much as Earlene.

It's like this. I'd like to tell you I'm one of those people who naturally decides to spend her free time helping the blind, or saving dolphins à la Hayden Panettiere, but the truth is I got into this whole retirement center thing for less-than-altruistic reasons. You see, pageant girls have to do community service. Well, you don't *have* to—it's not like a law or anything. But if you ever want to feel an actual tiara on your head . . . well, let's just say you better seriously look into getting a red-and-white-striped apron and heading down to the local hospital to pass out little plastic cups of water. Or finding some needy orphans or lonely old people or whatever. You know what I mean. Community service is what keeps us from being "just" a beauty pageant.

Anyway, so a few months ago Noralee, my executive director, decided it would look good if I "reach out to the elderly in the community," and she set up this whole me-reading-to-old-people thing.

I know. What the heck is an executive director, right? Basically, it's just a fancy title to describe the person in charge of a pageant. So, if I'm the reigning Miss Magnolia Blossom (which I am), and Noralee is in charge of the Miss Magnolia Blossom pageant (which she is), then that means Noralee is my executive director. Make sense?

Okay. So Noralee sets up this retirement center gig, and on the first day I show up wearing this really prim and proper black pantsuit. Because, you know, they're old. I thought it might look disrespectful or something if I went in jeans. And since I was already dressed up, I figured I might as well go the whole nine yards and wear my crown too.

Except as things turned out, wearing my crown wasn't exactly the greatest idea I ever had. Because about twenty minutes into my visit, Mrs. Ackerman (age 76, room 302) accidentally dropped one of her crochet needles and I bent down to pick it up for her. Which is when Mr. Zapatero (age 84, room 111) darted up, snatched my crown off my head, and *ran away* with it.

Well, as much as an eighty-four-year-old man in plaid bedroom slippers can run. It was more like a fast shuffle. But that doesn't matter. The important thing is that he was totally clutching my crown to his chest and laughing maniacally.

Shut up! It's not funny. He stole my *crown*, people. And it's not like you can exactly run down a little old man and tackle him. All I could do was stammer at him a few times and then watch helplessly as he shuffled/ran out of the common room.

Long story short, this really nice nurse named Carol eventually found my crown. On the head of this really nice old lady named Mrs. Finkel. Who turned out to be Mr. Zapatero's girlfriend.

You see, apparently, Mrs. Finkel's birthday was coming up and Mr. Zapatero wanted to get her a special present, so when he saw my sparkly crown . . . well, what he did was actually totally sweet.

Looking back on it, I mean. It didn't seem very sweet at the time.

I put my hands on my hips and narrow my eyes at Earlene, who is *still* laughing. Finally she reaches for the pad of visitor stickers. "You here to see Mrs. Huberman?" she asks casually, ripping off a sticker.

I nod stiffly.

"Aw, don't be like that. You know Miz Earlene's just joking with you." She hands me the visitor sticker along with a bright red lollipop.

"Thanks, Earlene." Grinning, I shove the candy into my pocket and slap the sticker on my shirt. How can I stay mad at her? She gave me a lollipop.

Officially stickered, I head off down the main hall to find Mrs. Huberman, who has basically become like my adopted grandmother. Mrs. Huberman is sort of like a celebrity at Willow Oaks because she's ONE HUNDRED AND ONE.

But that's not the impressive part.

The impressive part is that she's one hundred and one *and* she still has all of her original teeth.

I know that sounds like I'm being snarky, but I'm not. I've learned all sorts of things since I've been coming here. For instance, did you know that old people have sex? I don't mean old people in their thirties like my mom, I'm talking *old* people. People who have been getting the senior citizen discount at Denny's since way before I was born.

I know! I didn't either! But they totally do. Like, Mrs. Huberman's roommate, Mrs. Wright, is carrying on this torrid affair with Mr. Smythe, which is totally scandalous because Mr. Smythe's wife lives at Willow Oaks too. Of course, Mr. Smythe's wife has Alzheimer's, so she doesn't actually *know* she's his wife, but still.

Anyway, the point I'm trying to make is that old people may look boring, but they're actually cool. At least, the ones at Willow Oaks are, anyway.

Mrs. Huberman is in the dayroom, working on a ginormous jigsaw puzzle with a youngish-looking woman I've never seen before.

"Hi, Mrs. H!" I lean down and brush a kiss against her cheek, which smells like a mixture of talcum powder and the White Linen perfume her granddaughter, Izzie, got her for Christmas.

"Why, Presley! What a lovely surprise. We hardly ever see

you on the weekend." She beams up at me, delighted I've dropped in for an unexpected visit.

Except, of course, I *haven't* dropped in for an unexpected visit because it's not the weekend; it's Wednesday, the same day I always come. Mrs. Huberman never knows what day it is, but hello—ONE HUNDRED AND ONE, people. Give the woman a break!

I wave my hand dismissively. "Oh, well, I had some free time, so you know, I thought I'd come by."

Old people lesson number one: Don't correct them about stupid stuff like the date. It doesn't matter whether it's Wednesday or Saturday, and you'll just upset them.

"Wonderful." She gives me a big smile, then gestures to the woman across the table. "This is Lucinda, my wonderful new neighbor. She just moved into the room across the hall."

"Nice to meet you." I nod politely to Lucinda. Man, she's even younger than I thought when I saw her from the door. Barring plastic surgery and/or major laser resurfacing, I'd say she's not a day over sixty-five. That's practically jail bait by Willow Oaks standards. She's going to have to beat the old men off with a club. Luckily, hardly any of the old men can stand upright longer than five minutes, so she should be okay.

She smiles. "Likewise."

"Lucinda is going to go to the cafeteria and get us some pudding cups," Mrs. Huberman informs me. Mrs. Huberman is *addicted* to pudding cups. I swear she eats, like, three hundred a week.

"Speaking of, I'd better get down there," Lucinda says,

checking the expensive-looking gold watch on her wrist.

"No, don't get up," I say quickly as she starts to push back her chair. "I'll go get them." *Because then I won't have to do the cat jigsaw puzzle.* I know. That sounded mean, didn't it? But you have no *idea* how many jigsaw puzzles I've put together over the past few months. Millions and millions. They're Mrs. Huberman's favorite thing. Well, after pudding cups, of course.

On the way to the cafeteria, I'm cornered by the social director, Bethany, who gives me a stack of papers on the Ms. Willow Oaks pageant (don't ask), as well as Mrs. Smythe, who frantically asks if I can babysit Patricia while she goes to the grocery store.

Since Patricia is well-behaved due to the fact that she's a Cabbage Patch Kid and not the two-year-old Mrs. Smythe believes her to be, I graciously agree.

By the time I get back to the dayroom, I'm carrying so much stuff I'm having trouble walking. Which is unfortunate. Because a third person is now sitting with Lucinda and Mrs. Huberman at the jigsaw puzzle. A third person who looks a lot—no, who looks *exactly*—like Robbie Sweet.

Chapter Nine

How much do you feel in control of the course of your life?

oly—"

The rest of the expletive never makes it out of my mouth because one of the flip-flops I borrowed from Justine suddenly decides that it's a great time to get tangled up in the hem of my jeans and send me sprawling facedown on the floor next to Mr. Rudinski's wheelchair.

"Ow." I roll over on my back, holding my nose.

"Are you all right?" Mr. Rudinski peers down at me, his bushy gray eyebrows drawn together in a frown.

"I'm fine." I try to smile reassuringly, but it's hard to move my lips because it feels like somebody hit me in the face with a two-by-four.

Oh, wait. That was the floor.

Wincing, I pull myself up on my knees and start gathering up the mess. The pudding cups landed close to Mr. Rudinski's wheelchair, but the papers Bethany gave me are scattered all over the place.

"Looking for this?" a masculine voice asks.

No! Please tell me that's not who I think it is. Pleeeeease. I lift my eyes cautiously. Robbie is standing above me, holding Patricia by one of her fat, plush arms. He looks amused.

If this was a daydream, I would now make some sort of incredibly witty comment and impress him with my humor/brilliance. Unfortunately, it's not a daydream. It's real life. Specifically, *ital* real life, which means I just stare at him like an idiot.

He. Is. So. Hot.

You can't imagine. Well, okay, you probably *can*, but it still won't come close to the reality. No wonder Megan was upset when they broke up.

"Hello? Is this yours?" He waves Patricia in front of my face.

The movement snaps me out of my stupor. "Yes. I mean, no!" OMG, I don't want him thinking I carry a baby doll around. "She belongs to one of the residents," I clarify. I get to my feet and take Patricia from him, tucking her under my arm. "I'm babysitting."

"O-kay."

There's an awkward silence as we stare at each other.

"I'm Presley. We go to the same school," I blurt out.

"I know."

You do? He does? If I analyze this revelation too much, my brain will probably explode, so I go with the next obvious question. "Um, what are you doing here?"

"Visiting my grandmother." He jerks his chin toward Mrs. Huberman and Lucinda. "She just moved in yesterday."

"Oh." I try to look casual while I silently digest this information. Lucinda is his grandmother?

He gives me an appraising look. "Why are *you* here? Do you have relatives here too?"

"I come once a week to visit the residents." Then, in case he thinks I'm some kind of weirdo who hangs out in nursing homes because she has no life, I add, "I do pageants and we put a high priority on community service."

"How noble of you." His mouth turns up in a smirk.

"We try."

A laugh bursts out of his mouth. "I'm sure you do."

I don't know what to say to that, so I just stare at him. He gestures to the pudding cups in the crook of my arm. "So are you going to feed those to the doll, or do you have some sort of addiction, or what?"

He's teasing me. Robbie Sweet is teasing me. I wrack my brain for a witty response, but all that comes out of my mouth is, "No. They're for Mrs. Huberman and Lucin—your grandmother."

If he wonders how I came to be bringing pudding cups to his grandmother, he doesn't comment on it. "Let me help you, then," he answers, stepping toward me. As he reaches out to take the pudding from me, his fingers brush against my arm and a jolt of electricity—no, LIGHTNING—skitters through my body.

Except wait. I think lightning and electricity are the same thing. Isn't that why Benjamin Franklin ran out with the kite in the thunderstorm like a moron?

Whatever—it doesn't matter. The point is, even my *teeth* are tingling.

Robbie, on the other hand, appears not to notice the megahot chemistry crackling between us. He's too busy gawking at Mr. Rudinski.

"Dude, I think that dude's having a stroke or something."

"Huh?" I turn in the direction he's looking. Mr. Rudinski is sliding out of his wheelchair, trembling and gasping for air.

What? Like two minutes ago he was asking if *I* was okay, and now he's, oh, I don't know—DYING THREE INCHES AWAY FROM ME?

"Ohmigosh!" Reacting instinctively, I drop the remaining pudding cups and Patricia on the floor and rush over to his side.

Which, to be totally honest, is *completely* out of character for me. I mean, I'm not the person who jumps up and does the Heimlich when the woman at the next table at Olive Garden starts choking on her chicken marsala. I'm the person who spills her Diet Coke all over the table when she jumps up and shrieks, "Oh my God, she's choking! Somebody help her!"

Not that I ever did that, of course. I'm speaking hypothetically.

Yeah. Hypothetically . . .

I glance over my shoulder for a nurse or an aide or maybe a big red button that says PUSH IN CASE OF EMERGENCY, but all I see is Robbie. "Help me get him on the floor," I tell him, desperate.

I half expect him to refuse, but to my surprise he comes

right over. He slides his arm under Mr. Rudinski's back and eases him to the ground.

"Man, he doesn't look so hot."

That's the understatement of the century. Mr. Rudinski looks the furthest from "hot" as you can possibly get. He's stopped gasping and trembling, but now his eyes are shut and he looks sort of . . . blue.

"Ohmigod, I don't think he's breathing!" I drop to my knees and grab hold of his wrist to check for a pulse.

Nothing.

I feel the side of his neck. Still nothing.

As a last-ditch effort, I hold my finger under his nose to see if I can feel breath coming out. But again—nothing. All I can feel is a super-long nose hair.

Lucky for him, I never miss an episode of *Grey's Anatomy*. "Let's get some paddles!" I shriek. "We need to shock him!"

"Shock him?"

Robbie's bewildered tone jolts me back to reality. Right. I'm not actually on *Grey's Anatomy*. "I mean, he's not breathing! He needs CPR!"

I glance up at the faces of the people who have crowded around, hoping the CPR fairy—or, oh, I don't know, maybe a *nurse*—will appear, but I'm met with blank stares.

Okay. I guess that leaves . . . me. I am so dropping a nasty note in the suggestion box when this is all over.

"C'mon, we can do this." Robbie straddles Mr. Rudinski and poises his hands over his chest. "I'll do compressions and you blow in his mouth."

Oh, wow. For some reason it never occurred to me that Robbie would help. I immediately feel a rush of gratitude, but even so, I can't suppress my instinctive reaction.

"Why can't you blow in his mouth?"

"Because I'm doing compressions."

"I can do compressions."

"No, you have to blow in his mouth. You're a girl."

"What, so this is a gender thing?"

"Yes, actually. I'm not rubbing lips with another guy when there's a perfectly fine girl standing right next to me. Now, do you want him to die or what?"

The mention of the d-word propels me into action. I definitely do *not* want Mr. Rudinski to die.

Well, technically, I guess he's dead right now, but you know what I mean.

I kneel at the top of Mr. Rudinski's head as Robbie starts pushing against his chest.

"One. Two. Three. Blow!"

I obediently lean over and blow a stream of air into Mr. Rudinski's mouth. Then I pull back a few inches, waiting for him to sit up and cough the way people do on TV. Except Mr. Rudinski apparently doesn't watch much TV, because he just lies there. Not breathing.

"Okay, let's try again," Robbie orders. This time he does ten compressions instead of three, but when I blow in Mr. Rudinski's mouth, it's the same result. Which is to say, there's no result.

I look up at Robbie. "What should we do?" I say frantically.

"Just keep going."

I have no idea how much time passes before the (clearly horrified) nurse shows up. It feels like hours and hours, but I'm sure it's actually only, like, a couple of minutes. A second, equally horrified nurse is right behind her, trailed by a bored-looking orderly who looks like he'd rather be taking a smoke break out on the terrace.

I can understand why the nurses look freaked. When two teenagers are compelled to do CPR on one of your patients because you're MIA, you can probably kiss that pay raise/promotion good-bye.

"Thank God," Robbie and I say in unison.

OMG. Hunter and Lilly really are rubbing off on me. I'm talking at the same time as random people.

"Get back," Horrified Nurse Number One barks. "We'll take it from here." This command is followed by a death glare, as if she thinks Robbie and I are personally responsible for Mr. Rudinski's nonbeating heart.

Even so, she doesn't have to tell us twice; we practically leap away from Mr. Rudinski. "You're welcome," Robbie mutters.

Almost as soon as the nurses take over CPR, two EMTs show up with a stretcher and pack Mr. Rudinski off to the hospital in an ambulance.

"Do you think he'll be okay?" I ask one of the nurses as the white van pulls away from the building. (Robbie and I followed Mr. Rudinski out into the parking lot.)

"Beats me." He shrugs and follows the other nurses back into the building, leaving Robbie and me alone in the parking lot.

"Well, that was fun," Robbie says drily. "Maybe tomorrow

we can come back and operate on somebody with a penknife."

I know he's being sarcastic, but the "we" part of that sentence makes me feel way more tingly than it should.

"Or we could go to the pool and wait for somebody to drown," I suggest. "You know, to keep up our skills."

As far as witty comments go, it's not exactly, er, witty, but the laugh that comes out of his mouth is deep and musical.

Wait a minute—did I actually just say Robbie's laugh was "musical"? Yeah . . . let's pretend that didn't happen.

His laugh peters to a chuckle, and then his expression returns to normal. "So, I guess I'll see you around."

"You're leaving?" The question comes out way sharper and more pitiful-sounding than I intend. "I mean, uh, don't you need to tell your grandmother good-bye?"

"Nah. My mom and I are bringing her TV over later this evening, so I'll see her in a couple of hours."

The image of Robbie delivering his grandma's TV with his mom is such a normal, boring picture that for a second I can't think of a response. "Oh. That's cool," I say finally.

He grins. "Not according to Nana. When you came in and fell down, she was right in the middle of ripping me a new one because I didn't bring her TV last night and she missed *Lost*." He shakes his head. "Man, I've never been so glad to see somebody fall on their face in my entire life."

Okay, now there are *way* too many things swirling around in my brain. Nana? Did he just refer to his grandmother as Nana? OMG, that's so adorable. But the "never been so glad to see somebody fall on their face" part . . . not so much.

A wave of bummed-out-ness (hey, I coined a new word!) cuts into my adrenaline high. I know it's totally stupid, but I guess I was secretly hoping that he came over to help me up because he was so struck by my beauty, or he found my klutziness endearing or something. Or, worst-case scenario, just because he's a chivalrous guy. But it turns out he was just trying to escape from his angry grandma.

Oh, shut up. A girl can fantasize, can't she?

I manage to force out a lighthearted laugh despite the crushing blow to my make-believe life. "Anytime. Always glad to be of service."

"Thanks." He grins again and gives me a little half-salute/half-wave. "Well, see ya." He turns on his heel and starts walking toward the parking lot.

The abrupt good-bye catches me off guard. "Um, yeah, see ya," I call to his retreating back.

He gestures absently over his shoulder, not looking back. He's already on his cell phone talking to somebody. Probably his supermodel girlfriend. Yasmin. Who I totally made up in my head, but it doesn't matter because she probably exists in real life.

Sigh.

Chapter Ten

How did you prepare for this pageant?

ue to Hunter and Lilly's highly excitable nature (i.e., the one-hundred-percent chance that they will dedicate their lives to driving me crazy if I tell them what happened), I decide to keep the whole Robbie/Mr. Rudinski incident to myself. At least, I try to keep it to myself. But when Robbie gives me a casual "What's up?" and a chin jerk when we pass in the hall the next day at school, I'm forced to spill my guts.

"Um, what just happened?" Hunter demands.

"What do you mean?" I say innocently, trying to feign ignorance while simultaneously trying *not* to start jumping up and down screaming.

"Robbie Sweet just said 'what's up' to you."

"No, he didn't."

"Yes, he did. Just two seconds ago. I saw him."

"I think he was talking to somebody behind us."

"There isn't anybody behind us."

I glance over my shoulder to prove her wrong by pointing out all the people trailing on our heels, but she's right;

the nearest person is, like, a mile down the hall. Rats.

"And," Hunter continues, getting more excited, "you said hi back to him."

"No, I didn't." Technically, this isn't a lie. I said "hey." And how did Hunter even hear that, anyway? I practically whispered it.

"You did so." She lengthens her step and whips around in front of me, blocking my path. Her eyes are sparkling. "Are you using Lilly's idea? Did you ask him to the gala?" she asks eagerly.

"No! You're imagining things. And we're going to be late for class." I try to go around her, but she blocks me again.

Uh-oh. Now she looks all stern and Justine-like.

"Yesterday Robbie Sweet doesn't 'know you exist'"—she makes air quotes—"and today he's asking you what's up. Explain."

Wow. And she even *sounds* like Justine. I don't know whether to laugh or cry.

"All right, all right," I give in. "But not here. I'll write you a note in class."

I won't bore you with the details of Hunter's/Lilly's/Justine's reactions to my Robbie encounter, since I'm sure you can already imagine. Pretty much, it's exactly what I expect. Justine is amused, and Hunter and Lilly immediately start babbling about signs from God and how I *have* to ask Robbie to the gala now. I tell them I am pretty certain God has more pressing things on his mind than my dating life, but I don't think they're listening.

Anyway, enough of my drama-rama (yes! I've been trying to work that word into a sentence forever). I'm about to do Something Important.

Namely, go inside Becky's Bridal Boutique and pick up my new talent costume, which (fingers crossed) hopefully looks as fabulous as Becky promised it would.

Becky is this *amazing* seamstress who does a lot of work for pageant girls. Evening gowns, talent costumes, swimsuits—you name it and Becky can make it. Or alter it. Whatever you need. Her primary business is her bridal store, but her pageant stuff must be running a close second because I swear, everybody goes to her.

"HI! HOW ARE YOU TODAY?" Becky's assistant, Tess, shouts at me as I step inside the shop.

Tess shouts at everyone because apparently, when she was little, her brothers set off some fireworks too close to her head and now she's deaf on one side. That's what Becky told me, anyway. I try to limit my conversations with Tess to one- to four-word exchanges because otherwise I'd be deaf on one side too. I'm not kidding—she is *loud*.

"FINE. HOW ARE YOU?" I yell back. That's the other problem with talking to Tess; you practically need a megaphone to make her hear you. I gesture toward the back of the store where Becky does alterations. "I'M SUPPOSED TO TRY ON MY COSTUME."

She nods enthusiastically. "WE JUST GOT A NEW SHIP-MENT OF STRAPLESS BRAS YESTERDAY."

Er, right. Good to know. "GREAT. THANK YOU." I make a grateful expression and head toward the back as if she's just told me exactly what I wanted to know. Poor Tess—it must be awful not to be able to hear like everybody else.

(Interesting pageant trivia: Miss America 1995 was deaf. And get this—she did *ballet* for her talent.) (No, really. It's true. I read a book about her and everything.)

"Knock, knock." I tap on the wooden screen that hides Becky's messy work area from the rest of the shop, then step around.

She's sitting at her sewing machine, working on a . . . baby dress? Rats. I was hoping she might be working on somebody's evening gown so I could scope it out.

She glances up and smiles. "Right on time," she says approvingly.

I dart my eyes around the space. "Where is it?" I ask eagerly. Normally, I'd spend a few minutes making polite chitchat, but I can't stand the suspense. I *have* to see my costume.

I normally do a traditional ballet en pointe for talent (think flowy pink costume, classical music, my hair in a big bun), but this year I'm going to do a high-energy tap dance to a medley of Elvis songs, and my costume has to be just right if I'm going to pull it off. Because—and this is just between you and me—I'm not that great a tapper.

Don't get me wrong, I'm not, like, horrible or anything.

It's just that, according to my dance teacher, Miss Violet, I'm "more of a performer than a dancer." Which is basically a polite way of saying that I actually suck, but most people don't notice because I have a good stage personality. You know, I distract them with my charm and all that. And part of distracting people with your charm is having a flashy, cute costume—hence, why my costume has to be perfect.

Becky gestures to the row of hooks that holds all her completed projects. "It's in that white garment bag. Why don't you take it in the dressing room and—"

I don't hear the rest of the sentence because I'm already racing toward the dressing room with the garment bag flung over my shoulder. I bang into one of the stalls and yank down the zipper on the bag.

My squeal is instantaneous. "Ohmigosh, it's so cute!"

Becky has totally delivered on her promise—my costume is *adorable*. At least, it looks adorable on the hanger. Now if it will just look adorable on my body, everything will be perfect.

Nervous, I shed my clothes and wriggle into the black-and-white-sequined halter top and the black-rhinestone-studded dance pants. Then I suck in a deep breath and turn around to look in the mirror.

I'm not the kind of girl who ever looks at her reflection and thinks, *Man, I am so hot*, so when the first thing that pops into my mind is, *Hey, not bad*, I'm pretty excited. The dance pants flatter my hips and the top is super-sparkly. I angle to the side. And thanks to the thousands of crunches I've been doing over the past few weeks, I actually feel okay about it showing my midriff.

After a couple more minutes of scrutiny, I feel totally comfortable. I look good.

Excited, I open the door and go out to the ginormous three-way mirror where brides-to-be check themselves out in potential wedding dresses. Becky is waiting for me. "Well, what do you think?" she asks.

"I love it!" I run over and give her a hug. "You're amazing."

"I don't know about that." She laughs off the compliment, but I can tell from her expression that she's pleased. She steps back and motions to the carpet-covered block in front of the mirror. "Stand up there so I can get a better look," she directs.

I spend the next fifteen minutes trying not to fidget while Becky does some sort of sewing thing to the side of the top. Apparently, the seam isn't right or something. I don't know; it looks okay to me.

Finally she's satisfied that everything is perfect and I go to change. When I'm finished, I go to the front to pay my [wince] three-hundred-dollar balance. Becky's policy is half down at the beginning and the rest when you pick up, so if any of you are math challenged (or just not paying attention), that means I'm paying *six hundred dollars* for this costume. Do you know how many hours and hours of babysitting that is? A *lot*. And the sad thing is, that's not even expensive. I know a girl who paid three *thousand* dollars for her talent outfit.

Tess is still behind the counter, but now she's showing jewelry to a twentysomething girl and an older woman I assume is her mother. "THIS CHOKER IS NICE." She passes the girl a thick rope of pearls, then smiles as she catches sight of me. "DID YOU FIND A BRA?"

Oh, man. "Uh, YES." I nod, feeling my cheeks color. The girl and her mom are looking at me.

Luckily, Becky bustles up, saving me from further embarrassment. "C'mon, sweetie, I'll write you out a ticket." She greets the mom/daughter duo, then grabs a yellow pad off the counter and motions for me to follow her over to the little seating area where people can sit and look at different bridal catalogs. I guess she doesn't want to talk over Tess either.

She settles herself in a flowered armchair and starts writing. I swear, Becky must be the only shop owner in the world who still writes out receipts in longhand. And who doesn't have a credit card machine. Can you imagine? Apparently, she has a computer phobia or something.

I sit down in the chair across from her and start thumbing through a bridesmaid dress catalog.

"So," she says conversationally, still writing, "What's that boyfriend of yours up to these days?"

My hand freezes on a picture of two women in coordinating apple green strapless dresses frolicking around a tree. The question is totally innocent, but it hits me like a concrete block. Mostly because I've been trying to pretend like Gabe doesn't exist. Never existed. That *we* never existed. You know, like that movie where Jim Carrey and Kate Winslet hire those people to erase their memories of each other after they break up? *Eternal Sunshine of the Spotless Mind*? That's what I'm trying to do: erase Gabe from my mind.

In other words, I've progressed from repressing my emotions to flat-out denial.

"My John is always talking about that boy," Becky continues. "He even goes out to watch him at the ballpark sometimes. Says people ought to take advantage now, while it's free."

"My John" is Becky's husband, and he's not the only middle-aged sports-nut type who goes to Gabe's games. Gabe's got, like, a whole fan club of them. I think they secretly hope that when he becomes a professional player, he'll remember them and give them free tickets or something.

I murmur something unintelligible, hoping she'll drop the subject, but this is me we're talking about, so of course that doesn't happen.

She tears the receipt off the pad. "Will he be able to come watch you at the pageant, or does he have to stay in town for ball?" she asks, handing me the pink copy.

I clear my throat. "Actually, Gabe and I aren't together anymore. We broke up a few days ago." I restrain myself from telling her *why* we're not together anymore. Becky has a strict rule about not mentioning other pageant girls when you're with her. Period. Even if it's something nice, like *I really like so-and-so's new haircut*. She says that part of the reason people go to her is because they know she doesn't gossip.

"Oh!" Her face registers surprise, and then she immediately turns philosophical. "Well, that's the way romances go when you're your age, sweetie." She pats me on the shoulder. "You date for a while and then you break up. There'll be twenty more boys lined up to take his place."

Ha. If only it was that simple.

Chapter Eleven

What advice would you give on how to pick the perfect mate?

Thanks to Becky so insensitively reminding me of Gabe's existence, I immediately start obsessing about him again. And the more I obsess, the more furious I get. And when I call his cell phone and a robotic message informs me that "the number you have reached is no longer in service," I finally explode.

I mean, WTH? Blocking me from his Buddy List was bad enough, but this is totally ridiculous. What's he going to do next—get a restraining order?

Of course, there might be an innocent explanation for the number change that doesn't involve me. Maybe he lost his phone, or broke it, or maybe it got stolen, even.

But I doubt it.

This is the frame of mind I'm in Thursday afternoon when I ambush him at the City Sports Complex. As far as places to yell at my ex-boyfriend go, the local ballpark isn't exactly my first choice, but with Gabe blocking all forms of electronic communication and Megan hanging on him at school like an extra appendage, it's not like I have a lot of options.

His white Ford truck pulls into the gravel parking lot that borders the little kids' fields at exactly four twenty-nine. In addition to being Mr. Super Athlete, Gabe "gives back" by coaching Little League every summer, hence how I knew he'd be here right now.

I know—doesn't the "giving back" thing just make you want to gag? It makes me want to. Now, anyway. When we were going out, I thought it was sooooo sensitive and sweet. Funny how someone lying and cheating changes your opinion like that.

Gabe parks next to a minivan with a smashed-up front bumper and climbs out of the cab. That's my cue, so . . . wish me luck.

I get out of my car, slam the door, and stride confidently toward his truck.

At least, that's what I intend to do. What actually happens is more like this: I do a panicked lip gloss/hair check in the rearview mirror, fumble my way out of the front seat, wrestle with the door, which for some reason doesn't want to latch all the way, then run/walk toward him because, of course, by this time he's already walking toward the field.

Yeah, well, I never said I was going to ambush him *gracefully*.

"Hey, wait up!" I call to his quickly disappearing back.

He turns instinctively, but when his eyes light on me, it's obvious he wishes he hadn't. In fact, he looks like he wishes he could crawl into the bat bag slung over his shoulder and hide. But it's too late; I'm already on him, and he knows from experience I'm not too proud to take him down in a football tackle.

"Hey," I pant, coming to a halt beside him. My less-than-pretty exit from the car and dash through the gravel has left me out of breath and (I fear) slightly sweaty. I covertly check for forehead moisture.

Gabe watches me warily. "What are you doing here?"

Right. Like he doesn't know.

Instead of answering, I give him a don't-be-an-ass look and say, "Why is your cell phone disconnected?"

The question catches him off guard; this isn't what he was expecting me to lead with. He shifts his weight. "I got a new phone," he says uncomfortably.

"You switched numbers because you got a new phone? Don't you think that's kind of weird?"

"It's not—"

"Speaking of weird," I continue, talking over him, "did you know that I've somehow been blocked from your Buddy List? And your e-mail?" I shake my head in mock disbelief. "If I didn't know better, I'd almost think you were scared to talk to me."

He exhales heavily. "Look, can we talk about this later? I sort of have stuff to do right now." He motions toward the three little boys in red baseball uniforms playing catch in the field closest to us. As if to prove Gabe's point, one of the boys suddenly throws down his glove, rushes forward, and wrestles one of the other boys into a headlock. Apparently not wanting to be left out, the third little boy immediately jumps in too.

Gabe puts his fingers in his mouth and blows an ear-splitting whistle. The little boys break apart like they've been cracked by a whip. "Cut it out!" Gabe yells at them. He turns back to me. He's trying to look annoyed by their roughhousing, but I can tell he's secretly thrilled. He's probably just disappointed there wasn't any blood. Then he could have really gotten rid of me.

"I've got to go. The rest of the team will start showing up soon, and I've got to get things set up."

"Okay. I'll stay for the game and we can talk after," I say agreeably. I start toward the field.

"No!" He lunges for my arm like I've just announced I'm going to go beat one of the cute little boys with a baseball bat. "I can talk for a couple minutes," he concedes. "Let's just do it now."

I suppress a smile. I knew threatening to stay for the game would work. He wouldn't want it getting back to Megan that his ex-girlfriend was in the bleachers.

"Good," I say primly. "We can start with why you're acting like I'm some psycho stalker who you have to change all your info to avoid."

"I don't think you're a stalker," he protests.

I give him a sarcastic look. "Really? Then that explains why you've done everything short of getting a restraining order to make sure I can't communicate with you."

"It doesn't have anything to do with—"

"Are you sleeping with her?" I say bluntly. The best way to

get information out of Gabe is to randomly hurl stuff at him. Half the time you don't even have to listen to his answer; you can find out what you want to know just by looking at his expression. See? Like right now, for example. He looks like he's going to pass out, which means— "Ohmigod, you are, aren't you?"

I stare at him in horror, waiting (no, praying) for him to deny it, but all he says is, "C'mon, Pres, talking about that kind of stuff isn't going to help anything."

"You really are," I say slowly.

"Look, are we finished? 'Cause I *really* need to go now." He glances anxiously toward the field. More players have arrived, and now a couple of parents are on the infield.

I mentally curse whoever came up with the idea of organized sports for first graders. Whatever happened to playing ball with sticks and rocks in somebody's backyard?

I turn back to Gabe. "I need to know why."

"Because the game starts in thirty minutes, and they're waiting on me to start the warm-up."

"I know why you have to go," I snap. "I'm talking about why you . . ." *Left me for Megan*, my brain screams, but out loud I say, "Did this thing with Megan." I have to maintain *some* pride, after all. "And don't tell me it just happened or that it won't help anything to talk about it," I add.

He takes off his baseball cap and rakes his hand through his hair. "I know I've been a total jerk to you," he begins earnestly.

"JUST TELL ME WHY!"

My sudden explosion startles me just as much as it does

Gabe. Ooops. I didn't mean for that to come out quite so loud. Or angry-sounding. "Look, I didn't come here to try and make you grovel," I continue in a calmer, more normal voice. "I'm just trying to understand. I mean, we were together for a long time, you know? I need some kind of . . . closure." This is a complete lie, of course. I *totally* came here looking for groveling. Lots and lots of groveling. My whole goal was to make him feel like you-know-what.

"All right. I get it." He drags his hand across the top of his head again. It's a good thing he has a hat, because his hair needs some serious intervention at this point. "The deal with Megan . . . it was just a combination of a lot of things," he says miserably. "You and I were always fighting about stupid stuff, and we started spending more time apart, and then the season started and you didn't want to come to the games, and—"

"You said you were okay with me not going to all the games this season! You *told* me not to go." I clench my fists, trying to hold my temper. He's right about the fighting and not spending much time together, but the thing about his games is totally unfair.

We came to an understanding about baseball season waaaaay back in January, before the season even started. I was worrying about how I was going to manage school, his games, cheerleading, dance practice, *and* working extra to save up money for Miss Teen State, and he said—all sensitive and caring-like—"Baby, don't stress about my games. I'm a big boy. You should concentrate on your stuff."

"I know," Gabe says when I repeat his words to him.

"Then why are you acting like I suddenly turned into some kind of neglectful girlfriend who never paid attention to you?"

Once again his hand goes back through his hair. I'm starting to be seriously concerned for his follicles. "I don't know. When I said all that stuff, I didn't think it would be a big deal if you were off doing your own thing, but then when it actually happened . . . well, it was a big deal."

"So, what, you just decided to run off with Megan?" I can't keep the bitchiness out of my voice.

He has the gall to look offended. "I didn't *decide* to do anything. Megan started coming to some games, and then she asked if she could practice on me, and then one thing led to another, and . . . I don't know . . . it just sort of happened."

"What do you mean, she asked if she could practice on you? Practice what?" I try to imagine what Megan could want to practice "on" Gabe, but the only images that come to mind are way X-rated.

"Interviewing me. You know, because she wants to be a sportscaster. That's why she started coming to baseball games," he says. "She has to learn everything she can about all the major sports."

I'm sorry. You'll have to excuse me for a moment WHILE I ROLL ON THE GROUND LAUGHING HYSTERICALLY. *A sportscaster?* Please. Megan has as much interest in becoming a sportscaster as I have in becoming a rodeo clown.

"Wow, that's weird," I tell him, struggling not to laugh. "On her pageant bio she always says she wants to be a pediatrician." I refrain from mentioning that *everybody* says they want to be a pediatrician on their pageant bio.

He shrugs. "I guess she changed her mind."

Yeah, that's it.

There are sooooo many more things I'd like to say, but the Bad News Bears are restless.

"Coach Gabe! Coach Gabe!" A scrappy-looking boy whose uniform looks like it's about to swallow him alive runs up to Gabe and thrusts out his lip. "Jayden called me a butthead."

"You're not a butthead," Gabe tells him gravely. "I'll have a talk with Jayden, okay?"

Scrappy's face brightens. "Are you going to kick him off the team?" he asks hopefully. Clearly, he and Jayden aren't exactly BFFs.

"Uh, I don't think that will be necessary," Gabe tells him.

"Oh." He reaches up to hold Gabe's hand in that cute way that little kids do, and I reluctantly accept that I'm not going to get anything else out of Gabe. He has to go do his coaching thing. I *want* him to go do his coaching thing. Because it's kind of hard to hate someone who is standing in front of you holding hands and being all sweet and Big Brother–ish with an adorable little kid. And right now I really need to hate Gabe for a little while. Like maybe a decade.

"I'll talk to you later," I tell him while simultaneously vowing silently to never, ever talk to him again. Which, considering he's practically entered the Witness Protection Program to avoid me, shouldn't be all that difficult.

"Yeah. Talk to you later." He hoists Scrappy onto his back and sprints toward the field.

And that's that. The end. Relationship over.

I turn back toward the parking lot. This time when the tears spill over my lashes, I make no effort to stop them.

Chapter Twelve

How can we encourage the media to report more stories about the good things young people are doing?

ime: eight a.m. Place: the school parking lot. Mental status: mortified. Cause of mortification: see newspaper clipping below.

TEEN COUPLE AIDS AILING MAN

Robbie Sweet, age 17, and Presley Ashbury, age 16, were visiting Willow Oaks Retirement Center on Wednesday when they noticed resident Edgar Rudinski, age 82, struggling to breathe. Sweet, son of U.S. Senator Robert Sweet Jr., and a football standout at Lincoln High School, and Ashbury, the reigning Miss Magnolia Blossom, rushed to Rudinski's side, where they performed CPR until paramedics arrived. Rudinski was transported to Lincoln Memorial Hospital, where he is currently in intensive care. Of the heroic couple, Elinor Harrison, the director of Willow Oaks, commented, "It is refreshing to see young people demonstrate such amazing compassion and heroism. It gives me hope for the future."

I glance up from the article and look beseechingly at Justine. "This is a joke, right? Please tell me this is a joke."

"Nope," she replies cheerfully. "It's on the front page of today's paper. My dad noticed it when he was having his coffee."

"The front page," I repeat.

"Right next to the report about last night's council meeting." Justine is having trouble controlling her laughter.

I start to say that surely they have more important/interesting stuff to put on the front page of the paper, but then I remember where we live.

"It's a nice article," Justine points out.

"Yeah, it is. Except for the teeny-tiny part WHERE THEY CALL ROBBIE AND ME A COUPLE." I wave the clipping around. "What if he thinks *I* had this put in there? He knows I go to Willow Oaks because of my pageant community service. What if he thinks I called up the newspaper to try and make myself look good? And that I told the reporter person he's my boyfriend?"

Justine grabs hold of my arm. "First," she says calmly, plucking the paper out of my hand, "that's just the way they do newspaper headlines. It doesn't mean couple-couple. It means couple as in two. Second"—she shoves the paper into her purse—"I'm pretty sure Robbie Sweet has better things to do with his time than sit around analyzing a stupid article in our Podunk newspaper. And third, he's walking this way, so if you still feel freaked out, you can clear things up yourself."

"*What?*"

"Ciao!" Justine wriggles her fingers and disappears before I can do more than blink at her like an idiot.

I turn around slowly and look across the top of my car. Justine wasn't just trying to screw with my head; Robbie is heading straight for me.

Gulp.

I consider hiding underneath my car, but since he's looking at me looking at him, I guess that's not the best idea. Besides, I don't *know* that he's coming over here because of the article. Maybe he just wants to say hi.

Yes, that's it. I straighten up, feeling more confident. He just wants to say hi. I mean, really, he probably hasn't even seen that stupid article. If it wasn't for Justine, I wouldn't know anything about it either.

A few seconds later he's at my side. "Hey!" I say brightly.

He rips a rolled-up newspaper out from under his arm and thrusts it at me. "Have you seen what's in today's paper?" he demands.

Whimper. So much for the him-just-wanting-to-say-hi theory.

"I swear I had no idea—"

"My father is such a fucking asshole."

"—that they were going to . . . what did you just say?" I blink at him.

"I said my dad is an asshole." He slaps the paper. "I thought I made my point when I quit football, but no, he's still trying to pimp me out."

"Um, what are you talking about?"

He points to the paper. "You saw this?"

I nod.

"Yeah, well I hope it doesn't bother you, because tomorrow it'll be in the state paper and anything else my dad's asshat assistants can get it in. Dammit!" He balls his hand into a fist and punches the air in a really, really violent manner that makes me wonder if maybe I should get back in my car.

I feel behind me for the door handle. I don't do violence, thank you very much. Even from really hot guys and even if it's not directed at me. I had enough of that watching my dad freak out back before he was clean.

My thoughts must be obvious from the expression on my face because Robbie suddenly looks embarrassed. He blows out a breath. "I'm sorry," he says apologetically. "You must think I'm a lunatic."

Yeah, pretty much. "No, I don't," I say out loud. And, in his defense, he does look totally calm now. I let go of the door handle. I think I'm just overly sensitive about that kind of stuff.

He looks at the stream of people heading toward the school entrance. "Walk inside with me?" he asks, cocking his head toward them.

"Yeah, uh, sure." I hitch the strap of my messenger bag up higher and fall in step beside him. I'm curious to hear what he's going to say next, but before we've gone three paces, Romy pushes in between us like a human bulldozer.

"You need to be there at eight instead of nine tomorrow night," she informs me, apparently oblivious to the fact that

SHE'S THE RUDEST PERSON EVER. I mean, seriously, do I look like I want to talk about the stupid gala right now? Can't she see I'm busy? Not to mention, hello—text message, anyone? I hardly think she needed to track me down in person to tell me to show up an hour earlier.

I grit my teeth. "Fine. I'll be there." *Now go away.*

But of course she's not through issuing orders. "And bring some bug spray," she adds. "Last year I found a tick on my leg after I got home."

"Eight o'clock. Bug spray. I got it," I say tersely.

"But not the kind that smells like gasoline. Try to find some that smells good."

"Fine."

She glances over at Robbie as if she's just noticed he's walking beside us. "Are you going to the graduation gala?" she demands.

"It's not on my to-do list." He gives Romy a bemused look. "Although, all this talk of ticks and bug spray is making it sound awfully enticing."

Any moron with half a brain would get that he's being *sarcastic*, but apparently Romy isn't just any moron. "There's going to be beer, too," she tells him, totally serious. "And we have a designated driver system so people don't have to worry about getting home."

"That's great." Robbie smiles at her, then glances over and gives me a why-the-hell-is-she-still-here look. Which, of course, is exactly the same thing I'm wondering. Clearly, this calls for drastic measures.

I send out a silent apology to Nicole for ~~throwing her under the bus~~ the necessary, unavoidable action I'm about to take. "Hey, Romy, that was really sweet of you to let Nicole off the hook like that," I say loudly.

Her head whips away from Robbie so fast I'm surprised it doesn't snap off and go flying across the parking lot. "What do you mean, let her off the hook?"

"You know, about the beverage thing. She told me you said she didn't have to worry about it."

"Harrrr!" Romy charges off without waiting to hear another word.

Robbie stares after her. "Did she just say 'harrr'? Like a pirate?"

I giggle. "Uh-huh."

"O-kay." He turns back to me. I wait for him to say that he'll talk to me later since (thanks to Romy) we're already at the front steps and now the bell is about to ring, but instead, he plops down on the bottom step and pats the empty space beside him like we've got all the time in the world to just hang out and chat.

I look at the patch of concrete next to his thigh, then at the door, uncertain. If Mr. Smooter catches me out of class twice in one week, he'll probably make me go to, like, summer detention or something. But on the other hand . . . I look back at Robbie. He grins as if he knows exactly what's going through my mind and is enjoying my crisis.

Ugh! I swear, sometimes I really hate boys.

I move over and sink down pointedly beside him. "You

were going to tell me about your dad?" I say sweetly.

He laughs, delighted by my spunky personality, which he obviously notices more and more with our every encounter. "Dude, you've got a giant bug in your hair." He plucks what appears to be a cockroach with wings off my scalp and tosses it out onto the grass.

Or not.

"Thanks." I try to act like having bugs in my hair is no big deal. "So, about your dad . . . ," I prompt again. Maybe if he gets all worked up like before, he'll forget that my hair is housing insects.

His face darkens. "My dad is an asshole."

Right. I think I'm pretty clear on that part. "Because . . . ," I say meaningfully, cocking my head.

He rakes his hand through his hair, reminding me uncomfortably of Gabe. Except unlike Gabe, Robbie's dark hair falls perfectly, sexily, back into place, complete with the jagged lock that always hangs down in his left eye. Sigh. Life is so unfair. I bet a bug wouldn't even *think* about taking a stroll through Robbie's hair.

"Look, you know my dad is a senator, right?"

I nod. If another guy asked me if I knew what his dad did for a living, I'd say no because I wouldn't want it to look like I'd been scoping him out, but since Robbie's dad has a giant billboard that says ROBERT SWEET JR., U.S. SENATOR right next to Burger King, it seems sort of implausible to act stupid.

"Well, he's up for re-election next year, and he likes to use me as a campaign advertisement. You know, an I-must-be-a-good-guy-because-look-what-an-all-American-son-I-have sort of thing. So if I'm involved in anything that he can twist to his advantage, he likes to make sure people know about it."

"Are you saying your *dad* put that article in the paper?" I say incredulously.

"Hell yes, he put it in there! I'm sure he had one of his staffers dialing the phone as soon as he heard about it."

"Oh." This scenario is soooooo completely opposite of the scenario *I* was worried about that I'm having trouble coming up with something intelligent to say.

"I told Nana not to say anything, but she doesn't really get it."

OMG, he said "Nana" again. I think I may love him.

(Note: In case any guys are out there, I feel a responsibility to clarify that referring to your grandma as Nana in public only increases your hotness if you're *already* really, really hot. So if you're *not* really, really hot . . . well, you should probably leave the cutesy names to the professionals, okay?)

"That's understandable," I tell him, because . . . well, I can't think of anything else. But at least I've progressed to two-word answers. That counts for something, right?

"Yeah." He blows out a breath and stands up. "Anyway, it's not really that big a deal, I was just pissed off." He holds out his hand to help me up. "Sorry for unloading on you like that. And for making you late," he adds, glancing toward the building.

"It's fine. No problem," I murmur, letting him pull me

to my feet. At least, I *hope* that's what I murmur. It's sort of hard to concentrate because OMG, HE'S TOTALLY HOLD-ING MY HAND AND IT'S SO AWESOME I THINK I MAY PASS OUT.

But once again, Mr. Rudinski has to ruin my moment of ecstasy.

"Hey, that old guy is okay, right?" Robbie lets go of my hand. "I would've gone by to check on him, but I figured my dad would manage to get wind of it and send a news camera to the hospital or something."

Sigh. So much for hoping he might suddenly pull me into his arms and kiss me passionately. "It depends on your def-inition of 'okay,'" I answer, reluctantly returning from la-la land. "Apparently, he needs to have some sort of major heart operation, and the doctors are worried he might not make it through the surgery."

What, you didn't think I just went home and forgot about Mr. Rudinski, did you? Hello, unlike ~~Megan~~ some people, I do have a soul. That's actually what I did right after my show-down with Gabe—went to the hospital to visit Mr. Rudinski. Except I couldn't really visit him because he's in the intensive care unit, and you have to be a relative to go in there. Or so Mr. Rudinski's daughter told me. To be honest with you, she didn't seem to like me very much. It was almost like she was annoyed that her dad was still alive or something. Which totally doesn't make any sense. My mom said she's probably expecting a big inheritance and was disappointed that she's not getting it yet.

Whatever. I mean, what did she want me to do—apologize for *not* letting her dad die?

"That sucks," Robbie says sympathetically.

"Yeah, it really does." I try to think of something else to say—maybe something to make him feel better about his dad—but . . . yeah, I've got nothing. "Um, well, I guess I'm going to go in now," I say awkwardly.

"Okay, have a good day." He smiles and gives me that same little half-salute/half-wave thing he did at Willow Oaks.

Naturally, I assume he's going to go inside too, but when I turn and start up the stairs, I realize he's going in the *opposite* direction, back toward the parking lot. "Aren't you going to class?" I call after him, sounding exactly like a forty-year-old mom. Great. Why didn't I just tell him to be sure and wear a sweater?

He turns and grins at me, walking backward. "I might drop in later. Right now I've got to spend some quality time with my dad."

"Okay," I reply, still sounding like an idiot. But it doesn't matter, because, as always, he's already walking away, silver cell phone at his ear. How does he *do* that? And who is he always talking to?

Oh, right. Yasmin. The sultry, exotic supermodel who lives in an apartment in Italy with her two dogs, Max and Xavier. Every morning when she wakes up, she puts their diamond-studded leashes on them and takes them to the coffee shop around the corner, where she sits at an outdoor table sipping one of those tiny little espresso—What? No, I don't have too much time on my hands. I have no idea why you would say something like that. Geesh.

I have to go to class now. Yasmin is shooting an Armani ad during second period.

Robbie may be ticked at his dad, but when I check the message boards later that night, I wonder if maybe I should send him a thank-you note. Because thanks to the free publicity, I'm, like, a goddess now. Seriously. I have my own thread and everything. Check it out.

> **Felicity12:** Has anybody seen the article about Presley Ashbury in today's *Town Record*? She saved a man's life!!!! You can read the article on the *Record*'s website.
>
> **Tiarachick:** WOW!! How incredible is that?? I just went to the site and read the article and all I can say is . . . WOW!
>
> **Crown75:** I'm not surprised that Presley acted heroically. You can tell just by talking to her that she has a lot of character and integrity. I REALLY hope she wins Miss Teen State. She would be a great representative at Nationals.
>
> **Sparklebabe:** Everybody on the Presley train!!! Presley has been my pick for Teen State forever! I was soooo disappointed when she didn't win

last year. Hopefully, this year's judges won't be blind, deaf, and dumb like the ones last year. ☺

Hotman: What about the guy in the article? Is Presley dating him? Because I've heard that his dad might run for president someday.

Tiarachick: What does his dad running for president have to do with Presley? Who cares what his dad does?

Hotman: LOL—nothing, I guess. I was just thinking about how it would be cool if one of our pageant girls ended up being connected to the White House someday.

Sparklebabe: You guys, this thread is supposed to be about how Presley SAVED SOMEONE'S LIFE. Stop talking about stuff that's irrelevant.

Okay, okay. I'll stop torturing you now. You don't have to read the rest of it. But it is sort of cool, don't you think? Except it's also sort of embarrassing because deep down I know that I am so *not* a hero and totally don't deserve all the nice things people are saying. I mean, I spent, like, *two hours* washing my mouth out with Listerine after I blew into Mr. Rudinski's mouth in case he gave me any gross old-people germs. Does that sound like something a hero would do?

Exactly.

Not to mention that technically, Robbie and I aren't

even the ones who saved Mr. Rudinski. The nurses and paramedics are the ones who got his heart restarted.

And even if Robbie and I had saved him and I wasn't selfish and paranoid, hello—you don't do a good deed and then get off on people talking about how awesome you are. That, like, totally negates the whole thing.

Really, I feel like I should get on the boards and write a disclaimer or something.

You know, like *WARNING: I'm not nearly as good a person as you think I am.*

But it's not so much that I'm enjoying people thinking I'm some kind of super-awesome Good Samaritan. I'm enjoying the *effects* of people thinking I'm a super-awesome Good Samaritan, which are that (a) I look like an even better candidate to be Miss Teen State, and (b) OMG, can you imagine how completely ticked Megan is right now? I bet she has flames coming out of her ears.

No, I bet her whole *head* is engulfed in flames, like Nicolas Cage in that awful ghost-on-a-motorcycle total boy movie Gabe made me watch last year.

The muffled sound of "Sweet Home Alabama" makes me look up from my laptop. Justine is calling.

I scramble to the end of the bed and snag my purse off the floor to fish out my cell phone.

"Hola, Juan, vamos a la playa?"

As usual, Justine is not amused by my charming habit of answering the phone with random phrases from our oral

Spanish quizzes. "No, I don't want to go to the beach," she says wearily. "And I told you to stop calling me Juan."

"Can I call you Juanita?"

"I'm hanging up."

"No, don't hang up! I'll stop, I swear."

"Hmmph."

It's not much of a response, but at least she's still on the line. I swear, she has been so irritable the past couple of days. She says she's just stressed about finals next week, but I don't know . . . she's not usually this testy. Get it—"testy"? Because a final is a test and . . . never mind.

"My uncle said we can borrow his Navigator," Justine informs me, sounding slightly less miffed. "But he said if anybody pukes in it, he's going to make us detail it, buy new floor mats, and give him our firstborn children."

"That sounds reasonable."

When it comes to driving around large groups of inebriated teenagers, Justine's Prius and my Honda aren't exactly the ideal vehicles, so Justine came up with the idea of hitting up her uncle to loan us his ginormous shiny black SUV. You'd think Justine's parents would have a ginormous SUV, but they're "green" rich people. Hybrid cars, solar panels, free-trade coffee, compost piles—they're all over it. No SUVs allowed.

As for my parents—please. My mom drives a 1996 Camaro and my dad drives whatever belongs to his girlfriend of the moment.

Justine mimics a man's gruff voice. "And if we end up in jail, we better not be calling him to bail us out."

"No puke, no incarceration. I think we can handle it."

Justine laughs. "Definitely."

Chapter Thirteen

How do you handle rejection?

The weekend dawns gray and rainy, and for a few beautiful hours it looks like the gala may be rained out, but then just after lunch the storm clouds magically disappear and the sun comes out.

Rats.

Don't get me wrong, I like to hang out and have fun as much as the next person, but like I said earlier, this is the last weekend before Miss Teen State, plus finals start on Monday. So, you know, I sort of have stuff to do. But, as my mom would say, that's why God invented Red Bull.

And I guess she sort of has a point because by downing (an undisclosed number of) the little silver-and-blue cans (sugar free, of course), I manage to work out, practice my tap routine, do interview prep, study for chemistry and Spanish, *and* pack almost all of my pageant wardrobe into the long plastic boxes that are de rigueur for all serious pageant girls before it's time to meet Justine.

Thanks to my mega-productivity, I'm in a great mood as I drive across town to her house, but when I get there, I find

Justine curled up in the window seat of her bedroom wearing grubby sweats and the kind of expression normally reserved for people who have just been told they have six months to live.

"What's wrong?" I rush over to her, distressed. Justine *never* sits around moping about anything. When she's mad or sad or upset, she prefers to "express" her feelings (i.e., fling something highly breakable and expensive against the wall).

I'm not kidding. When we were in the third grade and her gerbil, Daisy, died, she smashed *six* porcelain figurines from her Precious Moments collection before her mom stopped her.

Justine just continues staring out the window like she doesn't even know I'm in the room. "Hey! Can you hear me?" I jostle her shoulder.

She turns her head and blinks at me. "Oh. Hey," she says in a lifeless voice. "I didn't hear you come in."

"So I noticed." I wedge myself in next to her on the blue-and-white cushion. Like the rest of her bedroom, the window seat is covered with books. And books. And more books. I call her interior decorating style "library chic." Except it's not a style; she actually reads all this stuff.

"What's wrong?" I demand. "Why are you sitting here like you're in a trance? And why aren't you dressed?" I gesture to her sweats, which—now that I'm practically sitting on her lap—I can see are not only grungy but also have what look like moth holes in them.

"Nothing's wrong. I was just thinking about something, that's all." She unfolds her legs. "I'll go change."

I fling out my arm, blocking her from getting up. "I know something's wrong," I persist firmly. "Tell me what it is."

I'm trying to act all do-what-I-say-or-die, but even so, I don't really figure she'll tell me anything. Justine is notoriously hard to ~~bully~~ persuade. So you can imagine my surprise when she slumps back resignedly and says, "Fine. I'll tell you the whole sordid story."

The whole *sordid story*? Did she really just say that? Because "sordid story" is how you describe, like . . . I don't know, having an affair with a married man twice your age and getting pregnant with his baby (i.e., things I'm totally unqualified to give advice about and/or make me really, really wish I'd kept my mouth shut).

"Okay," I croak, trying to look composed. "Tell me."

She exhales heavily. "I'll just show you. It'll be easier."

This time I don't try to stop her from getting up. She goes over to her gigantic oak desk (also covered in books) and opens the bottom drawer, where she keeps important papers.

I squeeze my eyes shut. OMG, she *is* pregnant with a married man's baby. And now she's going to show me the ultrasound picture. That must be what she's getting out of the drawer. And after she shows me the ultrasound, she'll start crying, and then she'll ask me what she should do, and I'll have to tell her I don't know. I mean, her parents would be freaked at first, but after a few weeks they'd probably—

"Here."

I open my eyes as she thrusts a white business-type envelope into my hands.

"It's all in there," she says morosely, gesturing to the envelope. "Read it."

Wow. I didn't know you had to read ultrasound pictures. I thought you just looked at them like regular pictures. What sort of stuff do they say, I wonder?

"Okay." My fingers are trembling as I open the flap and reach inside the envelope.

I stare at what I've pulled out. "It's a letter," I blurt out.

Justine gives me a weird look. "You were expecting a car? What else would you find in an envelope?"

"Er, right." Probably better not to mention that I was expecting to find a picture of her unborn love child. I angle the letter more toward the light and start to read.

Dear Ms. Renault,

Thank you for applying for the Director's Summer Program at the National Security Agency. Although your résumé was impressive, we regret to inform you that you were not selected for one of the twenty-four summer intern positions. Please know that this decision is in no way a reflection on your qualifications as a candidate, but rather the highly competitive nature of the program and our policy of giving preference to applicants who are already enrolled in college.

We wish you the best of luck and invite you to reapply for the program in the future.

My first thought when I finish reading is . . . well, nothing, frankly. I have no idea what any of that meant. I frown at Justine. "What is the National Security Agency?"

"The government's cryptology organization." She gives me a duh look, like this is something any random two-year-old in the park knows.

Right. The government's cryptology organization. How silly of me. Now everything makes perfect sense.

Seriously, isn't a crypt like a coffin? Is she saying the government has an entire *office* that studies coffins? That can't be right. It must be something else, like . . . the dead people *in* the coffins. Eeeeew! I knew Justine was watching too much *CSI*.

"So. You're upset because you wanted to study dead people this summer?" I say slowly, trying my best not to sound judgmental.

"Not crypts. Cryp*tology*." She stresses the last three syllables as if better enunciation will make me understand. "It's the practice and study of hiding information."

"You want to learn how to hide information?" Now I'm even more confused. I thought she wanted to be a doctor.

She grabs the letter out of my hand. "Forget it," she snaps disgustedly. "I knew you wouldn't understand."

"No! Wait!" I try to snatch the letter back, but she jams it under her arm and stalks back to her desk.

I slide off the window seat and follow her. "C'mon, Justine," I say plaintively. "Don't do this. Please talk to me."

She whirls around. "How can I talk to you?" she cries. "You're not even smart enough to read this letter! You can't comprehend anything that doesn't involve shiny rhinestones and pancake makeup!"

There's a split-second delay before the tears sting my eyes, kind of like that awful moment after you stub your toe, when the pain hasn't registered yet but you know it's about to hurt really, really badly.

Ouch. That was super-harsh. In all the time we've been friends Justine has never, ever made me feel like I was stupid. Until now.

Justine's angry expression immediately transforms to horror. She rushes back toward me. "Oh, God. Presley, I'm so sorry. I don't know what made me say something so awful. I didn't mean it." She places a hand beseechingly on my arm. "Please don't be mad at me. You know I didn't mean it."

It would be easy to say something nasty and storm out, but I don't. Because even though she just totally ruined my eyeliner and new gray shimmer eye shadow, I know that she's being sincere. She didn't mean what she said; she was just lashing out because she's upset and I'm the only one here. And since she's held my hand through more personal dramas than I can count, I'm going to suck it up and be a big girl.

"It's okay," I tell her. "I know you didn't mean it. I'm not mad." Then, struck by a flash of inspiration, I say, "You're right, you know. I'm *not* smart enough to understand a lot of the stuff you're interested in."

"That's not what I—"

"But," I continue, talking over her protest, "I do understand what it feels like to work hard for something and not get it." (I'm referring, of course, to losing a pageant, but in light of the shiny-rhinestone/pancake-makeup comment I figure I should leave that part out.) "And it feels awful. So even though I may not get all that stuff"—I gesture to the letter, which is still crammed under her arm—"I get that you're upset, and I want you to know that I'm here for you."

OMG, that sounded so mature and insightful! Maybe I could be a therapist someday!

I look at Justine, waiting for her to say something like, *Wow, you're so mature and insightful—I feel tons better just knowing I have you to lean on!*

She blinks at me, opens her mouth . . . then throws herself facedown on the carpet and starts sobbing uncontrollably.

Okay. So maybe I was a little premature with the therapist thing.

"They didn't want me," she wails. "I'm not"—*hiccup*—"good enough."

I stare down at her helplessly. Part of me wants to tell her to stop being such a drama queen, but another part of me understands why she's taking this so hard. I mean, if you've never, ever failed at anything in your whole life, I guess even a tiny rejection like this sort of smacks you upside the head.

See? Justine can talk about how pageants are stupid and evil and pointless all she wants, but maybe if she'd had the experience of watching some hideously ugly girl with a subpar talent and interview take a crown away from her a couple of times, she'd have a few more coping skills right now.

I'm just saying.

Deciding to take one last stab at playing therapist, I crouch down beside her on the floor. "You know that's not true," I say firmly. "They just didn't pick you because you're too young. They want people who are already in college." I may not know what cryptology is, but I at least understood that much of the letter.

"But if I was"—*hiccup*—"super-talented, it wouldn't matter how old I was. They'd"—*hiccup*—"take me anyway."

"You *are* super-talented. You're just the wrong age, that's all."

No response except for the gasping sounds coming out of her throat as she continues sobbing into the floor. If she keeps it up much longer, she's going to have a big carpet burn right on her forehead, and then what will she do? I don't know if concealer will cover that.

Not to mention that we need to be leaving for the gala *pronto*. She's going to have to pull it together.

Since providing mature insight and comfort hasn't exactly been a rip-roaring success, I decide to use the technique Justine uses on me when I'm upset: tough love. Also known as "get over yourself."

I clap my hands. "All right, that's enough of the pity party," I say briskly, standing up. "Go wash your face and change your clothes."

The sobbing pauses. "No. I'm not going."

"Yes, you are." I nudge her with the toe of my shoe. "Get up."

"No." She flips over on her back and stares up at me stubbornly. "I don't want to go. I want to stay here."

We don't have time to play the "yes, you are/no, I'm not" game, so instead of continuing to argue, I just grab her underneath her arms and haul her to her feet.

Mind you, I don't normally manhandle my friends because they refuse to attend social events, but this is For Her Own Good. If she's a no-show, Romy will demote her to alternate. And I'll have to drive drunk people home by myself.

"Hey! Let go!" She flails her arms and legs as I drag her across the carpet toward her giant walk-in closet. Since I'm still jacked up on Red Bull, this isn't particularly difficult, even with the aforementioned arm and leg flailing.

Persuading her to change her clothes and arrange her hair into a style that doesn't look like it was achieved by electrocution is a bit more challenging, but my determined caring and support eventually win her over.

Okay, so I *may* have dangled her iPhone over the open toilet and threatened to flush it if she didn't make herself look presentable, but that was just for dramatic effect. She knows I would never purposely drown expensive cellular equipment.

By the time we navigate the borrowed Navigator (ha-ha,

I just said "navigate the Navigator") into a secluded patch of grass next to a giant oak tree forty-five minutes later, Justine seems pretty much like her old self.

"I hope nobody parks by us," she says pensively as we climb out of the SUV. "Uncle Ronald will flip if anybody scratches his doors."

I glance around our current location, which, give or take a few dozen miles, is roughly fifty thousand miles away from the field where the gala is taking place and/or anything remotely resembling civilization. "Yeah, I think we're good," I say drily.

I mean, I'm all for keeping her uncle's vehicle out of harm's way and everything too, but parking on a different continent seems a little extreme. On the bright side, however, she's acting totally paranoid and worrying about something that's unlikely to happen, which means she's definitely back to her old self. Yay!

Not wanting to interfere with her recovery, I summon up my inner Mature Presley for a second time and follow her through the grass without so much as a peep of complaint. I'm going to be totally Zen for the rest of the night, no matter what happens. Yes, sir. I am the definition of "cool."

Chapter Fourteen

What's your idea
of a perfect evening?

I'm hot," I whine to Lilly two hours later. "And my feet hurt. And"—I duck my head to do a quick body odor sniff—"I reek."

Lilly rolls her eyes. "I told you that you were putting on too much bug spray. It's not like sunless tanner, you know. You don't have to spray it on every inch of your body. You're probably, like, damaging your nervous system or something." She looks away from me and motions to a group of sophomore girls hovering uncertainly around one of the ice chests we have circled around our lawn chairs like an old-fashioned wagon train putting up for the night. "It's okay," she calls to them. "You can help yourself."

Lilly and I are on "guard duty," which is short for "making sure the jocks don't load all the beer into their vehicles and take off." That's right. Not only does the cheerleading squad have to provide the alcoholic beverages, we have to work together in shifts to police their distribution. Sad but true. Speaking of—

"Hey! Put that down!" I spring out of my lawn chair and

charge toward two beefy football players who are trying to covertly carry off an entire ice chest.

"Awww, man." They release the chest, bummed that I've foiled their beer heist. Of course, truthfully, if they hadn't put it down, there's not a whole lot I could have done considering they're, like, three times my size, but apparently that thought hasn't occurred to them. I'd like to think it's because I exude a powerful aura of authority, but, yeah . . . they're just totally wasted.

I trot back over to resume my position next to Lilly, but before my backside has barely even grazed the seat, Lilly is already shooting out of her chair. "Drop it right now!" she shrieks. I turn to see who she's yelling at. Unbelievably, the *same* two football players are now trying to make off with an ice chest that's farther away.

"Awwww, man." Once again they give up their treasure without a fight, but Lilly goes over and gripes at them anyway, presumably to head off a third attempt.

I watch in amusement as they slink off in disgrace. It'll be at *least* thirty minutes before they come back.

Lilly comes back over and plops down in her lawn chair. "Next year I'm bringing one of those dart guns like they use on animals," she announces. "Then I won't even have to get up. I'll just shoot a tranquilizer into anybody who looks like they're up to something."

I picture Lilly in a khaki safari outfit taking down the football team's defensive line like they're unruly zoo animals, and I immediately burst into laughter. "The scary thing is, I actually think that's a good idea," I tell her.

"It is, isn't it?" Lilly laughs with me, but then something over my shoulder catches her eye and her face turns dark.

"What's wrong?" I say automatically. "I swear, if those football players are already back, I'm going to—"

"Don't look!" she says sharply, grabbing my arm as I start to turn in my seat.

I look at her hand on my arm, bewildered. "What are you doing?"

She leans over and puts her head close to mine. "Gabe and Megan just walked up," she says in a low voice. "They're over by Donovan's Jeep."

"Oh." Two seconds ago I was laughing and having fun, but now my shoulders slump as if somebody just dropped a hundred-pound weight on my back. As crazy as it may sound, I sort of assumed the graduation gala was one place I wouldn't have to worry about running into Gabe and Megan. Gabe *never* goes to parties during baseball season. Ever. He says he can't "afford the temptation." And as I mentioned before, Megan doesn't like to associate with the unwashed masses, which means she never goes to anything, period—baseball season or not. So, you know, the thought of the two of them showing up tonight pretty much never crossed my mind.

"What are they doing?" I ask Lilly weakly.

She shakes her head. "Nothing, really. They're just talking to Donovan and some people who are standing around him."

I snort. "You mean Donovan's *customers*?" Remember how I told you earlier about Gabe's friend Donovan, the drug dealer? Yeah, that's who we're talking about right now. Donovan the Drug Dealer . . . That has a nice ring to it, don't you think? Like *Bob the Builder*, this cartoon one of the little boys I babysit watches. Only, you know, with more mind-altering drugs and fewer animated characters teaching valuable moral lessons through the use of construction equipment. Maybe Donovan can work up an act while he's in prison.

"I can't really tell who it is." Lilly leans forward, squinting. "I'm not wearing my contacts. Hey, wait a minute." She swings her gaze back to me. "I thought Justine didn't drink."

"She doesn't."

"Then what's up with that?" She points past me, toward where Gabe and Megan are apparently standing.

I follow the direction of her finger, trying to ignore the ball of dread that has suddenly formed in my stomach.

Just as Lilly described, Gabe and Megan are standing by Donovan's Jeep, chatting it up with Donovan and some other people I'm too freaked out to look at long enough to identify right now. Because barely five feet away from Gabe, Megan, Donovan, and said unidentified people, Justine is sitting on the lowered tailgate of somebody's truck chugging what appears to be a Bud Light.

Wait—it gets worse. Guess who is sitting next to her on the tailgate?

Sebastian Laffoon. Otherwise known as the Pervert Who Gave Me the Disgusting Boob Picture During Detention.

The ball of dread in my stomach is replaced by frissons of panic that shoot through every part of my body. This is bad.

Very bad. Bad, bad, bad. Justine + Alcohol = I really wish I was somewhere else right now. Because awful things happen when Justine drinks. Embarrassing things. Things that require years of therapy to forget.

I know, I know. Now you want me to give you an example of an awful, embarrassing thing that's happened, but I can't. It's too traumatic (see therapy comment above). The most I can tell you is that the last incident involved a moving car, vomit, and a Chihuahua named Sami.

There. Now you have something to think about the next time you're bored.

Except wait, now you're probably thinking Justine's, like, some kind of raging alcoholic or something. She's totally not. It's just that the couple of times she did drink were so completely horrendous that they're indelibly burned into my memory.

"Presley? Hello? Are you alive?" Lilly nudges me in the side.

"I'll be right back," I say absently. Lilly says something else—probably protesting being left alone with the circling beer vultures—but I'm already striding toward ~~the Gates of Hell~~ Justine.

I have no choice, really. Even if she didn't turn into a raving lunatic who wreaks havoc on everyone and everything in her path after she's had a drop of alcohol, she's still not supposed to be drinking right now, tonight. She's a freaking *designated driver*, for Pete's sake. If Romy sees her, she'll demote her to alternate. *After* she kills her.

Speaking of Romy killing people for disobeying her orders—

"You and I need to have a little chat." Nicole steps in front of me, blocking my path. Her face is murderous. "Just what do you think you're playing at, spreading lies about me to Romy?" she demands.

Oooops. I was hoping Nicole might, er, forget about that little incident. And I don't exactly have time to go into the whole I-had-to-offer-you-up-as-a-human-sacrifice-as-part-of-the-greater-good conversation right now, so . . . "Iknowitwasreally-awfulofmeI'msosorryIunderstandifyouhatemelet'stalklater. Bye!" I dart around her and dash off before she has a chance to recover from my sudden projectile confession/apology. She doesn't come after me.

One down, one to go, I think grimly.

I'd like to tell you that I'm so overwhelmed with concern and worry for Justine that Gabe and Megan no longer seem important—and that I'm not even tempted to sneak a look at them when I walk by, but . . . yeah, I think you know me better than that by now. However, even though I'm tempted, I somehow manage to restrain myself from actually doing it. Yay me.

I reach Justine a beat later. As soon as she sees me, her face lights up like a gajillion-watt bulb. "Look, Thebathon! Ith Prethly!" She flings out her arms as if I'm going to leap into them and give her a big hug. A slug of beer sloshes out of the can in her hand and hits me in the eye.

Great.

"What are you doing?" I demand. I grab hold of her arm and try to wrestle the can away from her, but the only thing I accomplish with this slick move is transferring most of the contents of the can to the front of my tank top. Wow, even greater! Oh, well. Maybe it will mask the bug spray.

"What are *you* doing?" Justine counters, giggling like the whole situation is so hilarious she can barely stand it. Of course, in her defense, I don't know why I'm even bothering trying to talk to her logically. Once she makes the leap from happy-drunk to happy-speech-impediment-drunk, it's all over. Besides, I already know what she's doing. She's trying to drown her sorrow over that stupid letter.

"Yeah, what are you doing?" Sebastian seconds. He leers at me. "I don't remember anybody inviting you over here."

Rats. I was trying to pretend like he was invisible.

I give him a death glare. Unlike Justine, he appears to be totally sober. He also appears to be totally enjoying himself. And why wouldn't he be? This is probably the closest he's ever been to an actual girl.

"Shut up," I snap. "This doesn't concern you."

"Oh yeah?" He drapes his arm over Justine's shoulders and looks up at me defiantly. "I'd say you're the one it doesn't concern."

Eeeew! Sebastian Laffoon's *entire arm* is touching Justine. And his underarm! We're going to have to burn her whole outfit now. And her hair—his arm is touching her hair, too! Do you think they make some kind of medicated shampoo that kills pervert germs? Because otherwise we're also going to have to burn the bottom six inches of her hair, and I'm not sure if that would really be a good look for her.

If Justine was in her logical, non-wasted mind, she would have already leaped off the tailgate and raced down to jump in the river, like people on TV do when they're being chased by bees, but as it is, she merely pats Sebastian's face and says, "You're sexthy."

"Okay! Time to go!" I sling Justine's arm over my shoulders and yank her up before she can say anything else that's going to cause her severe mortification for the rest of her life.

"Hey!" Sebastian says indignantly. "What do you think you're doing?" Now that Justine has tossed out the "sexthy" comment, he's *really* not going to let us—well, her—go without a fight. He'd probably shoot me out of a cannon into outer space if he could manage it.

"Please"—*pant*—"Sebastian—" I struggle to stand Justine at least partially on her own two feet, but she keeps slipping out of my hands. Happy-speech-impediment-drunk has progressed to wet-noodle-drunk. "If Romy sees her like this"— *pant*—"she'll kick her"—*pant*—"off the squad."

I don't really expect this attempt at earnestness to make any difference, but to my surprise, his face sobers. "Really?" he asks seriously. "Romy would actually do that?"

A glimmer of hope blooms in my chest. Maybe he'll be reasonable and not make a scene after all. Maybe I can even get him to help me. Because I just remembered that Justine parked the Navigator in Siberia, and I don't think I'm going to be able to drag/carry her all that way by myself. I nod. "In a heartbeat."

"Hey, you wan thome?" Justine shoves the beer can into my face, flattening my nose. The few drops of liquid left in the can dribble down my face onto my chin.

Growl. "Sure," I say tersely. I wrap my hand around the can and tilt my head back as if I'm going to take a sip. Then, I snap forward and throw the can away from me with all the force I can muster.

A second later there's a light *clunk!* and I hear a startled girl's voice say, "Ow!"

My cheeks turn hot. Ooops.

Justine is oblivious to the whole thing. I guess the beer can isn't so appealing now that I'm wearing everything that was in it. She throws both her arms around my neck, almost toppling us over. "I'm thired," she announces.

Sebastian steps toward us. "Let me have her," he urges, holding out his hand. "I can handle this. She'll be fine."

Or maybe I could just hike out to the highway and see if any serial killers are driving by, and send her with them! It'd be about the same thing. Actually, I think I'd rather take my chances with the serial killer.

I shake my head. "No, no, that's okay. I can do it. She's pretty hard to deal with when she's dru—er, like this."

"I can do it," he insists. He tries to pull her out of my grasp, but I yank her back toward me. Justine lets out a squeal.

We're starting to draw attention to ourselves, but I'm at a total loss as to what to do. I have no idea how to make Sebastian go away. At least, not without making a major scene that will draw *everyone's* attention, including Romy's.

I'm about to try my death glare again (if I concentrate, maybe I can make it an extra-super-scary death glare), but then a miracle happens. A knight in shining armor swoops in and saves the day. Er, night.

Oh, all right. So Robbie isn't exactly a knight, but the Tag Heuer watch on his wrist is shiny, and I bet it cost at least as much as a suit of armor. Plus, I've always wanted an excuse to say that.

"What the hell are you guys doing?" Robbie looks back and forth between Sebastian and me as if we've both lost our minds. And, to be fair, I guess we do look a little strange, what with our little game of human tug-of-war and all.

Sebastian and I immediately start babbling at the same time.

"I have to get her to the car, but Sebastian won't—"

"I was minding my own business then Presley comes over and starts harassing my date—"

"Whoa, whoa, whoa." Robbie holds up his hands to cut us off. He arches an eyebrow at Sebastian. "Your date?" he says quizzically.

Sebastian blinks. "Yeah . . . my date." He stands up straighter, and I can almost see the little wheels turning in his little brain. Poor Justine. I can only imagine what sort of rumors Sebastian will have swirling around by Monday.

"Yeah, me and my girl," Sebastian continues, nodding toward Justine, "were just here hanging out, having fun, and then *she*"—he gives me a dirty look—"barges up and starts yapping about how nothing is any of my business and how she's taking her to the car and if I don't . . ." His voice trails off as he notices the look on Robbie's face.

"Get lost," Robbie says softly.

"Right," Sebastian stammers. He starts backing away. "I was just going . . . was just about to, er . . ." He gives up trying to make words come out of his mouth and turns and flees.

I stick my tongue out after him. Ha. Take that, "Mr. Sexthy."

I turn back to tell Robbie thanks, but before I can get a word out, Justine lurches out of my arms. But that's not the good part. After she lurches out of my arms, she staggers into Robbie, looks up at him with a dead-serious expression, and says, "I hath to pee." Then her eyes roll back in her head and she starts to crumple to the ground.

Wet-noodle-drunk has now turned into passed-out-drunk.

Robbie and I both reach out to grab her at the same time, but since she's basically sliding down his body, he beats me to it. "Man, how much has she had to drink?" he asks me, swinging her up in his arms like a doll.

I immediately consider pretending to pass out too, but decide against it when I realize I'd probably just end up eating dirt since he's already holding Justine. "Um, two beers, I think. No, wait—just one. I'm wearing most of the second one."

"She passed out from one drink? How is that possible?"

Under normal circumstances, I'd explain about Justine's

whole freaky intolerance thing, but the loud *Warning! Warning! Danger!* alarms that just started going off in my head are making it kind of hard to concentrate. Because I just spotted Romy talking to a group of people who are standing dangerously close to us. And even though she's laughing and looks completely involved in the conversation, she could totally glance over here at any second.

And Romy + glancing over here = bye-bye Justine's squad membership.

"Can you help me take her to the car?" I blurt out.

If my abrupt conversation shift catches Robbie off guard, he doesn't show it. "Yeah, sure," he says easily. His gaze swings over the rows of vehicles parked haphazardly around the party area. "Where are you parked?"

"Siberia— I mean, uh, you can't see it from here." No need to mention that the car is in another state until absolutely necessary, right? "C'mon, I'll show you." I grab hold of his shirt and start speed-walking toward the Navigator. At least, I hope I'm speed-walking toward the Navigator. To be honest with you, I can't exactly remember what direction Justine and I came in from. But it doesn't matter; the important thing is that we're walking *away* from the party (i.e., Romy).

"Have you got an appointment or something?" Robbie asks a minute or so later, after I almost mow over a sophomore girl getting out of a red Saturn. "Or are we, like, running from the police?"

Ooops. I guess I am acting a little crazy. I force myself to slow down to something resembling a normal pace. "Sorry."

I gesture to Justine, who now has drool dribbling out of the corner of her mouth. "It's just that if Romy sees her like this, she'll go ballistic. We're supposed to be designated drivers."

"Romy—that's the bug spray chick, right? The pirate?"

I nod. "Otherwise known as our cheerleading captain."

See what I mean about cheerleading not getting you anything at our school? I mean, wouldn't you think most—no, *every*—guy in school would be able to identify the captain of the cheerleading squad? Although, granted, I guess Robbie isn't exactly most guys. Speaking of which—

"Hey, what are you doing here, anyway?" I ask teasingly. "Did Romy really entice you with the bug spray?" Now that I've managed to get Justine (at least temporarily) out of danger, other, nonrelated thoughts are finally filtering into my brain. In other words, I've switched from *OMG, Romy is going to kill us! OMG, I have to do something!* to *OMG, what is Robbie doing here? OMG, what if he came here to see ME?! Is that possible? And if he* did *come to see me, what does that mean? Is he in love with me? Did he break up with Yasmin?*

He shrugs. "Nah. I just came to get spectacularly wasted and hopefully get arrested for DUI. I paid my cousin fifty bucks to come out in a couple of hours and help me drive my 'Vette into a ditch up by Highway 16 where the state troopers patrol. It shouldn't take long for one of them to spot me."

I wait for him to laugh or grin or otherwise indicate that he's, oh, I don't know—JOKING, MAYBE—but no. He just keeps calmly tramping through the grass as if he's just announced that he's paying his cousin to pick up his dry cleaning.

And maybe that is what he just said. Yeah, that's it. Dry cleaning, DUI. All the stress I've been under lately must be affecting my hearing. Nobody *tries* to get arrested for DUI. That's crazy. That's like *trying* to get an F on a test. Except worse, because if you fail a test, they don't lock you up in jail.

I laugh. "Ohmigosh, for a second I thought you said you were paying your cousin to help you get arrested for DUI."

"That is what I said."

I stop walking and whirl to face him. "What? Are you insane? Don't you know you can go to jail for that?"

He sighs. "God, I hope so. But with my luck, they'll probably just let me go after they run my plates. That's what they always do with my sister. Well, actually," he amends, "they don't let her go; they call my mom to come get her."

It's official: I am in Bizarro World. No, I'm the MAYOR of Bizarro World. Really, I should have an office and everything. With a little sign on the door that says WELCOME, PSYCHOS. PLEASE TAKE A NUMBER.

"I realize this may be a stupid question, but why, exactly, would you *want* to get arrested and go to jail? I mean, are you just trying to ruin your life, or are the voices talking to you, or what?"

"Presley, Presley." He shakes his head indulgently. "Nobody's trying to ruin anybody's *life*. I'm simply trying to . . . how shall I put this? Keep my dad on his toes."

"Keep your dad on his . . . *Oh*." I fall silent as everything finally clicks into place. "You're trying to get arrested to embarrass your dad," I say flatly.

He grins, pleased I get it. "The road goes both ways, you know what I mean?"

"Oh yeah. Real brilliant." I slant him a disgusted look and take off in a burst of speed-walking. God must feel at least a teeny bit sorry for me, because I think I'm actually going in the right direction. Yep. The Navigator should be popping into view any hour now. Which is good because suddenly Romy isn't the only person I want to get away from.

Chapter Fifteen

If you could go back and relive part of your life, which part would it be and why?

I know. I'm obviously defective or something. Nobody wants to get away from the Hottest Guy in the Universe. But don't worry, even carrying Justine, Robbie catches up with me in, like, three steps.

"Why'd you look at me like that?" he asks curiously.

"I don't know what you're talking about." I try to walk even faster, but it's pointless. He stays beside me easily. And (even more annoying) while I can feel rivulets of sweat running down my temples and the front of my bra, he still looks totally perfect.

"Are you . . . mad at me?" His voice goes from curious to astonished.

"No." I cut to the left as the giant oak tree where the Navigator is parked comes into view. "There's the car," I say briskly. "If you'll just help me get her inside, then I'll drive you back to the party. I wouldn't want to interfere with your plan to act like a total jackass."

Ooops. I didn't mean to say that last part out loud.

Okay. You're right. Yes, I did. Because even though Robbie

is so incredibly gorgeous it should be illegal, I can't STAND spoiled rich kids who don't appreciate what they have and do stupid stuff like PURPOSELY GET ARRESTED.

Don't get me wrong, I'm not trying to act like privileged kids don't have problems too. I know they do. And I know Robbie's dad is a jerk. But seriously, I thought Robbie was smarter than that.

"I knew it. You're mad at me."

"That's crazy. Why on earth would I be mad at you? I mean, it's not like you're acting disgustingly spoiled and immature or anything." I shove my hand into the pocket of Justine's jeans as we walk, searching for her uncle's keys. "I think purposely getting yourself arrested for DUI because you have some sort of stupid Oedipus complex about your dad is a *great* idea. Really fabulous."

Robbie gives me a strange look. "You think I want to kill my dad and marry my mother?"

"What are you talking about?" I say irritably. I've managed to close my fingers around the keys, but now my hand is stuck in Justine's pocket because she's wearing the super-tight Luckys I convinced her to buy at the Buckle a few weeks ago. Great. This is my reward for giving her good fashion advice. Now I'll probably have to have my hand amputated.

"That's what an Oedipus complex is," he answers. "When a boy hates his dad and wants to kill him so he can have his mom all to himself."

"It is?" I glance up, startled.

"Yeah, you know, from the Greek play *Oedipus Rex?*" A

smile is playing around the corners of his lips, as if he's trying not to laugh.

Rats! Is everybody in the whole world smarter than me? And isn't an Oedipus Rex a dinosaur?

Sigh. That's what I get for trying to use words I heard on *Oprah*.

I go back to trying to free my hand from Justine's pocket of death. "Well, what's it called when"—yank—"a rich, smart, good-looking guy who"—yank—"has everything going for him"—yank—"acts like a complete immature jackass?" *Rip!* I stumble backward as Justine's pocket suddenly splits away from her jeans.

I right myself and look back at the scene of the crime to survey the damage. Instead of a pocket, Justine now has a jagged piece of material flopping against her leg. But, on the bright side . . . I got the keys out! And, more important, now I don't have to get my hand amputated. I'll just tell Justine I was trying to give them that distressed look.

Apparently, being referred to as a jackass twice in one conversation is the limit of Robbie's good humor. He gives me a hostile glare as I hit the keyless entry and go to open the back door of the Navigator. "Look, just what is your deal?" he demands.

Sigh. I wish I knew. Because if I did, I'd beat my deal to death with a club so I could stop compulsively saying stuff that's going to make Robbie hate me.

"My deal is that you just told me you're going to do something completely stupid and self-destructive for a completely stupid reason." I swing open the door and gesture for him to deposit Sleeping Beauty inside. "I mean, what am I supposed to say after you tell me you're trying to get put in jail, 'Way to go! Awesome! I'll look for your mug shot in the paper'?"

More hostile glaring. Angling his body to the side, he leans in and lays Justine carefully across the beige leather seats. She immediately draws her legs up into the fetal position and starts sucking her thumb.

At least, that's what I'm going to tell her tomorrow, anyway. (Oh, come on! Look at all the hell she's putting me through. I'm at least entitled to torture her a little, right?)

He ducks back out, closing the door with a quiet *click*. His face is stony. "You don't know the first thing about my reasons," he says icily. "Or my relationship with my father."

Don't say it, don't say it, don't say it, I chant silently. "Are you referring to how I don't know that you feel like your dad loves his political career more than you? Or how I don't know that you resent the hell out of him for treating you like a commodity instead of a son? Or"—I slam my hand down on the Navigator's hood—"how I don't know that you're a walking cliché, a poor little rich boy getting in trouble with the law so his daddy will notice him?"

Great. So much for not saying it. What is *wrong* with me?

I wait for Robbie's reaction, my heart pounding painfully against my chest. Thanks to my little experience playing therapist with Justine earlier, I have no delusions about him suddenly going, *Wow, you just totally pinpointed all my deepest, darkest fears! Obviously you're my soul mate. Let's run away and get married!*

More like, *Who do you think you are? Go to hell. I hate you.* Or something along those lines. You get the idea.

But as things turn out, I end up *wishing* he'd just told me to go to hell.

He flashes his teeth. "You should be careful tossing out those walking cliché accusations. Because the poor girl from the wrong side of the tracks trying to use her looks to move up in society isn't exactly an original." He says each word softly and precisely, watching me with cold eyes as I absorb their meaning.

Unlike earlier when Justine called me stupid, this time there's no delay before the tears sting my eyes. It's instantaneous. Not so much because of *what* just came out of his mouth, but the *way* it came out of his mouth. I mean, duh—of course I'm hoping beauty pageants will help me move up in the world. That's sort of the point. I've never tried to pretend anything else. But to have somebody—especially Robbie—say it in such a cruel, condescending way . . . well, I sort of feel like throwing myself down on the ground and bursting into tears like Justine did in her room.

Or, alternately, starting up the Navigator and running him over.

Hmmn. Weeping in the grass or vehicular manslaughter? It's so hard to decide.

In the end I decide to go with something in between. "Go to hell." I give him a withering look, then stalk around the front of the Navigator and yank open the driver's side door.

Don't worry. I'm not going to run him over. I'm just going to leave. But I'm *not* giving him a ride back to the party. He can hoof it back on foot. And then he can go get arrested or jump off a cliff or do whatever asinine thing he wants. I don't care.

I mean, I'm not saying I handled the situation perfectly just now, but I had good intentions. What I said to him wasn't very nice, but I said it to try to help him, to show him that he's making a mistake. Whereas what he said to me was only meant to be cruel. And I've got enough people being mean to me already, thank you very much. I don't need another one, no matter how ridiculously hot he is.

So what I'm saying is . . . Yasmin, I apologize for giving you that extremely rare and highly contagious skin disease that requires you to live in a plastic quarantine chamber in the basement of a remote hospital in Uganda, which is what I did earlier today when I was packing my pageant stuff. You can have Robbie back now. I'm going to become a nun.

The next four hours are—not to put too fine a point on it—HELL. Because I have to:

1. drive Justine home and sneak her (barely conscious body) upstairs past her parents.
2. drive *back* to the party and sell Romy the only semi-plausible lie I can come up with (Justine tragically stung by a wasp, deathly allergic, blah, blah, blah).
3. haul ten thousand stupid drunk people around town by myself.

4. do all of the above while alternately fuming/trying not
   to cry about the Robbie-being-a-total-jerk thing and
   the Gabe-showing-up-with-Megan thing.

You'd think that by the time I peel the last drunk person out of my car (it seemed wrong to take the Navigator without Justine), all I'd want to do is go home and go to bed, but the thought of my empty house makes me feel even more depressed. I don't want to be alone. I want to talk to somebody. In other words, I don't care if I'm seventeen; a boy was mean to me and now I want my mommy.

Well, truthfully, I want Justine, but she's unconscious, so I have to go with my backup person. Not that my mom is going to pat me on the head and make me cookies or anything, but being around her will make me feel better.

When I get to the station, my mom—excuse me, Hot Holly—is in the DJ booth, punching the illuminated buttons on the phone. It's two forty-five, which means she's taking caller requests. She used to do request hour at the beginning of her ten p.m.-to-five-a.m. shift, but she pushed it back to two because—and this is an exact quote—"the public has shit taste in music."

The idea was that more people would be asleep at two a.m. and thus not calling her to request crappy music, but yeah . . . apparently the kind of ~~freaks~~ people who call in to radio stations at night are also the kind of people who ~~still live in their mom's basement even though they're thirty-five~~ don't exactly have regular bedtimes.

Not that there's anything wrong with calling in to radio stations. I actually call in to my mom's show myself. Of course, that's usually just to annoy her by requesting the Jonas Brothers, but still.

My mom's face lights up when she sees me standing outside the booth. I'd like to think it's because she's so thrilled to see me, but I suspect her excitement has more to do with the giant gas station cappuccino in my right hand.

She immediately presses a series of buttons then takes off her headphones and motions for me to come inside.

"Coffee delivery." I hand her the thick paper cup with a flourish.

"You're an angel." She closes her eyes and takes a long, grateful sip. My mom drinks coffee like other people drink water. Which used to worry me, but Justine says that coffee has a whole bunch of health benefits, so now I actually try to encourage her to drink it. Because God knows that's the *only* substance with health benefits that ever enters my mom's body.

My eyes flick to the overflowing ashtray at her elbow and I let out a sigh. "You know you're not supposed to be smoking in here." I scoop up the ashtray and dump it out in the little plastic trash can by the door. "This is a non-smoking building."

"What else am I supposed to do?" she complains. "It's not like I can go outside for a smoke break. I'm the only one here."

I toss the ashtray back on the table. "You could try not smoking at all."

Ha. Like that's ever going to happen. We have this conversation almost as often as the "could you please date a normal guy like an accountant" discussion with almost exactly the same results. In other words, *no* results. The closest my mom has ever come to quitting smoking was the time she ordered a *Quit Cigarettes the Easy Way* hypnosis CD off the Internet. A CD that she promptly decoupaged and started using as a drink coaster.

"Oh yeah. That's a great idea." She slants me a sarcastic look, but then her gaze turns into a frown. "What are you doing here? I thought you were going to a party."

I gesture to the big clock above the door. "Mom, it's almost three in the morning. The party is over."

"Oh." She purses her lips, and I can tell she's trying to keep herself from saying something un-mother-ish, like *When I was your age, we partied all night.* "Well, did you have fun?" she asks finally.

The question is all the invitation I need. I sink down onto the floor beside her chair and start spilling my guts. "No. It was awful. Gabe showed up with Megan, and Justine got really messed up and I had to hide her from Romy, and then this guy—"

I break off as she flaps her hand for me to be quiet. She slips her headphones back on and opens her mike. "That was back-to-back Velvet Revolver," she says in her throaty Hot Holly voice. "And now, boys and girls, we're going to take a little trip down memory lane, back to the nineties. Because Kurt Cobain may be dead, but his spirit still rocks. And, of course, by that I mean his *Teen Spirit*. We're going to start off a rock block of ten hits in a row with a little Nirvana." She flips another switch, then shoves her headphones back down on her neck. "Sorry," she says apologetically. "But now we have more time."

I blink at her. "His spirit still rocks?"

She shrugs. "I'm not feeling very creative tonight." She picks up the cappuccino and sips. "Go on with what you were saying. I want to hear about everything."

I suck in a breath and resume my recap of the evening. I intend to go into detail about Gabe and Megan and Justine, but somehow I only end up talking about Robbie. As in, I tell her *everything* about Robbie. Our CPR adventure, the newspaper article, his dad, Yasmin, his possible short-lived romance with Megan, his stupid plan to get arrested, the condescending and cruel way he talked to me. And then I burst into tears. Big fat tears that run down my face and drip onto my shirt. The kind of tears that destroy all your makeup—even your lipstick—and give you a bad case of the hiccups. Tears that, if Justine was here, would make her give me a hug and suggest that we go buy some prepackaged cookie dough and eat it raw, potential salmonella poisoning be damned.

But Justine's not here, so my mom dries my tears with her own unique brand of consolation. "Come on," she says, holding out her hand. "Let's pick out some angry rock songs and dedicate one to 'R.' There's no better therapy than telling someone to eff off with a screaming guitar solo."

And that, children, is how the little girl and her mommy ended up playing really loud rock songs with explicit lyrics until the sun came up. The end.

(Well, not the *end*-end. You know what I mean.)

Chapter Sixteen

Would you like
to be famous?

I want to die."

Justine slumps against the wall next to our locker on Monday morning looking like—well, death.

In other words, it's . . . Happy Hangover Day! Most people recover from their alcoholic indiscretions within twenty-four hours, but as we've already established, when it comes to alcohol, Justine isn't most people. Or any people. Seriously, I think a scientist should, like, study her or something.

I pat her on the shoulder and try to look sympathetic instead of disappointed. Because I have a *ton* of "Mr. Sexthy" jokes and assorted other embarrassing comments primed and ready to go, but I can't torture her in good conscience until she's at least semi-human. Not to mention that we need to have a *serious* conversation about appropriate ways to deal with rejection.

"Have you taken any ibuprofen?" I ask her.

She closes her eyes. "Yes."

"What about water? You know you have to keep hydrated."

"I drank four Aquafinas on the way to school."

"Oh." I try to think of something else that's supposed to be good for a hangover, but all I come up with is drinking a raw egg. Eeeew.

"Well, at least you won't have to fake feeling bad if you see Romy," I point out. "You are supposed to be recovering from a near-death experience, after all."

She opens one eye. "What near death experience?"

"You know, the wasp sting, your terrible allergy, how I had to rush you home so you could get medicine?" I wait expectantly for some sign of recognition, but her face is blank. "Justine! Didn't you read my note?"

Now her other eye opens. "What note?" she asks, frowning.

"The note I left for you after I saved your butt Saturday night." After I practically gave myself a heart attack dragging her dead weight up the three million stairs leading up to her bedroom, I wrote out a detailed note explaining our cover story. Because, you know, I didn't figure she'd be answering her cell phone, and I wanted her to be clear on the facts in case Romy decided to drop by her house the next day or something. Of course, now I can see the hundred or so flaws in that plan—particularly that Justine's parents wouldn't have gone along with it—but I was stressed at the time.

She blows out a breath and gives me a that-was-a-stupid-idea look. "I haven't exactly been up buzzing around my room," she informs me drily. "Where did you leave it?"

"I pinned it on your shirt with a hair clip."

"Oh." There's a beat of silence as she digests this. "Well, what did it say?" she asks finally, apparently unable to think of a comeback.

"You had to leave the party because a wasp stung you and you have a life-threatening allergy to wasps. I had to rush you home so your mom could give you one of those shots. You know, like that girl at cheer camp last year? The one who got stung by a bee and started, like, choking, but then her coach pulled that pen-thingy out of the equipment bag and jabbed it in her leg and she was fine? Romy didn't even give me a hard time," I add proudly. "She just said to make sure you didn't die because then we'd have an odd number and that would screw up all our formations." I wait for her to compliment my genius, but instead she looks mildly horrified.

"You told Romy I had an anaphylactic reaction?" she says incredulously.

I frown. Wasn't she listening to anything I just said? "No, I told her you got stung by a wasp and had to get a shot."

"Presley, people who have insect venom allergies severe enough to cause anaphylaxis requiring treatment with epinephrine usually have to—"

The bell for first period clatters loudly, cutting off whatever the heck it is she's talking about. How can she still sound like a human computer when she's hungover?

"Owwwww," she moans, clapping her hands over her ears as the shrill sound vibrates through the halls. The awful grimace on her face reminds me of this picture we studied in ninth-grade art called *The Scream*. It's this really famous painting by . . . uh, a painter. Probably a famous one. I can't remember. I think I got a D on that test.

"C'mon. We have to go." I motion to the flow of people heading down the hall, away from the lockers, indicating that we should join them, but she thrusts out her bottom lip.

"No. I can't go into that gym. I'll die."

I try to suppress my impatience. Not to sound insensitive or anything, but I'm sort of tired of babying Justine. "You have to go," I reply calmly. "They're taking roll, remember?"

Normally, we only have to show up during finals week if we have an actual test, but this year the principal—in all his infinite wisdom—decided that everybody except seniors has to put in a full week of attendance. Except he apparently forgot to mention this little detail to the teachers, and when they found out last week, they were ticked. Because, you know, they thought they were pretty much rid of us. So now anybody not taking a final is supposed to report to the gym.

I know. It's so inhumane. What do they think we are—cattle?

"Pleeeease?" Justine drops her hands from her ears and looks at me pleadingly. "Do you know how loud it's going to be in there? My head will explode. Besides, there's no way they can take attendance with that many people."

Wow. This isn't just Hangover Day; it's Opposite Day. *Justine* wants to cut class. Er, gym. Fake class. Which brings up a good point: Why *should* we go sweat in the gym all day? It's not our fault the principal is an idiot.

Besides, Justine looks so pitiful I have to do what she

wants. "Okay," I concede. "But where are we going to go?"

"The library," she answers immediately. "So I can sleep in one of the study rooms."

"Good idea." Ms. Windsnap, the librarian, is roughly two thousand years old; she wouldn't notice if a herd of purple zebras stampeded through the library, much less a couple of unauthorized students hiding out in a study room. Although calling them study "rooms" is a little grandiose. They're more like study closets.

Our plan decided, we leave the locker bay and walk toward the library at roughly the pace of a snail gliding through molasses. Justine may be able to use big words like "anaconda reactor" (or whatever it was she said a minute ago) when she's hungover, but her ability to walk upright is seriously questionable. We haven't even gone ten feet before I'm carrying her purse, her backpack, and half her weight.

As we crawl along, I find myself glancing at the faces of passing guys, subconsciously looking for Robbie. Well, okay. I guess it's not subconscious since I know I'm doing it. *Why* I'm doing it, I have no idea. Robbie is a senior; there's no reason he would be strolling by. Like I said, the seniors are already through with school. They don't have to endure finals week.

Not to mention that I don't care if I ever lay eyes on Robbie again. He's dead to me, just like Gabe and Megan. Or so I'm telling myself.

When we (finally) get to the library, Justine immediately goes into a darkened study room and curls up on the floor, using her backpack as a pillow and my jean jacket as a blanket. I try to stay in the room with her, using the light from my cell phone to look over my English notes, but after fifteen minutes my fingers and toes feel like they have frostbite. The air conditioner vent takes up all of the tiny ceiling, and it's *freezing*.

I glance over at Justine. She looks pretty cozy under my jean jacket. Hmmn. Should I steal it back from her?

No, that would be mean. I guess I'll just go out into the library. It's at least a few degrees warmer out there.

I slip quietly out of the room and wind my way through the tall oak bookshelves toward the row of student computers near the checkout desk. Obviously, Justine and I aren't the only ones who weren't thrilled about the idea of spending all day in the gym, because there are quite a few people milling around.

I find an unoccupied computer and sit down to check my poor, neglected e-mail. With everything that's been going on, I haven't looked at it in forever. Not that I get a lot of important messages or anything, but sometimes my dad e-mails me from the road.

Sure enough, when I open my account, I find a message from him hidden among all the penis-enlargement/Viagra/Canadian-pharmacy/meet-singles-in-your-area advertisements.

Hey, baby!
Hope you and your mom are doing okay. Me and the band are good.
Luv ya,
Eddie

As you can see, my dad is a man of few words. But, oh well. At least I know he's alive.

I send him a reply, then close out my e-mail and cruise over to see what's happening on the pageant boards. When the home page comes up, I'm surprised to see that the newest thread is titled "Presley Ashbury Shocks Pageant Watchers."

Huh? Are they talking about the thing with Mr. Rudinski? I thought all that had died down.

I click the link, and my stomach flutters as a photo starts to load. I lean forward. By the time the picture finally appears, I'm so keyed up I can't immediately process what I'm seeing.

"Oh. My. God." I gape at the screen, my heart thudding in my ears. It's a picture of Justine and me, obviously taken Saturday night. Which wouldn't be a big deal except it was apparently snapped AT THE EXACT MOMENT I WAS PRE-TENDING TO DRINK SOME OF JUSTINE'S BEER.

I clutch the edge of the table. A million thoughts flood my brain simultaneously, the predominant one being *How can I kill Megan and not get caught?* Because even though the picture was posted by (shock) "Anonymous," I know it was her. Duh—of course it was her. Who else would it be? She was practically stand-ing right by us. She must have taken the picture with her phone.

Okay. Deep breaths. Maybe it's not as bad as I think. I reach shakily for the mouse and scroll down.

Crownguru: Unbelievable! She should be disqualified from competing at state.
Queenoftheworld: I agree with Crownguru. What

kind of an example does this set for other girls?

Tiarachick: It's common knowledge that Presley is a party girl. I'm surprised it's taken this long for the truth to come out.

A party girl? Are they serious? The most risqué thing I've done in recent memory is change lipstick shades. They're acting like I spend my weekends shooting footage for *Girls Gone Wild* or something.

The rest of the thread is more of the same, with one particularly supportive person suggesting the police should charge me with a minor in possession offense.

Right. So much for it not being that bad.

If I was a selfless person, I'd turn off the computer and keep this to myself, but selflessness has never been one of my strong points, so I go drag Justine out of the darkened study room so she can share in the mortification.

"I don't want to look at anything," she whines as I push her down in front of the computer. "I want to go back to sleep."

"Trust me. You want to look at this." I click the mouse and bring the screen back up.

She stares blearily at the picture. "Those girls look sort of like you and me."

I sit down in the chair next to her. "They *are* you and me, idiot. Somebody took a picture of us Saturday night." I know, I know. The idiot part was uncalled for, but I'm stressed, okay? I'll apologize later.

Whatever is left of Justine's hangover disappears instantly.

"What? Whose page is this?" She yanks the mouse out of my hand and starts clicking it furiously. One of the million or so things she likes to obsess about is the possibility that she'll somehow end up on somebody's MySpace page in a way that's unflattering and/or embarrassing and that a college admissions person will see it. Apparently, she saw a news program about people getting their applications rejected over stuff like that or something. I don't know.

"It's not on anybody's page," I tell her. "This is the pageant message board."

"Huh?" She gives me a confused look. "Why would somebody put a picture of us on a pageant message board?"

"Not somebody. Megan," I correct. "She's trying to make me look bad. All the judges and directors read the boards, so now they're all going to think I'm some kind of trashy slut. It actually doesn't have anything to do with you. You just happened to get caught in the picture."

Of course, technically, it has everything to do with Justine since THIS IS ALL HER FAULT, but saying that would just make her feel bad. I mean, it's not like she purposely got drunk and caused all this to happen.

"Oh." She frowns, digesting this information.

"Read the rest of it," I tell her, gesturing to the screen. "You'll see what I'm talking about."

"They're ripping you to shreds," she says a few moments later when she finishes reading.

"Gee, you think?"

"Well, aren't you going to defend yourself? You need to get

on there and explain. Tell them none of that stuff is true."

I give her a pitying look. Ahhh, to be so naive. "If I try to defend myself, it'll just make it worse."

"But there must be something you can do," she protests.

"Yeah, there is." I reach over and close out the screen. "I can drop out of the pageant."

"You wouldn't." Justine looks at me as if I've just announced I'm going to cut off one of my arms.

"Yes, I would. I am."

"No, you can't quit," she says urgently.

Hello—is this the same girl who once said I was pimping myself out for a bunch of chauvinist men? Shouldn't she be, like, encouraging me to drop out?

"Why can't I?"

"Because that would be like letting Megan win."

"She has! Don't you get it? My pageant career is over. Done. Finished. Obliterated. This will just get bigger and bigger."

She scrunches up her face. "But that's so . . ."

"Unfair? Tragic? Wrong?"

". . . gutless," she finishes.

"Gutless?" I echo incredulously. I throw up my hands. "Well, what am I supposed to do?" I cry. "Megan hasn't left me with much choice. And don't take this the wrong way, but . . . why do you care if I quit? I mean, you hate pageants. It seems like you'd be happy."

She gives me a wounded look. "You think watching my best friend get screwed over makes me happy? Especially when it's my fault?"

"It's not your—"

She cuts me off. "Yes, it is. If I hadn't acted like such an idiot, Megan wouldn't have been able to take a picture of you like that." She lifts her chin stubbornly. "I caused the problem and now I'm going to figure out a way to fix it. You're not dropping out."

I'm pretty sure that having a drunken photo of yourself plastered on the pageant message board falls into the category of Things That Can't Be Fixed Ever, but I don't want to burst the delusional happy bubble that her brain is apparently floating around in.

"Right. Let me know how that works out," I tell her.

"Shhhh." She motions for me to be quiet, then closes her eyes, concentrating. "I'm thinking." She squeezes her eyes shut, apparently concentrating. After a moment her eyes fly open. "I've got it," she says excitedly. She leans forward and grabs the mouse again. "This might actually turn out to be a good thing."

"A good thing? How do you figure that?"

"Because people love it when other people screw up. It's the Britney Spears Syndrome. You know?"

"O-kay," I say slowly, totally clueless as to where she's going with this.

"But what do people love to watch even *more* than somebody screwing up?"

"Sports?"

She rolls her eyes. "No, not sports. Success stories. You know, the welfare mom who makes a million dollars on Ebay, the amputee who climbs a mountain, the people on *American Idol*."

"I'm not exactly an ampu—"

"And do you know what else people love?" she continues, talking over me.

"Chocolate?"

"The repentant sinner!" She gives me a triumphant look as if everything should now make perfect sense.

"The repentant sinner," I repeat.

"Yeah, you know—the malefactor who wants to make amends."

"Right. The malefactor. That's just what I was about to say."

She slants me a look. "Don't be snippy. This is going to work."

"*What's* going to work?" I cry. "I have no idea what you're talking about."

"Okay. Remember when there was that big scandal about Donald Trump firing that Miss USA for taking drugs?" She frowns. "Tamara or Tanya . . ."

"Tara Conner," I supply.

She nods. "Right. Tara Conner. Anyway, so Donald Trump was going to fire her, but then he changed his mind and sent her to rehab, right? And when she got out, she went on a lot of talk shows and got a lot of publicity."

"Yeah, so?"

"So, you can do the same thing Tara Conner did."

"You want me to go to rehab?" I say incredulously.

She rolls her eyes. "Of course not. I'm not talking about that. I mean how she went on TV and got a lot of publicity. You could do that too."

"Oh, sure," I say sarcastically. "I'll just call up Larry King and see if he can fit me in on his show tomorrow night. Or would Barbara Walters be better?"

"Ha-ha, very funny. You know that's not what I meant."

"Actually," I counter, "I have no idea what you meant. What kind of TV are you talking about? I mean, who on earth would put me on the air?"

"KPTV is always scrounging for stories. They'd put you on in a second," she answers.

"And what would I say? That this whole thing is just a big misunderstanding? Who's going to believe that?"

She shrugs. "Nobody."

"Exactly," I say, relieved she's finally starting to get it. "Nobody."

"Which is why you're not going to say that it's a big misunderstanding," she continues. "But that you did it, you realize it was wrong, and now you want to prevent other teens from making the same mistake. Who's more qualified to tell people not to drink? Some girl who has never done anything, or somebody who has actually been in the throes of addiction?"

"The throes of addiction?" I exclaim incredulously. "Are you out of your mind? That makes me sound like Amy Winehouse or something."

"Okay, okay," she says quickly, backtracking. "We don't have to go that extreme. You could just talk about how you were influenced by peer pressure and how you regret it. Or you could turn it into a protecting-yourself-online issue. Instead of preaching against underage drinking, you could talk about how teens need to be careful not to put themselves into situations that could result in embarrassing photos or information about them circulating around online."

This suggestion is marginally less mortifying, but I'm still not interested. "No way, Justine," I say, shaking my head. "I mean, I get what you're trying to do and everything, but the whole idea seems like it has major potential to blow up in my face."

"Well, do you have a better idea?" she challenges.

Changing my identity? Moving to another state? Having Megan killed? Something tells me Justine won't go for any of these suggestions, so I say, "Er, I could drop out of the pageant?"

She tucks her hands under her arms and imitates a chicken flapping its wings. "Bawk, bawk, bawk."

"You don't have to be mean."

She drops her hands. "Look, at least think about it. I can't guarantee you'll win the whole pageant, but I promise it'll get you further than doing nothing."

I give her a suspicious look. "Define 'further.'"

"To a greater extent or more advanced degree," she replies automatically.

"Thank you, Miss Webster's Dictionary. I can see you're really going to be a big help."

"Oh, c'mon. Lighten up," she says teasingly. "This is going to be fun."

I blink at her. "Fun? Did the alcohol damage your brain or something? What about this situation could possibly be fun?"

"It's a challenge. Challenges are always fun."

Oh yeah. This whole thing is just a regular party waiting to happen. Yippee.

Chapter Seventeen

Do you believe in the power of forgiveness?

My mom's plan for handling the photo situation is much more straightforward than Justine's. "I'm going to rip every single hair out of that conniving little bitch's head." She paces agitatedly in front of the living room couch, oblivious to the ash dropping from her cigarette onto the carpet. "Every single one. She won't even be able to get extensions after I'm through with her."

Side note: This is the upside to your mom getting knocked up at her junior prom and giving birth to you when she's seventeen—she doesn't act all shocked by the behavior of actual teenagers and refers to your enemies as things like "conniving little bitches." Of course, the downside is that she's too busy changing your diapers to go to college, so you end up living in a crummy rent house, eating Ramen noodles, and spending every night praying that you'll somehow manage to win enough beauty pageant money to go to college because you're sure as hell not going to get any academic scholarships with a 1500 on the SAT and you can't afford a student loan and if you don't get out of the crappy cycle of almost-poverty that you were born into you might throw yourself off a bridge and . . . what were we talking about again?

Oh, right. My mom going to prison.

"Yeah, somehow I don't think my mom getting arrested for ripping out my competition's hair would exactly improve my tarnished image," I say drily.

"It couldn't make it any worse," she shoots back. Which, excuse me, does anybody else think is totally hilarious? I mean, that my *mom* is worried about my beauty pageant image? The same woman who wanted to get matching mother-daughter tattoos for Mother's Day?

Lucky for me, Jed is here, kicked back in our ancient plaid recliner, ready to smooth things over. See? I *told* you she was going out with him again.

"Baby, you need to chill out." He swings his gaze away from the TV to my mom. The motorcycle show he's watching has gone to commercial, so, you know, he has a couple of free minutes to butt into my life.

Sigh. Actually, Jed's not all that bad. I'm just in a really crummy mood for reasons I assume are obvious.

My mom scowls at him. "I don't like people messing with my kid." She pauses by the end table next to the couch and (thankfully) crushes her cigarette into the top of an empty Diet Coke can. "It pisses me off."

OMG, I think I'm going to cry! That's, like, the sweetest thing my mom has ever said to me! I spring off the couch and fling my arms around her neck. "That's, like, the sweetest thing you've ever said to me!" I cry.

"What are you talking about? I say sweet things to you all the time," she says irritably. "Didn't I just tell you a few days ago that your face is the perfect shape to pull off an eyebrow ring?"

"Yes," I say, laughing. I pull away from her, wiping at the tear in the corner of my eye. In our own weird, dysfunctional way, we just had a Hallmark moment.

"Baby, can you bring me some chips?" Jed asks from the recliner.

My mom whirls around, putting her hands on her hips. "What do I look like, your maid?" she demands. "Get your own chips."

"But you're already standing up, so . . ."

I don't hear the rest of the argument because I'm too busy fleeing to my bedroom. Stupid bickering over chips is my cue to exit stage left.

Except when I get to my room, I immediately wish I had stayed in the living room. Because my cell phone is going off in my purse and the ring tone is the Miss America theme song. Which means the person on the other end of the line is Noralee, my executive director. And, given the timing of her call, I highly doubt she's phoning to discuss whether I should wear my hair up or down during evening gown.

Gulp.

I cross quickly to my bed and pull my phone out of my purse. It's *so* tempting to just hit the decline button, but I force myself to resist. That would just be postponing the inevitable. Not to mention that it would probably really tick her off.

I flip the phone open. "Hey, Noralee! What's up?"

"Would you like to explain the appalling picture on my computer screen?"

Okay. So much for pleasantries.

"Really, Noralee, it's not what it looks like," I begin earnestly, but apparently she intended the question to be rhetorical.

"Do you have any idea how much time and money I have dedicated to you over the past year?" she continues angrily. "Do you?"

"You have no idea how sor—"

Her voice gets even shriller. "And the only thing I asked in return was that you behave like a lady. But apparently, that was too difficult for you."

Okay, wait a minute. I'll be the first to admit that Noralee has a right to be upset, but she's acting like I've just been sitting back with my feet kicked up all year, which is *so* not true. I mean, yes—she has been a totally awesome director and everything, but I'm not exactly a slacker here.

"I *have* behaved like a lady," I say forcefully. "That picture isn't what it looks like." I proceed to tell her the whole story, which—granted—sounds insane. I mean, it didn't sound insane when I was talking to Justine, or my mom, but that's because they know me. And the real Megan. Unlike Noralee, who only knows the fake, pageant Megan. Who, in the version I'm telling to Noralee, is merely "some person." Because there's *no way* Noralee is going to believe that Megan is trying to sabotage me. Megan's mom and sister were Noralee's queens a hundred million years ago, so Noralee thinks Megan is God's special gift to the universe.

After I finish, there's a reeeeeally long silence. "Um, are you there?" I ask uncertainly.

A weary sigh comes across the line. "I think your only option is to resign your title quietly."

What? Her words hit me like a punch to the gut. I mean, I'd be lying if I said the thought of Noralee yanking my crown hadn't crossed my mind, but I never dreamed she'd present it as my first option. I thought we'd at least, like, discuss stuff, you know?

"Oh," I say weakly.

Her voice softens. "I know it sounds like I'm being harsh, dear, but this is really for your own good. If you go to Miss Teen State, it will only keep things stirred up. This way, you can lie low and give the whole nasty business a chance to blow over. And you don't have to worry about the title," she adds reassuringly. "I just talked to Felicia Snow, and she's more than happy to take your place at State."

Wow. Now I feel like someone punched me in the gut, knocked me down, and stomped on me. Noralee already called my first runner-up? Before she even talked to me?

"What if I don't want to resign?" I say defensively. Yes, I know I told Justine I was going to drop out, but now that Noralee is trying to *make* me drop out, I suddenly don't want to.

Noralee obviously can't comprehend such a crazy scenario. "I'm not sure what you mean, dear."

"I mean, are you asking me to resign or telling me to?" I pause, taking a deep breath. "Because if you're asking, then the answer is no. I don't want to give up my title. I want to go to State."

Even as the words are leaving my mouth, I can't believe I'm saying them. Teen queens are notorious for clashing with their directors, but I've never challenged any of mine about anything *ever*. The directors talk to one another, so if a queen is hard to deal with—not showing up for appearances, squabbling about wardrobe, or just generally being rude—word gets around.

"But that wouldn't be in your best interests," Noralee protests. "Not to mention you wouldn't have the slightest chance of winning. Before, yes, but now . . . well, you'd be lucky to even make Top Ten."

"I know."

"Then why in the world do you still want to go?"

Because I'm insane? I take another deep breath. "Well, my friend has this idea about how I could maybe turn this around to my advantage. Of course, it's probably a really long shot," I add quickly. "But I'd at least like to try."

"What sort of an idea?" Noralee asks dubiously.

"Er, we haven't exactly worked out all the details yet." I'm not *about* to tell her Justine wants me to go on TV. She'd be over at Felicia Snow's house before I could even hang up the phone. "Please. At least give me a chance," I say plaintively. "You know how hard I've been working to get ready for State. Just give me a few days to try and salvage things."

There's another reeeeeeally long silence. Finally Noralee says, "All right," she says reluctantly. "I'll give you *one* chance. Don't make me regret it."

"I won't," I say fervently. "Thank you soooo much."

We hang up a few minutes later (once Noralee is finished making it clear that Felicia is still on standby), and I immediately dial Justine's number.

For better or worse, I guess I'm about to have my fifteen minutes of fame.

Chapter Eighteen

If you were on a TV talk show and could get one message across to viewers, what subject would you choose?

As soon as Justine finds out I want to attempt the Tara Conner mea culpa (that's Latin for when beauty queens try to distract people from the fact that they screwed up big-time by going on TV and looking sweet and photogenic), she gets on the phone and calls everybody in the free world, trying to make it happen.

And, unbelievably, the local news station, KPTV, agrees to go along with our insane plan. Although, I guess it's not really *that* unbelievable. I mean, KPTV isn't exactly giving CNN a run for its money, you know? It's more like glorified public access. Well, minus the glorified part.

"Isn't that the boy who used to bag groceries at the IGA? Since when is he a news reporter?" My mom hits the pause button on the DVR remote control and glances over at the couch where Justine and I are perched nervously on Wednesday night, watching my television debut.

"Mom!" I wail. "Let it play, okay? We can talk after."

"Fine, fine." Rolling her eyes, she turns back to the TV and aims the remote. A second later the screen unfreezes and we're once again watching [deep theatrical voice here] *Kyle Kennedy, KPTV's investigative reporter*. A hard-hitting newsman who has never in his life asked people if they preferred paper or plastic.

Oh, all right. So my mom's right; he used to be the bag boy at the IGA. But that was eons and eons ago. Like, at *least* six months, maybe even a year.

Kyle smiles into the camera and starts his spiel, which ~~Justine totally wrote~~ he wrote completely by himself with no help from anyone. Just like ~~Justine totally wrote out all my answers and made me memorize them~~ I prepared all of my answers myself.

"Over the past few years the pageant world has been plagued by a string of scandals," he intones. "From underage drinking to topless photos to criminal assault, these days it seems you can barely turn on the TV or pick up a newspaper without seeing a story about a beauty queen who has fallen from grace."

A montage of video clips of fallen beauty queens flashes across the screen: Tara Conner, Katie Rees, Amy Polumbo, Elyse Umemoto, Vanessa Williams, Ashley—wait a minute. Vanessa Williams? Why did Justine—er, Kyle—put her in there? Those lesbian pictures are *so* twenty-five years ago. This is supposed to be about recent scandals.

The video ends and the screen switches back to Kyle. "I'm here tonight with Presley Ashbury, a local title holder who, just a few days ago, found herself at the center of her own scandal when someone posted a compromising photo of her on a popular pageant website."

The camera pulls back and I appear on the screen next to Kyle. Per Justine's orders, I'm wearing my pageant interview suit with my hair pulled back in a low ponytail at the nape of my neck, and I have almost *no* makeup on. However, I do have on Justine's double-stranded pearl necklace. Supposedly, this ensemble makes me look conservative and demure, but (gag) it also makes me look like a thirty-year-old woman. Not to mention . . . OMG, the bump on my nose really *is* big, isn't it?

Horrified, I cover my face with my hands and peek out through my fingers at the screen. OMG, it's HUGE!!! I look like Owen Wilson's long-lost twin sister. And our TV isn't even high-def. Forget what I said about the deviated septum thing. I'm going in for a nose job as soon as possible. Which, if by some miracle this all works out and I somehow manage to win Miss Teen State, will be in about a week.

What? You didn't know that state-level prize packages include the complimentary plastic surgery of your choice? Of course you didn't. It's kind of a dirty little secret, what with the pageant being a *scholarship* competition and all. Funny how that works, isn't it?

I'm so upset by my newly discovered deformity that instead of watching the rest of the interview, I flee to the kitchen and eat TWO Double Stuf Oreos.

Thus, for your convenience, below is a transcript of the rest of my interview with Kyle:

KYLE: Now, let's talk about this photo. It's a picture of you drinking alcohol, is that right?

ME: Yes, I'm drinking a beer.

KYLE: Even though you're underage.

ME: Yes.

KYLE: Is that something you do a lot? Drinking?

ME: No. Gosh, no. I never— The picture we're talking about is not an accurate representation of who I am at all.

KYLE: But you admit that this is something that happened. You admit that you've engaged in underage drinking.

ME: I admit that I was at a party and I was curious and that I used very, very bad judgment. I made a mistake. And I regret it so much. Because, you know, I've let a lot of people down. I've let myself down.

KYLE: I spent some time, earlier, looking at the website where this picture of you is posted, and there are a lot of people commenting that they think you should be disqualified from competing in the state pageant because of this. That you should lose your crown. Have any of the officials from— What is the name of the title you represent?

ME: I'm the reigning Miss Magnolia Blossom.

KYLE: Have the officials in charge of the Miss Magnolia Blossom pageant talked to you about removing your title?

ME: Well, obviously, they're not happy about what's happened, but like I said, this in no way represents who I am. And all the people involved with the Miss Magnolia Blossom pageant know that. They know me. They know I'm a good person.

KYLE: Do you feel like you've learned anything valuable from this experience? Or is it something you'd rather just forget about?

ME: I have learned so much from this experience. And even though it's been really embarrassing and I've felt a lot of shame, I actually see this as a good thing, believe it or not. I see this as an opportunity for me to help others.

KYLE: Help others in what way? Do you mean speaking out against underage drinking?

ME: Certainly, that's something I would love to be involved with. I definitely hope to do that. But even more than that, I'd like to educate teens about protecting themselves online. I'm not talking about cyber-predators . . . I mean, a lot of teens just don't think, you know? They're clowning around with their friends, they take some stupid pictures, post them on their Facebook pages, and then *bam!* The next thing they know, a college admissions counselor is looking at those same stupid pictures and sending them a rejection letter.

KYLE: Quickly, because we're almost out of time, what is the most important thing teens can do to protect themselves?

ME: Think before you click. If it's not something you want the whole world to see, don't post it. I just launched a website called howtoprotectyourself.org where people can go for more information.

KYLE: Great. Thanks for talking with us.

ME: Thank you so much for having me.

My big TV interview doesn't exactly make me famous or do much to squelch the talk on the boards (if anything, it creates *more* talk), but it's worth every bit of the horror of seeing myself (i.e., my NOSE) on TV because it convinces Noralee to let me keep my crown and go to State. I'd like to say she makes this decision because she's so impressed by my ingenuity and determination, but, yeah . . . I'm pretty sure she just feels sorry for me. After all, she's met my mom. And dad. When they were drunk. They were also screaming and throwing things at each other, but that's a story for some other time.

Or not.

The rest of the week passes by in a blur of finals, weighted sit-ups, and last-minute packing. I go to great (some might say ridiculous) lengths to avoid coming into contact with anyone or anything that might make me feel bad. Which, at this point, encompasses pretty much everything in the known universe. Gabe, Megan, Robbie, the message boards, the TV, my makeup mirror, the bathroom scale. I may as well go live in a plastic bubble.

On Friday afternoon, Hunter and Lilly leave for Michigan with their parents, and then on Saturday, Justine and her parents leave for Central America. Hmmn. Which family is going to visit relatives and which family is going to help build a well to provide clean drinking water to an impoverished village plagued by flies and disease? Bet you can't guess!

And then [drum roll] it's THE DAY. Sunday. The first day of the pageant. Rehearse on Sunday and Monday, compete on Tuesday and Wednesday. I don't know what idiot decided on that schedule, but there it is. Not that it matters for the contestants, but I imagine most of the parents have, like, you know, jobs? I guess the pageant people just figure they can take vacation days.

True to her ~~threat~~ promise, my mom enlists Jed to be my escort for Arrival. And get this—she even buys him a *suit*. Well, okay, so she doesn't exactly buy it. She borrows it from her boss. And, okay, so maybe it's a couple (or four) sizes too small, but still. You have to give her credit for trying.

I tell you this not because I think it's so fascinating, but to explain why I am currently sitting in the backseat of a yellow monster truck with orange flames painted on the sides. That's right. I'm arriving at the pageant in a monster truck. With flames. Named Old Yeller.

Who says God doesn't have a sense of humor?

A regular, local pageant is normally a one-day kind of thing, but in addition to lasting four days, Miss Teen State is held in this touristy town near the center of the state. Which means that not only do contestants have to compete against each other, we also have to share hotel rooms with one another. In case you've never seen thirty-two pageant girls being unloaded in front of a hotel, let me give you a mental image of what it looks like: Armageddon.

"What the—" Jed starts in surprise as he swings Old Yeller left at the stoplight and the Majestic hotel comes into view.

My mom makes a face at the line of high-end luxury cars and SUVs crammed bumper-to-bumper under the covered driveway of the hotel and snaking out into the street, blocking traffic. "It's always like this," she tells Jed disgustedly. "Last year it took us forty-five minutes to get up near the front door."

"You're kidding." Jed glances at the clock on the dash and then over his shoulder at me. "What time did you say you're supposed to be in there, kiddo?"

That's Jed's new nickname for me: kiddo. Normally, I would pitch a fit, but this morning he gave me a hundred-dollar bill in case I need anything while I'm gone, and a few days ago he put a new transmission in my mom's Camaro.

In other words, he's been acting really decent, and I'm starting to get the sneaking suspicion that he's actually serious about my mom.

I glance at the piece of paper on my leg, even though I've already memorized every word of the itinerary the Miss Teen State office sent out to all the contestants. "Contestants shall check in at the registration table in the lobby between one and two p.m.," I read aloud.

"Oh." His brow creases. The clock on the dash already says one-thirty. "Well, maybe I can nudge a few cars out of the way. Get us up there quicker." He turns back around and reaches for the gearshift to put the truck in drive.

I have a sudden vision of Jed flooring the accelerator and roaring over the tops of all the vehicles in front of us. "No! That's okay!" I'm so flustered I'm practically shouting. "I'll just get out here and go on in and register. Then maybe by the time I'm finished we'll be closer to the front of the line. And if not, then we can just dump my luggage on the sidewalk or in the lobby and I'll get it later."

"But you'll get sweaty if you walk from here," my mom protests. The hotel's front door isn't *that* far away, but I'm one of those lucky people who sweat if the temperature gets above sixty-five and/or from the teeniest bit of physical exertion. It's *so* annoying.

If I ever get rich, the first thing I'm doing is getting those Botox injections under your arms that, like, paralyze your sweat glands. Ooooh, and laser hair removal. No more shaving *or* wearing deodorant. Can you imagine? Heaven.

"It's okay," I reassure her. "I put on about half a bottle of Secret Platinum this morning." Which was a waste of perfectly good deodorant since nothing can make a dent in my sweating problem, but I have to at least go through the motions, you know?

My mom says something else, but I've already got my door open. Smoothing the skirt of my dress, I suck in a breath and free-fall to the pavement, trying to look graceful, confident, intelligent, elegant, and pleasant all at the same time. Just in case. You never know when a judge might be skulking around. Which is why, from this moment on, I'm no longer Presley Ashbury, high school student. I'm Presley Ashbury, Beauty Queen.

Presley Ashbury, the Obvious Choice for Miss Teen State.

Presley Ashbury, Future Miss America Contestant.

Presley Ashbury, the Trashy Drunk Girl Who Will Inevitably Bring More Shame on the Pageant System.

No! I force the thought out of my mind. I have to stay positive, act confident, no matter what. Pageant girls can smell weakness as easily as they can spot fake boobs.

"I'll be right back," I yell to my mom and Jed, reaching up to slam the door behind me. My voice is barely audible over the roar of the truck's engine, but my mom gives a little wave, so I guess she gets the idea.

Needless to say, everybody within a ten-mile radius is gaping at me (what, hasn't anybody seen a girl get out of a monster truck before?), but I pretend not to notice, even though I can feel my cheeks burning. Taking a deep breath, I start toward the hotel. Normally, walking isn't something I think about all that much (kind of like breathing), but as soon as I get to a pageant, it suddenly seems like it requires the coordination of an Olympic gymnast. *Shoulders back, stomach in, chin up, palms open at sides facing hips, place one foot directly in front of the other, swing arms, sway hips, lift from the rib cage*—by the time I reach the front door, I'm exhausted.

I'm also feeling distinctly damp under my armpits. Sigh. Maybe instead of Botox injections, I could just, like, have my sweat glands removed altogether. I make a mental note to ask Justine if you can live without your sweat glands.

The scene inside the hotel is just as crazy as the scene outside. Maybe *more* crazy, even. Teenage girls in strappy high-heeled sandals and chic dresses from Caché and

White House | Black Market are swarming over the lobby like well-dressed, spray-tanned locusts.

Well, I guess the cute black girl over by the elevators doesn't have a spray tan, but still. She's the only person who doesn't have one. If the emergency sprinklers in the ceiling suddenly came on, everybody in the room (except for afore-mentioned black girl who—curse her—I just realized looks like Halle Berry's little sister) would dissolve into a dirty brown puddle on the floor. Me included.

Although, my "spray tan" is actually Fake Bake mousse I bought off the Internet and applied with plastic gloves, rather than an actual fifty-dollar airbrush tan from a salon, but what-ever. My tan looks just as good as everybody else's, if I do say so myself.

In addition to being super-spray-tanned, everybody has acrylic nails (on their fingers and toes), all painted in the req-uisite French manicure. I swear, someday I'm going to show up at a pageant with my nails painted, like, neon orange. Although, heck—even a medium shade of pink would be a scandalous show of individuality. (Yeah, all that "Be yourself!" stuff is a total sound bite.)

For every teenage girl in the lobby, there's also her mater-nal counterpart, generally a middle-aged woman in a taste-ful pantsuit from Talbots or Ann Taylor. (For the record, my mom is wearing a halter top and jean skirt from Forever 21, even though I literally *got on my hands and knees* and begged her to wear something else.) The funny thing about see-ing all the moms up close and personal is that you can tell *exactly* what each contestant is going to look like in twenty or so years. And let me tell you, some of them should be very, very scared.

"Hey, Presley!"

"Presley, your hair looks adorable!"

"It's so great to see you, Presley!"

"I *love* that dress. Where did you get it?"

~~Vultures~~ Girls attack me from all sides as I make my way toward the white-draped registration table. You know what I'm talking about—when people act all happy and delighted to see you, but they're secretly just checking you out. I play along, flashing my best pageant smile and generally acting like everyone who comes up to me is my long-lost BFF. And, to be fair, there are some girls competing this week who are actually nice. It's just that I haven't seen any of them yet.

When I *finally* make it to the registration table, it's ten minutes before two.

"There you are, Miss Magnolia." The plump chaperone behind the table smiles at me. Her name tag identifies her as Lola. "We were starting to get worried." She hands me a glossy blue folder embossed with my name and a giant tiara.

(Quick pageant trivia: The four points of the Miss America crown stand for success, style, service, and scholarship. That's right. It's not just sparkly and cute, people. It has meaning.)

"The traffic in front of the hotel is crazy," I say apologetically. I'm trying my best to act normal and polite, but it's hard because all I can think about is ripping open my folder. Because two critical items are inside said folder: my contestant number and the name of my roommate.

The roommate thing is obviously super-important because, duh, nobody wants to share a hotel room with some awful chick for four days. Although, I'm pretty easygoing, so it's not really that big a deal who I'm paired with. I mean, you can get along with anybody for four days, you know? But the contestant number—that's HUGE.

At least, it's huge in my opinion, anyway. Some people will tell you it doesn't matter whether you go first, or last, or in the middle, but I'm sorry—they're smoking crack. It matters. Going first is the kiss of death. You always, always, *always* want to be as close to the end as possible. Judges give higher scores to later contestants. No, really—they do. I've seen it happen *so* many times. Don't get me wrong, I'm not saying that it's impossible to win or do well if you have a low number. I'm just saying that it's harder.

"Yes, one of the mothers was commenting on that earlier," Lola replies. "She was worried that her husband might lose his temper and start yelling at some of the other drivers."

I consider telling her that there's a distinct possibility that the man who drove me here might lose his temper and start *running over* some of the other drivers, but I manage to hold my tongue. Instead, I just thank her, step away from the table, and ~~snap my folder open so fast I almost rip it in half~~ calmly open my folder to peruse its contents.

My heart practically lifts to the ceiling when I see my contestant number. *Thirty-one!!!* I'm the next-to-last contestant!

I drop my eyes eagerly to the next line.

WHAT??!!

I stare at the two words printed after "Roommate's Name," stunned. Oh no. No, no, no, no. This is *not* happening. It's a mistake. *Please* say it's a mistake. It has to be.

I squeeze my eyes shut, praying that the neatly typed letters will magically transform into other, different neatly typed letters, but when I open them again the name is exactly the same: Megan Leighton.

I'm sharing a hotel room with Megan. For *four* days.

Thirty-one girls in the pageant besides me. Thirty-one potential roommates. And I end up with Megan.

I don't know whether to laugh or cry. Or throw myself off a bridge.

And to make things oh so much worse, Megan is number thirty-two, which means she's the *last* contestant. Suddenly my number thirty-one doesn't seem all that great.

"Finally! I've been looking for you everywhere!" A voice cuts through my misery, and I'm startled to find myself being hugged by a tall blond girl I've never seen before.

"I'm sorry, do I know—," I begin, but then she releases me and I finally get a good look at her face. *"Sadie?"*

She laughs. "Pretty different, huh?" she asks, patting her Marilyn Monroe blond curls.

"I'll say." The last time I saw Sadie, her hair was tawny brown and hung stick-straight to the middle of her back. "It looks great, though," I add quickly, in case that sounded snarky. "Very Gwen Stefani."

Sadie (more formally known as Sadie Lee Deveraux, Miss Peach Festival) is one of the nice pageant girls I mentioned earlier. In fact, she's actually my BPFF (Best Pageant Friend Forever). We always hang out when we're at pageants together, and we also have a pretty good e-mail relationship.

She makes a face. "According to my mom, it looks very trashy Playboy Bunny–ish. She cried for a whole day when she first saw it."

I cluck sympathetically. Poor Sadie. Picture the most obnoxious, pushy stage mother you can think of, then multiply that by a million and you'll have a teeny-tiny idea of what Sadie's mom is like. Seriously, Sadie doesn't even like being in pageants. She just does them to please her mom. Which is a shame because she's really good. She can sing just like Reba McEntire.

Not that I ever listen to Reba McEntire, of course. That would be crazy. She's a country singer. My parents would disown me.

And Sadie's pretty and has a good personality, but . . . you can tell her heart isn't in it. I mean, she always performs perfectly and everything, but there's no spark.

"Of course," she continues, "she might have been crying because that was also the day I told her I was taking classes at the beauty college."

"Beauty college?" I repeat quizzically. "What's that?"

"You know, hair dresser school." She pats her curls again, giggling. "I was sort of a class project."

"But how are you going to school for that? I mean, you're still in high school."

She shrugs. "My school has a program where upperclassmen can leave at lunch to go to work or take college classes." She points to my folder. "Ooooh, what number did you get?" Apparently, she's tired of talking about hair.

"Thirty-one."

"Thirty-one! Ohmigosh, that's so awesome! You're the next-to-last person." She pauses, noticing my expression. "Why aren't you excited? You look like your dog just died."

"I wish," I say dejectedly.

"You wish your dog just died?"

"What?" I blink at her, startled, and then I realize what I said. "No, no! That didn't come out right. I don't even have a dog! But if I did have one, I would never want him, or her—it—to die because . . ." My voice trails off. Sadie is staring at me like I'm a lunatic. Probably because I'm acting like a lunatic.

"Megan is my roommate," I blurt out.

To a regular person this statement would be meaningless, but luckily, Sadie isn't a regular person. She gives a horrified gasp. "You're rooming with Megabitch? Oh, Presley, I'm so sorry. What rotten luck."

Ha. That's the understatement of the century. Notice how she automatically knows who I'm talking about, even though I didn't say a last name and there are at least two other Megans competing in the pageant? That's because there's only one Megan who strikes fear in the heart of everyone. There's only one Megabitch, which, by the way, is Megan's nickname on the pageant circuit. Fitting, don't you think?

"You have no idea," I mutter.

A few feet away a woman who looks exactly like Sadie, minus the Marilyn curls and plus twenty or so years, starts beckoning frantically at us.

Well, not us. Just Sadie.

"Um, I think your mom wants you," I tell her.

"Yeah. I better go." Sadie sounds less than thrilled. "But we'll talk later, okay?"

"Definitely."

She pats me on the shoulder. "And don't worry about the roommate thing," she adds reassuringly. "As long as you sleep with one eye open, I'm sure everything will be fine."

Chapter Nineteen

What do you think of America's obsession with reality shows?

Considering the way my luck is going so far, I fully expect to see Gabe decked out in his navy blue suit and tie, standing next to Megan at Arrival, but God must not totally hate me, because it turns out that she's being escorted by a distinguished-looking middle-aged man who looks like he just came off the set of a soap opera. Her dad, of course. Gag. Is there any aspect of Megan that isn't flawless? I mean, even her family is perfect, for heaven's sake. They look perfect, anyway.

Whereas my family . . . yeah, not so much.

"Are you okay?" I ask Jed in a low voice as the line edges forward.

He pulls at the knot in his borrowed tie, which looks more like a noose instead of an article of clothing. "Yeah. I'm good," he says hoarsely.

I give up a silent prayer of thanks to whoever decided to introduce us in alphabetical order according to our titles, instead of by our contestant numbers. Because Jed already looks bad enough without having to stand next to Megan's George Clooney lookalike father.

I know. That sounds terrible, doesn't it? But it's true. And it's not just that Jed's wearing clothes that don't fit—even if he had on a custom-made suit, Jed looks about as natural in dress clothes as a grizzly bear in a tutu.

Somehow, though, he manages to keep it together. Although, when we get to the bottom of the staircase after my name is announced, he does sort of growl at the photographer who takes our picture. (Jed isn't a fan of having his picture taken, apparently.)

Oh, well. I guess it could be worse. He could have, like, punched him in the face.

I sneak several surreptitious glances at the crowd, looking for Gabe, but I don't see any sign of his tousled blond head. Hmmm. Trouble in paradise, I wonder?

Awww. That would be too bad. Not.

Once all the contestants are introduced, we're given a few minutes to say good-bye to our parents and then we're herded into a big conference room for orientation. Also known as "the part where the pageant director threatens to hunt us down and kill us slowly if we do anything to screw up the pageant and/or make it/her look bad."

"Presley, over here!" Sadie calls as I come through the door. She's already sitting down in the back row. The Halle Berry lookalike is sitting next to her, looking like—well, Halle Berry.

Hmmn. Is it wrong to hate somebody you've never even spoken to?

Just kidding. I'm not *that* shallow. Still, I hope she's way far away from me in the lineup. I've got enough stuff going against me without having to go head-to-head in a bathing suit with a chick who looks like a gorgeous movie star.

I push the thought out of my mind and hurry over to slip into the empty seat on Sadie's other side. "Thanks," I say gratefully. "I was hoping we'd get to sit together."

"No problem. Hey, have you met Eve yet?" Sadie gestures to Halle. "Her family just moved here from Louisiana a few months ago." She leans back in her chair so that Halle—Eve—and I can see each other better. "Presley Asbury, Eve Samuels. Eve Samuels, Presley Ashbury."

"Hi, it's so nice to meet you!" The words come out of my mouth a little too enthusiastically, probably because I'm try-ing to compensate for my earlier, uncharitable thoughts about hating her.

She smiles shyly. "Thanks. You too." Her voice is so soft it's almost a whisper, and I immediately feel even more like a jerk. She may be stunningly beautiful, but she's also clearly dying of nervousness.

"Eve is my roommate," Sadie informs me. "She's num-ber fourteen and I'm lucky number thirteen. And last week I broke my makeup mirror, so now all I need is to, like, walk under a ladder or find a black cat or something. My mom says I should never go to Vegas because I'm a magnet for bad luck."

Ha. Sadie's mom obviously needs to spend a few days with me.

I spend the next couple of minutes quizzing Eve about her pertinent info (age: fifteen; talent: violin; pageant experience:

did some locals in Louisiana, but this is her first time at a state contest), but that's as far as I get before two women with identical highlighted blond hair and annoying fake smiles go to the front of the room and call for quiet.

Meet Suzette Cartwright-Thompson and her daughter, Claire, otherwise known as the co-tyrants of the Miss Teen State pageant.

I'm sorry. I mean the co-*directors* of the Miss Teen State pageant. Not that there's much difference. Suzette "inherited" the pageant from her brother a few years ago, and she basically runs it like her own little monarchy. There's a board of directors, which is supposed to be kind of like a checks and balances system, but that's a joke. The entire board is made up of her friends.

"Welcome to Miss Teen State, girls," Suzette says brightly. "I'm so excited to see everyone . . ." The rest of what she says sounds like "blah, blah, blah," because I stop listening. Everything we need to know is in our folders, so paying attention would be a waste of perfectly good brain cells.

Ditto for when Claire takes the microphone a few minutes later. So instead of paying attention, I torture myself by staring at the back of Megan's perfect French chignon (because of course she's sitting in the first row, gazing up at Claire like she's Jesus preaching from the pulpit) and thinking about the upcoming few days.

". . . The show will be called *Queen Scene*, and it's tentatively scheduled to air on MTV sometime next spring."

The word "MTV" brings me abruptly out of my stupor.

"What is she talking about?" I whisper to Sadie.

"Shhh!" Sadie flaps her hand at me. Her face is flushed, and she's straining so far forward I have no idea how she's managing not to fall out of her seat onto her butt.

"You'll be getting more information tomorrow and later in the week," Claire finishes.

The instant she steps away from the microphone, the room explodes into excited chattering and squealing.

I whirl around to Sadie. "Will you please tell me what's going on?" I beg. "I wasn't listening."

"Ohmigosh, it's unbelievable. This is the most exciting thing ever." She looks at Eve. "Don't you think this the most exciting thing ever?"

Eve nods.

"*What* is the most exciting thing ever?" I say desperately.

Sadie beams at me ecstatically. "MTV is going to do a reality show on the pageant!" Sadie answers.

"What?" I instinctively whip my head around, looking for hidden video cameras. "How can they do that? Don't we, like, have to sign a release or something?"

"No, not this pageant, the national pageant," Sadie clarifies. "It's going to be a documentary type thing. They're going to pick three different states and film their Miss and Miss Teen titleholders as they prepare for their national contests and then during the actual pageants themselves."

"So . . . there will be six girls in all? Three Misses and three Miss Teens?"

Sadie nods. "Exactly."

"But how do we know which states it's going to be?" I ask, still confused.

"That's just it—we *don't* know." Sadie bounces excitedly in her seat. "They haven't picked them yet. They're sending scouts to all the state pageants to check things out and see which winners would be best for TV."

Eve starts to say something, but her words are cut off when ~~Satan~~ Megan suddenly swoops in and throws her arms around me like a giant, bloodsucking bat.

Except bats don't really have arms, do they? They have wings. Oh, well. You know what I mean.

"Here you are, roomie!" she squeals. "I've been looking for you everywhere!"

My first instinct is to shove her away or maybe scream for somebody to bring a crucifix or some holy water or something, but then I notice a couple of chaperones giving us aren't-they-adorable looks, and understanding dawns. Megan is *trying* to get me to do something like that.

Because then I'll look bad in front of the chaperones.

Ha. Well, I've got news for Megan. Two can play at this game. "Sweetie! It's so good to see you!" I fling my arms around her neck, making sure to smash her hair the same way she's smashing mine. Of course, no doubt when we pull away from each other, her hair will still look perfect and mine will look like I just finished a cross-country ride on the back of a Hell's Angel's motorcycle, but still. I have to try.

Sure enough, when we break apart, Megan's chignon looks exactly the same. She looks over at Sadie. "Hi, Susie!" she says brightly.

"Hi, Marcy!" Sadie shoots back, not missing a beat.

Purposely calling people by the wrong name is one of Megan's favorite tactics of psychological warfare. Although how she can pull that stunt on Sadie with a straight face, I have no idea. They've been competing against each other since they were *babies*, for heaven's sake. Does she really think Sadie is going to believe that she doesn't know her name?

Annoyance flickers across Megan's face, but she quickly covers it. "And who are you?" she asks sweetly, turning away from Sadie and zeroing in on Eve.

Eve's chocolate-colored eyes widen in surprise. Or possibly terror. I'm not sure. Either way, she looks panicked to be the sudden focus of Megan's attention. "Eve Samuels," she replies.

"What's your title?" Megan continues the interrogation, her gaze sliding down Eve's green-and-white sundress to her Jessica Simpson peep-toe pumps and then back up. I can practically hear the wheels turning in her brain: *Where did she come from? Why wasn't I notified about this? Just what I need, a gorgeous black girl. She'll be in the Top Five for sure. And if she can belt out a Whitney Houston song and talk like a white person, she might even have a chance at winning. God, I hate minorities.*

Don't get me wrong, I'm not a racist or anything. I'm just trying to tell you what Megan—what *everybody*—is thinking about Eve. At least, everybody who's noticed her. And what I just said, as awful as it sounds, is *exactly* what they're thinking.

I promise. Because minorities are big. Big, big, big. Judges love them. And the ones who don't love them fake it lest they be branded as politically incorrect assholes who fly the Confederate flag on their front porches and think all illegal immigrants should be rounded up and burned at the stake.

So, you know, anybody who can check anything other than the little box beside *White/Caucasian* generally starts out with a leg up on the other contestants. Preferably a light-skinned brown leg like Eve's because (to paraphrase Jack Nicholson in *A Few Good Men*) deep down, in places they don't talk about at parties, the judges don't want a queen who looks *too* black. Or Hispanic. Or Asian. Or whatever.

Just ask the talented, adorable, sweet (and black) Miss State who made the mistake of including the beautician who relaxes her hair in her list of onstage thank-yous when she was giving up her crown a couple of years ago. I swear, if you'd heard the way people were whispering about it in the lobby afterward, you'd have thought she thanked Osama bin Laden or something.

"I'm Miss Hay Belle," Eve tells Megan proudly.

Megan's face immediately relaxes. "Oh," she says knowingly. "You're one of *those*."

"Those what?" Eve says blankly. She frowns as if trying to work out a super-hard algebra problem in her head.

I'm suddenly overcome by the urge to throw Eve over my shoulder like a caveman and take her somewhere far, far away. Because she seems like a really nice girl—possibly even a fragile, sensitive girl (in which case I should definitely throw her over my shoulder and take her far away)—and she obviously has no idea that she's swimming in a pool filled with big hungry sharks. And now Jaws has scented blood and is going to take a bite.

Megan laughs. "Oh, you know," she says breezily, making a dismissive gesture with her hand. "There are always five or six girls from closed Podunk prelims like Hay Belle. My mom keeps telling Suzette that she ought to shut those hick contests down because the queens they send to state are always so embarrassing, but Suzette is too soft hearted. Not that you'll embarrass anyone, of course," she adds smoothly. "I'm sure you'll do a lovely job."

At first Eve looks confused by Megan's answer, but then understanding dawns, and she looks crushed.

You see, preliminary pageants are like doors; they're either closed or open. An open prelim means that anyone can enter. You don't have to live in a certain county or go to a certain school—as long as you're between the ages of thirteen and seventeen and have never been married, been pregnant, or possessed a penis, you can compete.

(I'm so not making the penis thing up. That's really in the contract. You have to affirm that you are "not now nor have ever been a member of the opposite sex.")

Closed prelims, on the other hand, only allow contestants from designated geographical areas or schools to compete (and no, the penis thing doesn't fly with them, either). Which means that they're usually smaller and less competitive than open prelims. And in the case of a prelim like Miss Hay Belle, which is in a, uh, less *advantaged* part of the state, the competition is pretty much nonexistent. As in, you could dress up a monkey and enter it, and it would probably win.

In other words, Megan basically just told Eve that she sucks.

"Shut your face, Megan," Sadie snaps. "I'm sick to death of your crap, and so is everybody else. If you feel threatened by Eve, that's your problem."

Megan rolls her eyes. "Oh, please. I'm not even going to dignify that with a response."

"Nobody asked you to." Sadie grabs Eve's hand, then turns to me. "We're going to our room to unpack. I'll call you later."

And before I can throw my arms around Sadie's legs to stop her, she and Eve are gone. And I'm alone. With Megan.

"We should go unpack too," Megan informs me nonchalantly. She looks totally unruffled by Sadie's angry departure. In fact, she looks quite pleased with herself.

"Great," I muttered. "I can't wait."

Megan and I determinedly continue our BFF charade all the way through the lobby and on the crowded elevator ride up to the fifth floor, but the instant our hotel room door closes behind us, we drop the act and resume our normal personalities.

"This is my bed," Megan announces imperiously. She picks up a hot pink duffel bag monogrammed with the word "Queen" and tosses it onto the bed closer to the bathroom.

Our luggage, delivered by hotel porters while we were at

Arrival, is stacked haphazardly by the dresser. "Whatever." Shrugging, I pluck my suitcase from the pile and place it on the other bed. If she thinks I'm going to haggle over stupid stuff like the beds, she's smoking crack. In fact, I'm not going to haggle over anything with her. I'm going to be polite and civil if it kills me. Not because I'm such a saintly person, but because she's probably just trying to provoke me into saying something nasty so she can secretly tape it and, like, put it on YouTube or something.

"This place is a dump," Megan says disdainfully. She kicks off her shoes and reaches around behind her to unzip her dress. "Homeless people live in nicer alleys."

"I think it's nice," I disagree, even though she's right, the Majestic is a dump. It's one of those hotels with a nice lobby and downstairs, but the actual rooms are throwbacks to the Stone Age. No Internet, no cable, no hair dryer, and carpet that's showing bare patches. And get ready for this: *One* electrical outlet. That's right, one. And I don't mean, like, there's one outlet in the room and one outlet in the bathroom. I mean there's one outlet period. The TV and lamp are plugged into it.

It's impossible. The only reason this place is still in business is because it's some kind of important historical landmark or something. Apparently, a lot of people are really into that kind of thing, which I totally don't get. I mean, hello—what's more important? History or having somewhere to plug in your Chi iron?

Exactly.

All I can say is thank God for whoever invented power strips, because thirty-two beauty queens trapped together in a building with a shortage of electrical outlets is the kind of volatile situation that could lead to carnage and possibly even death.

"Of course you do." Megan sniffs. "Compared to the hovel you live in, I'm sure it's like being at the Ritz." The dress falls off her shoulders and lands in a puddle at her feet. She steps out of it, then carelessly kicks it away like it's an annoying piece of debris blocking her path.

I swallow hard. That's a seven-hundred-plus-dollar dress, and she's treating it like a piece of trash.

"Are you getting a good look, you little perv?"

"Huh?" I glance away from the crumpled-up dress and back at Megan. Who is completely naked except for a tiny little pink thong with black bows at the hips.

"Go ahead, get a good look," she sneers. "See what Gabe left you for."

At first I have no idea what she's talking about, but then her meaning registers. Eeeeew! Does she think I'm looking at her? Like, *looking* looking at her?

"You're disgusting." Dropping the lid to my suitcase, I grab the ice bucket off the dresser and slam out of the room. As far as indignant exits go, it's not that impressive, but I don't exactly have much to work with.

When I get back to the room, things are better. And worse. On the positive side, Megan is now wearing pink velour sweatpants and a tank top.

On the negative side, the room looks like an entire Sephora store exploded in it.

I halt inside the door, dumbstruck by the vision in front of me. *How did she unpack all this stuff so quickly?* I wonder incredulously. I mean, granted, I didn't exactly rush back from the ice machine, but I haven't been gone *that* long.

"What are you doing?" I demand, finally finding my voice.

"Unpacking." She pulls three boxes of protein bars out of the "Queen" duffel bag and lines them up on top of the TV.

"Unpacking what—your entire house?" I move into the room. "Hello, you're not in a private room here. I need somewhere to put my stuff too."

"I saved you a hanger," she says innocently. She gestures to the single wooden hanger hooked over the closet doorknob.

"Ha-ha. Very funny." I stomp over to the dresser and start gathering up bottles.

"Hey! Those are mine," she exclaims indignantly. "Put them down."

I continue piling things into my arms, ignoring her. I know I said I wasn't going to haggle about anything with her, but this is different. If I don't stand up for myself now, she'll monopolize everything—the vanity, the bathroom, the one measly electrical outlet. By the end of the week I'll be sleeping out in the hall. Well, assuming she hasn't smothered me with a pillow in my sleep first.

Megan's voice comes again, more threatening. "If you don't put my stuff down this instant, I'm going to Yvonne."

The mention of Yvonne stops me in my tracks like a stray bullet. Yvonne is the head chaperone, and she's been in the pageant system for roughly ten thousand years. Which means she knows Megan's mom, and Megan's aunt, and Megan's sister, and Megan's fourth cousin sixteen times removed, and—you get the idea. Last year there was even a rumor going around that Yvonne went on *vacation* with Megan's family to Bora Bora. (Which I thought was a made-up place, but according to Justine actually exists.) I have no idea if that's true or not, but either way, Yvonne and Megan's family are definitely like this [picture me crossing my fingers]. In other words, if Megan decides to go play the poor helpless victim to Yvonne, I'm screwed.

I know. It's so totally unfair. But that's the way it is. You see, the chaperones aren't just glorified dorm mothers whose only power is calling lights out and deciding who gets the Neat as a Pin award at the end of the pageant. Noooooo. They have *way* more influence than that.

They lunch with the judges, take them around town to see the sights, hang out with them at the hotel bar. And the whole time they're doing these things together, they're talking. About the pageant. And by "pageant" I mean the contestants.

Get the idea? If the chaperones hate you, or decide that you're a troublemaker, they can totally screw you with the judges. The same goes for the board of directors. If a girl ticks off somebody on the board, she can kiss her chance at the crown good-bye, because the board officials hang out with the judges too.

Megan can tell from my expression that I've caught on. "I'm glad we have an understanding," she says smugly.

It takes every ounce of self-control I possess not to punch her in the face. Fuming, I storm into the bathroom and sit down on the closed toilet lid.

Megan has taken over all the counter space in here too. My eyes travel over all the bottles and tubes. Hair spray, Fake Bake, cellulite cream, Firm Grip, Crest Whitestrips, Vaseline, Static Guard, lint roller, Band-Aids, electric toothbrush . . .

Electric toothbrush? I swing my gaze back to the blue-and-white brush. It's one of those hundred-dollar deals that get rid of plaque or give you superpowers or whatever it is they do. My mouth curves up in a smile.

Now, for the record, what I'm about to do is wrong. Wrong, wrong, wrong. Immature. Dangerous, even. I should be ashamed of myself for even thinking about doing something so awful.

I pause, waiting to be afflicted by appropriate feelings of shame.

Yeah . . . not so much.

Standing up, I pluck Megan's toothbrush off the counter. Then I turn back to the toilet and lift the lid, grinning like a maniac.

As far as my next move—well, let's just say that a Sonic-care toothbrush is good for cleaning more than just teeth.

Chapter Twenty

What is your favorite TV show?

Sleeping with one eye open is a lot harder than it sounds because of the whole, you know, sleeping thing, so when the alarm on my cell phone wakes me at six fifteen the next morning, I actually feel happy. I'm alive! Megan didn't kill me in my sleep!

I hit the disable button and glance over at Megan's bed. Empty. Rats. She beat me awake.

From behind the closed bathroom door I can hear the shower running, so I get out of bed and start doing the parts of my morning routine that don't require a bathroom, trying to ignore the weight on my bladder. If I was rooming with Sadie or somebody normal, I'd just see if the door was locked and—if not—go in and pee, but since Megan already basically accused me of being a lesbian, busting in on her when she's in the shower doesn't seem like the best idea.

Switching on the TV, I take the ironing board out of the closet and set it up in the space between the double beds. Thanks to Megan hogging every millimeter of the room, including all the drawers, all my clothes look like crap. They're still in my suitcase, which is presumably where they'll stay unless Megan suddenly develops a conscience.

She did (begrudgingly) let me hang my evening gown and talent costume in the closet. Wow. I'm so impressed.

Not.

I up the volume on the TV and fit my khaki shorts from Express over the nose of the ironing board. For rehearsals, contestants are required to wear an "official" pageant T-shirt with either shorts or capri pants. Each day is a different color; today's T-shirt is pink.

I think it's supposed to promote a sense of unity or something like that, which is a total joke. The only thing it promotes is a mini competition to see who can look the best.

You know what I'm talking about. If you have a super-toned stomach, you tie it up with a ponytail holder so it shows your midriff. Or you wear it with teeny-tiny shorts and heels to show off your legs. Or you tie the sleeves up with ribbons to make it sleeveless. Or maybe you wear it with an awesome belt—the possibilities are endless.

It doesn't matter what you look like at rehearsal, of course, but it's a chance to psych out your competition. Or so the theory goes. I've never had much luck psyching out anybody.

Once I'm dressed, I spend several minutes obsessing over footwear (sandals or tennis shoes?), and then when that's resolved (sandals, definitely), I obsess over my jewelry. Earrings or cuff bracelet? Both? Neither?

I hold a silver hoop up to my face and peer in the vanity mirror critically, but the pressure in my bladder makes it impossible to concentrate. I seriously need to go.

Laying the earring down, I go over to the bathroom and rap on the door.

"Hey, can I get in there for a minute?"

No answer. The shower is off now, but I can hear the faint clinking of bottles as she does . . . whatever it is somebody like Megan does in the morning. Moisturize with chicken blood? Recite ancient voodoo curses? Practice scathing insults and dirty looks in the mirror? It's a mystery.

I knock louder. "Hello—I need to use the bathroom."

This time her curt voice comes from the other side of the wood. "Go away. I'm busy."

I blink at the door. Busy? What's she doing in there, writing a book report?

"Well, when will you be unbusy?" I persist. "Because you've been in there forever and I need to pee."

"When I feel like it," she shoots back.

I start to say something mean, but then the memory of last night's impromptu toilet cleaning pops into my brain. OMG, what if I caused her to get infected with some lethal toilet germ and now she's in there, like, throwing up her internal organs or something? I'd be a murderer.

I press my face into the crack above the doorknob. "Um, is everything okay? I mean, are you feeling okay?"

"Why wouldn't I feel okay?" she replies hatefully. "I'm about to beat you, aren't I?"

Never mind. She's fine.

"Look, I really, really need to go, so could you finish up? Like now?"

"No."

I take a deep breath. Obviously, it's time to use the finely honed communication skills I've learned from competing in pageants. "If you don't unlock this door in the next three seconds, I'm going to pee on your shoes." (Hey, I never said they were *mature* communication skills.)

Unfortunately, Megan doesn't seem fazed by the prospect of me ruining her shoes. "Go ahead," she laughs. "Pee on my clothes, too. The more I have to tell Yvonne, the better."

"Aaargh!" I kick the bottom of the door. Which is a pretty stupid thing to do since I'm wearing open-toed sandals. "Ow, ow, ow." I hop on one leg, clutching my throbbing toes.

"Destruction of hotel property is grounds for expulsion from the pageant, you know," Megan singsongs.

I make a not-very-nice hand gesture (that, for the record, I never, ever use in real life. Well, except for now. But she deserves it) at the closed door and turn back toward the room. My eyes swing to the digital clock on the nightstand. Six forty-five! OMG, I'm going to be late!

Panicked, I snatch up the complimentary canvas tote bag provided to all contestants and scramble around the room gathering up the stuff I need for the day—room card, tap shoes, bottled water, protein bars. Being late to rehearsal—even by a second—is basically the same thing as waving a giant flag over your head that says "Don't pick me! I'm totally irresponsible!" Or that's the way the chaperones make you feel, anyway.

Which is exactly why Megan decided to take up permanent residence in the bathroom, I realize as I let myself out of the room and sprint toward the elevators. She's trying to make me late.

Ha. Well, I've got news for her. Two can play at that game. Tomorrow I'll get up at five a.m. No, four a.m.—heck, I'll stay up all night, if that's what it takes. I'll make a pallet on the floor in front of the bathroom. No, I'll sleep *in* the bathroom.

Except wait. Isn't that what I was trying to avoid last night when I made my pathetic attempt to stop Megan from taking over the room? Is she trying to do some sort of weird reverse psychology thing on me? Am I wasting way too much time and energy obsessing about this when I need to be focusing on the actual competition?

Right. Don't answer that.

The elevator pings to announce that we've arrived at the hotel lobby, and, pushing the whole mess out of my mind, I dash through the doors, rip through the bathroom next to guest services like a tornado, then race across the enclosed bridge that connects the hotel to the convention center.

When I arrive in the cavernous auditorium, the stage is already a sea of pink T-shirts and chaos.

"Everybody, listen up, please! All eyes on me, lips zipped! We have a lot of work to do!" an ultra-tan guy in a sleeveless black T-shirt and khaki cargo shorts calls out as I steal unobtrusively up the steps and slip into the front row of girls standing onstage. I was hoping to stand next to Sadie and Eve during rehearsal, but now, thanks to Megan, I don't have time to figure out where they are.

Oh, well. I guess it doesn't matter. Blaine is just going to move everybody around anyway. Blaine being the ultra-tan guy, by the way. Otherwise known as the pageant choreographer. Who is, of course, gay because beauty pageants are magnets for gay guys. (Hey! That's like a little rhyme! "Pageants are magnets." I crack myself up.) Seriously, if there were no gay guys, pageants would be extinct in, like, a week.

"I have exciting news for you girls," Blaine continues as the stage falls quiet. "The theme for this year's pageant is going to be"—he pauses for effect—"*Dancing with the Stars*! Isn't that fabulous?" He beams at us, clearly waiting for us to break into ecstatic applause, or, I don't know, start jumping up and down, but everybody just sort of stares back at him. A few people smile politely, but that's it. Not because there's anything wrong with *Dancing with the Stars*. It's just that all pageant production numbers are dorky. It doesn't matter what they are. Personally, I'm just thrilled Blaine didn't pick *High School Musical*. Do you have any idea how many times I've had to sing "We're All in This Together" over the past two years?

"Yay! That is such a great idea!" Somebody near the middle of the stage suddenly starts clapping wildly. I don't even have to look to know that it's Megan.

A moment ago Blaine's smile was wavering, but now it returns full-force. "I'm glad *somebody* appreciates it," he says raking his eyes over us pointedly. He motions to Megan. "Come up here, darling."

There's a rustling as people shift to let her pass, and then Megan steps gracefully out of the crowd and goes to stand next to Blaine. She looks incredible, thanks to her hostile take-over of the bathroom. Her hair is swept back low on the nape of her neck with multiple bands of delicate Grecian braids interspersed on the sides. In other words, she obviously sub-scribes to *In Style* magazine too because last month they had an article called "Grecian Braids are Hot, Hot, Hot!" and they showed Jessica Alba and Heidi Klum wearing the exact same hairstyle.

Blaine sweeps Megan into his arms as if preparing to ballroom dance. "The opening number will consist of me and the current Miss Teen State doing the tango while you girls dance around us with beautiful red roses in your mouths," Blaine informs us. "But as you know, Katy won't be here until this afternoon, so for right now Megan can fill in."

I blink at him. I'm sorry, did he just say we were going to dance around with ROSES IN OUR MOUTHS?! Are you freaking kidding me? Suddenly *High School Musical* doesn't seem so bad.

We spend the next four hours painstakingly learning our moves for the opening number while listening to Blaine's run-ning commentary on Megan's "racehorse legs," her "natural gracefulness," and her "long lines." In fact, if Blaine's boy-friend, Darin, wasn't sitting in the front row of the auditorium intently texting on his BlackBerry, I'd swear the whole gay thing was just an act.

By the time Blaine dismisses us for lunch, I have permanently removed *Dancing with the Stars* from my list of must-see TV. Which stinks because *DWTS* is one of my very favorite shows. But I have no choice; Blaine has ruined it forever. And I'm sorry, but he only picked that theme so *he* could be onstage and get attention. It's so obvious.

I find Sadie and Eve and we make our way to the convention center's banquet room, where a buffet lunch of lasagna, green beans, and big fat buttery rolls is spread out for the contestants. That is the hilarious thing about Miss Teen State. You starve yourself for months, kill yourself in the gym, and then when you get here, they try to shove BUTTERED ROLLS down your throat. I mean, are the people who plan the menus really that sadistic or do they just not get it? The latter, I hope, but gee . . . sometimes I wonder.

Sadie takes one look at the steaming buffet pan filled with gooey lasagna, then whips a box of Zone bars out of her tote bag. She shakes the yellow box at me and Eve. "Anybody want one?"

"I do," I say quickly, even though I have Zone bars in my bag too. But mine are fudge flavored and Sadie's are chocolate mint, my favorite.

Sadie hands me a yellow-wrapped rectangle, then looks expectantly at Eve. "Eve? You want one?"

"Sure," Eve answers, but I see her eyes go longingly toward the lasagna.

Guilt niggles at my stomach. Eve would probably eat from the buffet if Sadie and I weren't here. Are we putting unfair peer pressure on her? I don't want to be responsible for, like, turning her into an ana or anything. The thought of anorexic girls reminds me of something I noticed in rehearsal.

"Ohmigosh, have you seen Georgia Ketchum?" I whisper to Sadie as we move to the drinks table.

She reaches for a glass of unsweetened tea. "Yes, I saw her earlier," she murmurs. "Poor girl. She looks awful, just like a skeleton."

Eve frowns at us. "Who are you guys talking about?"

"Look. Over there." Sadie nudges her until she's looking at the table where Georgia Ketchum is sitting. "The girl who is wearing the big silver cross," she whispers, which is totally unnecessary since only a blind person wouldn't be able to figure out which of the five girls at the table we're talking about.

Georgia Ketchum used to be a cute, normal-sized girl with milky skin and bouncy blond hair, but now she looks like a bad Halloween skeleton. Apparently, about a year or so ago somebody told her that her swimsuit score was holding her back and that she'd score higher if she lost about five pounds. So she went on a diet. Except instead of losing five pounds, she lost about *fifty* pounds.

And now she looks so awful, I feel actual physical pain every time I see her. It's like, I just want to grab her and shove a cheeseburger down her throat, you know?

"Oh yeah," Eve says in recognition when she sees Georgia's emaciated figure. "I noticed her yesterday." She shakes her head sadly. "Why don't her parents send her to a rehab clinic or something?"

Sadie pops a piece of Zone bar into her mouth. "They have. Twice. Believe it or not, she used to look worse."

"You're kidding." Eve looks horrified by this revelation.

"Well, it *is* a complex psychological illness requiring both medical treatment and behavioral therapy that addresses underlying issues of control and self-perception," I tell her because, apparently, Justine has somehow taken over my body.

Sadie and Eve are impressed. "Wow, is your platform about eating disorders?" Sadie asks me.

I shake my head. "No, it's the importance of cherishing the elderly. I have no idea where that came from."

"O-kay." Sadie glances at her watch. "We've still got forty-five minutes before we have to be back for afternoon rehearsal. . . . What do you say we stop by the gift room?"

"That'd be fun," Eve agrees, brightening. "I just need to grab something first, okay? I'll be right back." She takes one last glance at Georgia, then hurries back to the buffet table and shoves a giant dinner roll into her mouth.

Sadie turns to me. "Is that okay with you?" she asks. "Going to the gift room? I don't want to be a Bossy Bess or anything."

A Bossy Bess? I've heard of Pageant Pattys and Chatty Cathys, but that one must have slipped past me.

"Yeah, sure. It's fine," I lie. Truthfully, the gift room is the *last* place I want to go, but I don't want to be left alone in here with all the circling vultures. And I saw Megan heading back over the bridge to the hotel earlier, so no way am I going back up to our room.

Besides, we haven't even been here twenty-four hours. How much stuff could possibly be there yet?

A whole friggin' lot, I realize fifteen minutes later when we step off the elevator onto the second floor of the convention center.

"Whoa." Eve stops in her tracks, gazing in amazement at the two long, sagging tables in front of us. "Are you sure this isn't for a wedding or something?"

I shake my head. "Nope. This is the gift room. Well, the gift *area*," I amend.

"Whoa," she says again, apparently too shell-shocked for anything beyond that.

And what we're looking at *is* pretty unbelievable. But I haven't really explained the gift room, er, area yet, have I? Oops, I'm sorry.

It's like this: Long, long ago in a kingdom far, far away some well-meaning mom started a tradition whereby people send contestants gifts every day of the pageant. I'm sure it started out as no big deal, just sweet little gestures like a nice Hallmark card or a good-luck helium balloon, but somewhere along the way it turned into MAJOR LOOT.

I'm talking humongous flower arrangements, gift baskets, jewelry, spa gift certificates, elaborately wrapped packages from boutiques with names like Spoiled and Classy Chic. Last year one girl even got a *car*. (No, really. I swear. Her parents sent her this black velvet box with a red bow, and when she opened it up, there was a shiny silver key with a picture of a brand-new Mustang.)

Which is great and all, but the thing about presents is that they don't just magically poof out of the air. Somebody has to send them to you. In this situation, usually your parents. So if your mom and dad have no idea this whole gift table thing exists and no money to send you anything even if they did . . . well, you can see why I wasn't exactly jumping up and down at the thought of coming here.

I know, I know. Get out the violins. Woe is me. But really, I'm not whining. I don't care whether I get presents or not. However, I *am* human, and let's face it—even if you don't give a flip about getting a present, it's still not fun to stand around listening to a bunch of spoiled girls say things like "Ohmigod, can you believe my mother sent me *another* pair of Sevens? I told her I wanted a new nano."

"Look what I got!" Sadie calls out, lifting up a huge arrangement of pink and yellow daisies from the end of one of the tables. "It's from Mi-Mi and Pi-Pi."

"Wow, that's beautiful," I tell her. I'm not even touching the Mi-Mi and Pi-Pi thing.

Squeals pierce the air as more girls get off the elevator and start claiming their loot. Sadie rakes it in, finding two more flower arrangements, a bottle of the new Sarah Jessica Parker perfume, and a wooden cuff bracelet with matching necklace. Even Eve has something waiting for her—super-cute Victoria's Secret pajamas from her aunt Linda.

I'm over by the window discussing the merits of Cinderella Hair vs. Great Lengths extensions with a girl named Brandi when Sadie suddenly calls out, "Hey, Pres, there's something here for you. Aren't you even going to come look at it?"

"Huh?" I look at her blankly.

Sadie motions to me excitedly. "Come and open the card. Everybody's dying to know who they're from."

"I'll be right back," I tell Brandi apologetically.

"Look, there must be some kind of a mix-up," I start as I reach Sadie, but before I can get the rest of the sentence out, she shoves the most enormous arrangement of red roses I've ever seen in my life into my hands.

"Aren't they gorgeous?" she gushes.

I set the roses back on the table with a *thunk*. "Yes, they're beautiful, but they're not mine."

She snatches up the little white envelope that's affixed to one of the stems. "Then why does this say 'Presley Ashbury'?" she asks, squinting at the name printed on the envelope.

Hmmm. Good question. Maybe Noralee felt guilty for giving me the cold shoulder at Arrival yesterday, so she decided to send me a present? And somehow the card to her present accidentally got stuck on the roses?

Yeah, that's it. It has to be. I mean, don't get me wrong. I *wish* they were my roses, but let's get real. Who is going to send me roses? My parents don't have that kind of money, and Justine would never, ever send me a good-luck present at a beauty pageant. Plus, she's not even in the country. And Hunter and Lilly are in Michigan.

"I bet Noralee bought me something and the cards got mixed up," I tell Sadie. I scan the loot left on the table, looking for a more plausible package. "There." I point to a pink stuffed cat in a princess dress. "I bet that's it. That looks like something Noralee would buy."

Eve picks up the cat. "But this says 'Good Luck, Caroline.' See?" She turns the cat around so we can see the bright pink words embroidered on the front of its dress.

I frown at the cat. Rats. It would have looked so cute on my bed. "Okay, well maybe that bath set thingy," I amend, pointing to a basket of pastel bottles from Bath & Body Works.

"Because your mom and dad are so proud of their 'duckie girl'?" Sadie asks, reading from the card attached to the handle of the basket with a ribbon.

"Uh, no." Double rats. And there was an Henri Bendel candle in there too.

I look around the rest of the table, completely flummoxed. "Which one is it, then?"

Sadie rolls her eyes. "Hello—it's the roses."

"But I don't—"

"Why don't you open the card?" she interrupts before I can issue another denial. "Maybe it will say something helpful like 'Enjoy the beautiful roses and stop acting like a dork.'"

Oh. Right. The card. I knew that. I break the seal on the envelope and pull out the little square of cardboard. The handwriting isn't Noralee's neat, schoolteacher cursive, but a barely legible scrawl.

You're right. I am a jackass.
Give me a second chance?
Robbie

I have to reread the three sentences about ten times before my brain finally processes their meaning. *Oh. My. God. Robbie sent me flowers.*

Chapter Twenty-one

Define "beauty."

No, not flowers. He sent me roses. RED roses. The kind of roses you send to your wife, or your girlfriend, or someone you have a crush on. But Robbie doesn't have a crush on me. That's impossible. I'm making too much out of the color thing. He probably just asked for a nice arrangement and that's what the florist shop decided to send. It doesn't have any hidden meaning. And the thing he wrote on the card about giving him a second chance—that just means he hopes I accept his apology. He's not saying he wants to see me again. Is he? IS HE?

These are the thoughts that run through my head roughly sixteen million times throughout the rest of the day. Over and over and over again—I can't think about anything else. Because, needless to say, I am FREAKED OUT.

In fact, I'm obviously freaked out to the point of mental impairment because it's now eight p.m. and I am sitting in a chair in Sadie and Eve's hotel room letting Sadie "experiment" with my hair.

"Is he somebody you met on the Internet? A friend of

the family? A guy from school?" Sadie peppers me with questions about Robbie's identity as she teases my hair with a metal comb that could double as a lethal weapon.

"I already told you," I say impatiently. "He's just this guy I had an argument with. He's trying to apologize. It's no big deal." Normally, I'm an open-book type of person, but for some reason I don't want to tell Sadie and Eve about Robbie.

"No big deal?" She pulls the comb away from my head and props her hands on her hips. "Honey, those roses cost two hundred dollars if they cost a dime. That's at *least* a medium-sized deal. And in my book it's a super-huge deal."

I shrug.

She rolls her eyes and resumes teasing my hair to the ceiling. "They're not from your ex, are they? What was his name—Gabe?"

"No." The denial comes out sharper than I intend and Sadie gives me a strange look. "Er, what exactly are you doing to my hair?" I rush on, hoping to divert her attention. Because Robbie isn't the only thing I haven't told her about; she's in the dark about Gabe, too.

I mean, she knows we broke up, obviously, but she doesn't know about him and Megan. I've started to tell her a million times since she flagged me down yesterday at Arrival, but . . . I don't know. I just can't seem to force it out of my mouth. It's too embarrassing.

I know, I know. That's a stupid way to feel because Sadie is my friend—and so is Eve—and I know they would be totally sympathetic, but I can't help it.

"I'm making it higher," Sadie answers as if this should be perfectly obvious.

I reach a tentative hand up to the top of my head. "Higher? It feels like it's practically Marge Simpson hair as it is."

"The higher the hair, the closer to God," she says primly. She plucks a missile-sized can of Aqua Net off the dresser and aims it toward my head.

I glance over at Eve, who is propped up on her side on the bed, reading *People* magazine. "Save me. Please."

She laughs. "No way. You're on your own. She already threatened to give me bangs."

"I did not threaten!" Sadie says indignantly. "I *offered*. 'Threaten' sounds so . . . threatening. Besides, I need the practice." She jams her finger down on the nozzle and blasts me with about a thousand gallons of Aqua Net.

When she's finished permanently damaging my lungs, she once again returns to her favorite topic of conversation. "Well, are you at least going to call and thank him?" she asks, stepping back to survey her handiwork.

"Thank him?" I echo stupidly.

"Yeah, you know, that thing you do when somebody gives you a present?"

"Uh, I haven't really thought about it," I say truthfully.

She makes an exasperated sound as she tosses the Aqua Net into the wicker basket of hair care products at her feet. "Well, aren't you going to?"

I have a brief mental image of calling Robbie to say thanks and then stuttering like an idiot. Or worse, calling Robbie and then not being able to say anything at all. Not to mention I don't even have his cell phone number.

"No, I'll just, er, tell him thanks the next time I see him." Which will be precisely never since he's going off to college in three months.

"Okay, if that's what you want to do," Sadie answers in a tone of voice that implies I'm a total idiot if that is, in fact, what I want to do. "Come and look at your hair," she urges, motioning for me to go in the bathroom with her.

I follow her eagerly, grateful to finally drop the subject. At least, I hope we're dropping the subject.

She flips on the light and pushes me in front of the mirror. "Do you like it?" she asks breathlessly.

I blink at my reflection, temporarily speechless. I look like I'm balancing the Empire State Building on my head. Except taller. With wings.

"Well?" she prompts. "Do you?"

I swallow hard. My initial instinct is to just let out a bloodcurdling scream, but that would probably hurt Sadie's feelings. Besides, she hasn't done anything that can't be fixed with a little water and a hundred or so bottles of shampoo.

"Er, yeah, it's great," I croak. "It's very . . . high."

I wait for her to call my bluff, but instead, her face lights up. "I knew you would love it! Do you want me to do it like this tomorrow night? You're wearing your blue evening gown, right? This would look so good with it."

"Er, I'll have to ask Noralee," I hedge. "She wants me to

wear my hair down, and she's pretty strict about that kind of stuff." If Sadie was anybody else, I'd suspect that she was trying to sabotage me by making my hair look hideous, but she's sincere. She's just a horrible hair stylist.

"Okay," Sadie agrees easily. "You can ask her and then tell me tomorrow."

"Right. I'll ask her first thing tomorrow," I promise. Which is a big fat lie, but what am I supposed to do—tell Sadie I hate my hair? She'd be crushed.

As much as the idea of going up to my hotel room makes me want to fling myself out into traffic, nine p.m. bed check is fast approaching, so I reluctantly say good-bye to Eve and Sadie and ride the elevator back to the fifth floor.

The first thing I notice when I walk in the room is that Robbie's roses are no longer on the windowsill next to my bed. Nor are they on the nightstand, or the dresser, or the TV, or any of the other places a person might put a flower arrangement. In fact, they're not anywhere.

The second thing I notice is that Megan is draped across *my* bed on her stomach, wearing nothing but a towel and giggling to somebody on her cell phone.

I have no idea what the third thing I notice is. I'm too preoccupied with numbers one and two.

I put my hands on my hips and peer down at her threateningly. "Get off my bed," I order. "And tell me what you did with my flowers."

My voice is surprisingly scary-sounding, but Megan just rolls over on her back and looks up at me irritably. "Hello—

I'm talking to my *boyfriend* here. Do you mind?"

Great. So she's lying half naked on *my* bed talking to *my* ex-boyfriend. Except the funny thing is . . . I don't really even care. I mean, I want her off my bed, obviously, but I don't care that she's talking to Gabe. Right now I'm only worried about Robbie's flowers.

"Yes, I do mind," I shoot back. "Where are my flowers?"

Megan ignores me. "What did wu say, Baby Bear?" she coos into the phone. "Mama Bear was distwacted."

Even royally ticked, this brings me up short. Did she actually just call Gabe *Baby Bear*? And herself *Mama Bear*? There are so, so many things wrong here. I don't even know where to start.

I do, however, know how to be persistent. "Where are my flowers?!" I screech, kicking the mattress.

Megan pulls the phone away from her face. "For heaven's sake, they're in the closet," she snaps. "Stop acting like a psycho. Nice hair, by the way."

I ignore her mocking look and go quickly to the closet and yank open the door. The vase is sitting on the floor next to a pile of Megan's dirty laundry.

That's right. My beautiful two-hundred-dollar roses are keeping company with Megan's dirty thong underwear. Not only that, they look like Megan played soccer with them before she dumped them by her Cosabella unmentionables.

I close my eyes and count slowly to ten, trying to control the fury lashing at my insides. *Just two more days, just two more days,* I chant silently. *Two more days and this will all be over.*

At least I was smart enough to hide Robbie's card inside the obligatory Bible in my nightstand. Who knows what Megan would have done if she'd seen that? Something tells me she would have destroyed more than my flowers.

When I finally get my anger down to nonhomicidal levels, I turn back to the room. The two bears have apparently said their good nights because now Megan is standing in front of the dresser mirror carefully pulling a wide-tooth comb through her wet hair. Except—wait a minute. Why is she doing that awkward pause thing at the top of her head? It's like she's combing around a barrette or a ponytail holder or something. Almost like—

"You have hair extensions?" I gasp.

She whips toward me. "What? Who told you that?" she demands sharply.

"Nobody told me. I can tell by the way you're combing around the bonding."

For a teeny-tiny second I see something that looks like fear flicker in her eyes, but then it's gone and her mask of evil is back. "Well, Sherlock Holmes," she says haughtily, turning back to the mirror, "I hate to disappoint you, but your detective skills need a little work. Everybody knows my hair is natural."

Which is exactly what I'm getting at. Megan (and everybody else) is always making this huge deal over how Megan's hair is so long and so beautiful and so shiny and so bouncy and so *natural*. "The only girl onstage whose follicles actually grew from her own head," somebody wrote on the message boards after Miss Teen State last year. And it's all a big fat lie! Megan has normal hair just like everybody else!

I don't know if it's all the stress getting to me, or if I'm just relieved to find proof that Megan is mortal, or what, but for some reason this thought strikes me as unbelievably hilarious and I dissolve into giggles.

"What are you laughing about?" Megan gives me a death glare, but I'm too far gone for it to have any effect. Megan Leighton has hair extensions. Megan Leighton has hair extensions. I want to run down the hall screaming it out loud.

Disgusted, Megan throws her comb down on the dresser, then stomps into the bathroom and slams the door. A moment later I hear the electric *buzzzzzzzzzz* of her toothbrush, which immediately sets me off again.

"Shuth up!" she yells through the door in a garbled voice.

"Okay, okay." Forcing my laughter down to a barely audible snicker, I pluck up Robbie's roses and return them to the windowsill, pausing first to break off one of the blooms and slip it under my pillow like a little kid leaving a tooth for the tooth fairy.

I know. I'm a dork. But maybe it'll bring me luck or something. And by "luck" I mean "maybe Robbie will call and tell me that these flowers aren't just an apology and that he's really madly in love with me."

With the good-luck bloom safely under my pillow, I turn my attention to trying to arrange the rest of the stems so that they look marginally less pitiful. I think Megan really *did* play soccer with them. That's how bad they look.

Have I mentioned that I hate Megan? Intensely?

Right. Just checking.

As I do my best to hide the worst of the damage, I think about Megan lying on my bed, cooing to Gabe in baby talk. Or, more specifically, I think about my nonreaction to Megan lying on my bed cooing to Gabe in baby talk. Because I wasn't just putting on a brave face. It really didn't bother me. Even now, thinking about it, I don't feel upset. It just seems, well, really, really hilarious, frankly. I mean, *Mama Bear and Baby Bear*? Come on! Could anything *be* more hysterical?

I feel a giggle trying to burst out of my throat and quickly choke it back. Megan's hair extensions are one thing, but if I allow myself to let loose over the two bears, I'm afraid I might really and truly die laughing. Literally.

Not to mention, what's wrong with me? Why aren't I upset? Fourteen days ago I couldn't even think about Gabe and Megan without feeling like somebody reached into my chest and ripped out my heart with their bare hands, and now the only emotion I can conjure up is amusement? How is that possible?

As I'm pondering this question, something Justine said wriggles its way into my thoughts. At lunch the day after Gabe dumped me, what was it she told me? Something about how Megan had done me a favor because I'd lost interest in Gabe anyway? And I basically told her she was crazy, but now . . .

OMG, Justine was totally right, I realize, startled. I *had* lost interest in Gabe. That's why I'm not upset. I'm already over him. And there's no way I could already be over him unless I wasn't that into him to start with.

Wow. *Justine* is the one who should be a therapist. Forget hiding information in coffins or whatever the heck she was so upset about not getting to do this summer. She needs to get a TV show like Dr. Phil. I mean, she knew what was up and I didn't even have a clue.

Abandoning the flowers, I instinctively go for my purse to get my cell phone and call her, but then I remember that she's in Central America saving the world.

Rats. If I call her there, it'll probably cost, like, a thousand dollars. I only have the bargain basement cell phone plan. And that's assuming I could actually get her. Do they even have cell phone towers in Central America? Isn't that one of those places where the people live in, like, grass huts and stuff?

Bummed, I drop my purse back onto the floor next to my bed. Oh, well. It's not like I could've really talked to her, anyway, not with Megan in the bathroom just waiting to eavesdrop.

The thought of Megan eavesdropping immediately makes me want to call Robbie (per Sadie's instructions to thank him), but only for about half a second. As much as I'd LOVE for Megan to hear me talking to the hottest guy ever, I can't be sure that it wouldn't blow up in my face. (Reference earlier comments regarding possible muteness and/or stuttering.) And, of course, there's the teeny-tiny matter of his cell phone number. Specifically, that I have no idea what it is.

Besides, I think later that night when I'm curled under the covers, stroking the velvety bloom hidden under my pillow, *if my lucky rose works, maybe Robbie will call me.*

Chapter Twenty-two

In what way could you be a role model for today's youth?

If I kept a journal like Justine does, this is what my entry would look like for today: *Today is private interview. Feel like might puke. Hopefully not on judges.*

"How do you feel about the Patriot Act?" the balding judge asks me, peering over the tops of his seriously outdated glasses. According to my contestant folder, his name is Thomas Benfield, but I have taken the liberty of giving him a new name: Mr. I-Hate-Your-Guts-Why-Do-You-Keep-Asking-Me-These-Impossible-Questions? But that's a little long, so I'll go with Mr. I-Hate-Your-Guts for short.

"I feel that the Patriot Act is very important," I say confidently, even though I have absolutely no idea what the Patriot Act is. Something to do with 9/11, maybe? For some reason that sounds right, but I'm not sure.

I'm sure you've already figured this out, but on the off chance you haven't, I'm currently in the middle of my interview with the judges (i.e., 30 percent of my final score). And frankly, it's not going all that well. Mostly due to Mr. Smarty-Pants-How-Do-You-Feel-About-The-Patriot-Act-Here.

A lot of people think pageant interviews are nothing but stuff like *What's your favorite ice cream flavor?* or *If you were an animal, what animal would you be?* but that's *so* not true. The judges ask you serious questions. But this guy is over the top. I mean, he's already asked me how I feel about stem cell research, prayer in public school, and whether I think it's okay for women to work outside the home if they have small children. I think he can give it a rest.

"*Why* do you think the Patriot Act is important?" he presses because, of course, there's no way he's going to let me off that easy.

I tighten my hands on the sides of the podium, praying for divine inspiration. The first rule when answering a pageant interview question is to reverse it and repeat it back, so I say slowly, "I think the Patriot Act is important because . . ." I hesitate and for a split second I'm terrified that I'm going to have a Miss South Carolina 2007 Teen USA moment (see hilarious video on YouTube), but then by some miracle, divine inspiration really does strike. "Because it helps protect our country and its citizens from dangerous threats," I finish.

I hold my breath, waiting for some sign that I have just royally screwed up—maybe the Patriot Act is about giving kittens good homes—but he merely nods and starts writing on his clipboard.

I exhale quietly. Whew. I feel like I just dodged a bullet.

In addition to Mr. Patriot Act, there are two other judges: a smiling, middle-aged woman with frosted hair, who (so far) has only asked me softball questions about school and my plat-form, and a young, intense-looking guy in a bright purple tie who has yet to utter a peep. Which is probably good because I do the whole picture-your-audience-naked thing to make me less nervous, and he's actually kind of hot. So, you know, that might be kind of distracting.

"I see on your fact sheet that you're a cheerleader, Presley. Is that something you've been doing for a long time?" The woman judge—Janet, I think her name is—takes over the questioning, and I feel like running over and kissing her. Because the chick monitoring the timer in the back of the room just gave me the two-minutes-left signal, which means that if I can just manage not to say anything stupid for the next one hundred and twenty seconds, I might make it out of here with a pretty good score. Maybe even a *great* score.

"Yes, I've been a cheerleader at school since the sixth grade," I answer, practically beaming at her. No, not practi-cally. I *am* beaming at her. I can feel my face glowing. "And before that I was involved in the peewee cheerleading pro-gram that my hometown's community center sponsors," I continue, trying to take up time. "Peewee cheerleading is a great way to introduce young girls to the sport, plus it teaches the value of teamwork at a young age. And it's a great way for kids to be involved in their community, not to mention a great way to get lots of good exercise." Now I'm just spewing out b.s., but I don't care.

One minute left.

The monitor holds up one finger and my heart soars. Sixty seconds!

I continue beaming at Janet, waiting for her to ask me what I like best about cheerleading or maybe something about my other extracurricular activities, but the next question comes from Mr. Hot Purple Tie judge who has apparently decided that he's not mute after all.

He clasps his hands behind his head and leans back in his chair. "How do you feel about underage drinking?" he asks curiously.

My beaming, glowing expression immediately turns into a deer-caught-in-the-headlights expression. I blink at him, trying to gather my wits, while simultaneously trying to decide if this is a loaded question (i.e., does he know about my message board infamy?).

"I'm sorry, do you need me to repeat the question?" he prompts politely.

"No, no, it's fine," I say quickly. I clear my throat. "I think underage drinking is a serious issue that can have very serious consequences. I also think it's something that happens way more than most adults realize." I pause. All three of them are leaning forward, listening to me intently, and I suddenly have the overwhelming sensation that if I can't come out with whatever it is they're hoping to hear, the rest of the interview may as well have never happened.

The monitor motions to me again. *Twenty seconds.*

I gulp in a breath and rush on. "This is actually an issue that's very close to my heart because it's something I have struggled with personally. When you're in high school, it can be very easy to give in to peer pressure and do things that go against your values. That's one of the reasons why I'm so passionate about becoming Miss Teen State. Teenagers need role models they can relate to, people who understand the problems they struggle with on a day-to-day basis. They're not looking for some perfect Barbie doll with a crown on her head. They want a real person who knows where they're coming from, a person who has made mistakes, learned from them, and wants to share those lessons with others. And as Miss Teen State, I know I can be that perso—"

"Time!" The monitor cuts me off before I can get the word "person" completely out of my mouth, and that's it. For better or worse, my interview is over.

After my interview I feel like I could sleep for about a thousand years, but I have to make do with a handful of almonds and a gulp of water because then it's time to get ready for The Show. As in, the part of the pageant that's open to the public. Tonight is the talent preliminary, which means—well, duh. You know what it means. We're competing in talent. All THIRTY-TWO of us.

Did I mention that whoever designed this year's schedule is possibly a recent parolee from a mental institution? Because having thirty-two contestants do talent on the same night is *insane*. Who wants to sit through that? I mean, I *adore* watching pageants, and even I start getting edgy after about the fourteenth or fifteenth contestant. Thirty-two is unthinkable.

And I was so elated over being next to last . . . oh, well. At least if the judges are asleep when my turn rolls around, that means they'll be asleep for Megan's turn too.

By the time I make it to the giant dressing room back-stage, the place is a whirlwind of activity. Girls are running around in Spanx and Velcro rollers, taping their boobs, stretching, warming up their voices, wriggling into dresses, touching up their makeup—it's typical prepageant madness in all its glory.

I find Sadie and Eve near the middle of the room, taking turns zipping each other into the black strapless dresses we're supposed to wear for the opening number.

"Oh, thank goodness," Sadie exclaims when she sees me. "Do you have any extra Spanx?"

I nod. "Probably. Let me go find my stuff and I'll look." I drop my tote bag on the ground next to Sadie's and go in search of the long plastic boxes containing my pageant wardrobe and essentials, which pageant volunteers carried over earlier today.

By the time I find the boxes and drag them back, the crisis is over; another girl has already found an extra pair of Spanx and loaned them to Sadie.

And now we're at a crossroads. At this point, I can either (a) give you a play-by-play of everything that happens over the next three or four hours even though you've already seen it in a dozen bad pageant movies, or (b) I can skip to the good parts.

I vote (b).

• • •

Three hours, thirty performances, and one intermission later, and finally Chuck, the over-blow-dried, annoying emcee, says . . .

"Our next contestant will be performing a tap routine to an Elvis Presley medley. Please join me in welcoming contestant number thirty-one to the stage—Miss Magnolia Blossom, Presley Ashbury!"

The audience breaks into obligatory welcoming applause, and at the stage director's signal I run out onto the stage and hit my opening pose. (Yes, it's the famous Elvis stance—head down, leg cocked, attitude on.) My prop, a straight-backed wooden chair, is already in place just to the left of center stage.

As the auditorium falls silent, Elvis crackles to life on the speaker system. *"The warden threw a party in the county jail . . ."*

I launch into motion, throwing myself into the dance with every particle of my being. Not just because I'm desperate to get a good score (although, of course, I am), but because— well, I really, really love to dance. I know that sounds stupid and cheesy, but it's the truth. I love to dance. And I especially love to dance in front of an audience. Remember how I told you about my dance teacher saying I'm more of a performer than a dancer? Well, that's why I always score high in talent, even though I'm just an average tapper. It's because I love what I'm doing and the audience can tell.

My shoes beat out a bold, satisfying rhythm on the stage floor. The floor mikes they set up to magnify dancers' taps are a hit-or-miss kind of thing, and tonight the amplification system is working perfectly. I sound like a Rockette.

If you can't find a partner, use a wooden chair.

That's my cue. In one lithe movement, I grab the chair, step onto the seat, and start tapping.

The audience immediately breaks into a cacophony of applause and whistles, sending an adrenaline rush through my body. If the audience is impressed, hopefully that means the judges are impressed too. And I *do* look pretty cool, if I do say so myself.

(Shhh. Do you want to hear a secret? This might look like a regular old kitchen chair, but actually, Miss Violet, my dance teacher, had her husband build it especially for me. It's wider than a regular chair, which is why I can tap on it. But the audience and judges don't know that. They just think I'm awesome. Isn't Miss Violet a genius?)

My last (and hardest) move is a toe touch off the chair onto the stage, and then I hit my final pose and the song is over.

The audience applauds enthusiastically. I try to check the judges' expressions, but the stage lights are so bright in my eyes that the whole audience, including the judges' table, is just a big sea of darkness.

Seeing the emcee's signal, I quickly release my pose, bow, and sashay sideways off the stage, waving to the audience with both hands. I'm so happy I'm practically vibrating. And to make the moment even more perfect, Megan is standing in the wings, waiting to go on next, which means she saw my whole performance up close and personal.

As I reach the shadows, I see her standing in the fold of the curtain, watching the stagehands roll out the grand piano for her solo. She's wearing a gown I've never seen before—midnight blue velvet with a plunging neckline and one of those trains that drapes over the back of the piano bench. I'm sure it's brand-new and expensive.

"Good luck," I tell her chirpily.

"I don't need luck," she retorts. "Unlike *some* people, I have an actual talent, not just smoke and mirrors."

"I know. Good thing the judges can't tell the difference, huh?"

She doesn't get a chance to come back with an insult because just then Chuck booms, "Our final contestant this evening is a pianist who will be playing George Gershwin's 'Rhapsody in Blue.' Please give a big round of applause to contestant number thirty-two, Miss Diamond Hills, Megan Leighton!"

Megan gives me one last death glare, then throws her shoulders back and sweeps onto the stage.

I move to the spot in the fold of the curtain that she just vacated. I don't know why I'm bothering to watch her. I've seen her talent so many times I could probably do it myself.

Walk gracefully across stage to piano while smiling beatifically at judges? Check.

Take seat on bench making sure to drape train over back with dramatic flourish? Check.

Bring hands down on keys with exaggerated gesture as background music starts? Check.

Sway dramatically during the entire two minutes of playing? Check.

End with impressive-looking maneuver that involves running hands up and down piano keys really fast? Check.

Slide off piano bench and take a bow as if just finished playing Carnegie Hall? Check.

Yeah, that's pretty much what just happened. And now Megan's going to be coming off the stage, so I've got to get out of here. I don't want her to know I was watching.

Whirling around, I slip out of the curtain and hurry toward the dressing room to find Sadie and Eve.

Chapter Twenty-three

How do you use your beauty and how is it used against you?

When I wake up the next morning, I'm surprised (and delighted) to discover that Megan is mysteriously missing from the room.

Marveling at my good fortune, I stumble blearily into the bathroom and turn on the sink to start my morning routine. Brush. Floss. Wash face. Witch hazel toner. Moisturizer. Eye cream. I make it all the way to my Smashbox makeup primer before I notice that something about my reflection doesn't look quite right.

Now, before I go any further, I feel the need to emphasize that I am *so* not a morning person. If you see me before ten a.m., I'm pretty much like this: "Durrrrrrrrr." I don't really hit my stride until about noon. Which explains why I make it all the way to the Smashbox before I notice that my hair is brown.

Let me say that again. MY HAIR IS BROWN.

I shoot off the closed toilet lid I was using as a make-shift vanity stool and blink stupidly at my reflection. My eye-catching (freshly highlighted just for the pageant) blond hair has somehow been transformed into dull clumps of medium and dark brown locks. Which, in case you're wondering, is *not* a good look for me. I'm not the kind of girl who can pull off being a brunette.

Don't freak out, don't freak out, don't freak out, I chant silently. I sink back down on the toilet seat, willing myself to keep it together. If I can stay calm and figure out how this happened, then maybe I'll be able to fix it.

No, not maybe. I *will* fix it. Because there's no way I'm going out onstage tonight looking like a goth vampire in a sequined dress.

I suck in a deep, calming breath and run through everything that happened last night after the pageant. I came back here, texted Hunter and Lilly, took off my makeup, washed my hair, exfoliated— Wait a minute. Washed my hair? Oh my gosh, I am *such* an idiot.

Swearing, I yank open the plastic shower curtain and fumble around all of Megan's crap on the ledge of the tub, looking for my shampoo bottle. When I find it, I unscrew the cap and dump a big glob into the palm of my hand. At first glance it looks perfectly normal, but when I bring my hand up closer to my eyes, I think I can see fine streaks of brown running through the clear whitish liquid. However, it smells fine. Like peaches and cream, the same way it always does. Whatever Megan used, she was clever about it.

I spend the next thirty minutes standing under a stream of scalding hot water, scrubbing my hair with everything I can think of—the complimentary hotel soap, Megan's kiwi-scented bath gel, even toothpaste. The only thing I *don't* put

Julie Linker

on it is actual shampoo. Obviously, my shampoo is poisoned, and I'm too paranoid to use Megan's on the off chance that she anticipated I would use it and thus doused it with a little brunette surprise too.

As I scrub, I fantasize about bringing my shampoo bottle to the pageant officials and having it tested for hair dye like that Miss Puerto Rico who had her evening gown tested for pepper spray after she broke out in a rash while she was wearing it during competition. It would come back positive, of course, and then Megan would be banned from pageants forever. Maybe the police would even bring some kind of charges against her. Surely ruining somebody's hair qualifies as assault or something, right? They'd read her her rights, then put her in handcuffs and—oh, who am I kidding? That's never going to happen. If I took my shampoo bottle to the chaperones or the pageant board and told them what happened, they'd just look at me like I was crazy.

When I run out of alternative grooming products to put on my hair, I get out of the shower and help myself to Megan's ionic blow dryer. Needless to say, when I finish drying my hair fifteen minutes later, it's still brown. Because, duh—no way Megan would use something that would wash out. That would be too easy.

And that's when the panic sets in. Desperate, I wrap a bath towel around my head turban-style, throw on my clothes, and rush out of the room. Sadie may not be the greatest at updos, but maybe, hopefully (fingers crossed), she can do something to help me.

• • •

254

"I think she needs more eyebrow pencil." Eve steps back and surveys me as if I'm a piece of artwork she's thinking about buying.

"Yeah, I do too." Sadie nods and obediently leans forward to sketch the kohl pencil in her hand across my eyebrows for the third time.

Despite Sadie's and Eve's heroic efforts, I am still a brunette. Sadie even called one of her beauty school teachers for help, but it was no use. You need special chemicals to go from brown to blond, and—gosh darn it—somehow all three of us forgot to pack any. Go figure.

So now we've moved on to Plan B: make me look less hideous.

"There," Sadie says, pulling the pencil away with a flourish. "How does that look?"

"I don't know," I answer. "I can't see."

"Shhh. I'm talking to Eve." Sadie shushes me distractedly with her hand. Her eyes are on Eve's face, waiting for her opinion.

I close my mouth and slump back against the chair with a resigned sigh. I'm starting to think Sadie and Eve are a little *too* into this. It's like I'm their human Barbie doll or something.

Eve eyes me for a long moment, then pronounces, "That's perfect. Exactly right."

"Yay!" Sadie exclaims, clapping her hands excitedly.

"Can I look in the mirror now? Please?"

"Oh, I guess." Laughing, Sadie moves out of the way so I can stand up.

When I go over to the dresser mirror and peer at my reflection, I barely even recognize myself. I look like a completely different person. Instead of my normal light pastel makeup, Sadie has lined my top lashes with the same dark brown kohl pencil she used to fill in my eyebrows, brushed a dark gray shadow over my lids, highlighted my cheeks with bronzer, and smoothed a deep berry color onto my lips. My hair is swept back into a tight chignon and actually looks almost glossy thanks to the half bottle of shine serum Eve rubbed all over it.

Sadie comes up behind me and peeks over my shoulder. "Well, what do you think?"

"I don't know," I say uncertainly. "I look so different. What if the judges don't even recognize me?"

"They're not picking you out of a police lineup," she answers logically. "You'll have your contestant number on, plus the emcee announces everybody by name. Surely they can figure it out."

"And if they figure it out, then what will they think? What kind of girl dyes her hair a different color in the middle of a pageant? They're going to think I'm schizophrenic or something."

"No, they won't," Eve protests. "You're being paranoid."

Sadie's head bobs up and down in agreement. "Besides," she adds, patting me on the shoulder, "You don't have another choice."

I'm lying on Megan's bed in a towel, waiting for my self-tanner to dry and plotting various ways to bring about Megan's ruin-ation, when I hear the sound of a key card in the door. And guess who walks in? Why, it's the conniving bitch herself! Back to the scene of the crime. I honestly didn't think she had the guts.

My first instinct is to leap off the bed and shove her across the room, but I force myself to stay where I am. I'm not going to give her the satisfaction of seeing me lose my cool. (Plus, the pillows I'm lying on are from her bedroom at home, and I want to smear as much tanning lotion as pos-sible on them.)

"Where have you been all day?" I ask casually, folding my arms behind my head.

"Out." She moves into the room and smirks openly at my hair. "I see you got the special shampoo I left for you."

This statement is so completely the opposite of what I'm expecting to come out of her mouth that for a moment I'm speechless. "You admit that you did this?" I ask incredulously, reaching up to touch my hair.

"Of course I admit it," she laughs. "Why wouldn't I?"

Right. Why wouldn't she? It's not like I can do anything about it, after all. "What about the picture of me on the mes-sage boards? Are you going to admit to that too?"

She puts her hand to her mouth in mock sheepishness. "Ooopsie! You're right! I think that was me too."

"And Gabe?" I say sharply. "Do you have any feelings for him at all, or was he just an 'ooopsie' too?"

Her face falters for the barest instant, but then she lifts

her chin. "Gabe has never been anything more than a means to an end."

"A means to *what* end?" I cry. "Are you really that desperate to win this stupid crown?"

"Yes, I am. Because whoever wins this 'stupid crown' is going to be on MTV."

I roll my eyes. "Oh, please. There's a three in fifty chance of MTV picking our state. No, a three in fifty-*two* chance," I amend, remembering the District of Columbia and Virgin Islands. "I'd hardly say that's a sure thing."

Megan laughs. "Actually, it is. Suzette and Claire have already got the contracts for *Queen Scene* sitting on their desks."

"How do you know that?" I say skeptically.

"Because MTV has already flown my sister out to LA, you idiot. This has been a done deal for weeks."

I start to ask her what her sister has to do with anything, but then I remember that Caitlyn is Miss State. Remember how I told you that Megan's older sister is a favorite to win Miss America? Yeah, that would be Caitlyn.

And then it all falls into place. MTV flew Caitlyn to LA because she's already been selected as one of the three Miss queens who are going to be profiled on the show. Which means that whoever wins the crown tonight is automatically going to be on the show too. Suzette and Claire lied when they said MTV hadn't made any decisions yet. They've known this whole time. More important, *Megan* has known this whole time. There's just one thing that doesn't make sense.

"Why are you so worried that I'm going to win? Your mom and Suzette are BFFs, and we both know that Suzette and Claire aren't exactly troubled by a lot of pesky morals. I'm sure they'll see to it that the scores come out in your favor tonight. They've probably already got your name engraved on the plaque."

"Yes, well, that was the plan until one of the scheduled judges pulled out a couple of weeks ago and that idiot, Claire, replaced her with *Thomas Benfield*." Hatred practically drips from her lips as she pronounces the name. "He's the most hard-assed judge in the system."

I suddenly feel a wave of love for Mr. Patriot Act.

"So," Megan continues, "I had to take matters into my own hands."

"Let me get this straight." I swing my legs around so that I'm perched on the side of the bed. "Suzette was going to rig the pageant in your favor, except Claire screwed up and accidentally put a judge they couldn't bully on the panel. And when you found out you couldn't count on your win being preordained, you started this whole . . ." I search for a word to describe all the stuff she's done. "I don't know—*quest* to make me drop out of the pageant? You don't even know if I'll win. I could come in dead last. And it's not like you couldn't beat me without cheating," I add. "You've placed higher than me plenty of times."

"Plenty isn't the same thing as *all*," Megan answers. "And unbelievable as it might be, the fact is that judges *have* chosen you over me before. Not often," she adds swiftly. "But still. I couldn't take the chance."

What does she mean, "not often"? I've come in ahead of her lots and lots of times. I mean, yes, she probably has more wins overall, but the "not often" thing—that's her rewriting history.

I don't pursue the point, however. Instead, I say, "But what about the other contestants? It's not like getting rid of me would automatically put the crown on your head. Or have you been working your special little magic on everybody else too?"

Her mouth curves up. "I might have done a few little things here and there. Nothing compared to all the time and energy I've devoted to you, though. Suzette thought you would be the biggest threat. Apparently, Thomas Benfield has a thing for rags-to-riches girls. Suzette said if you did your whole poor-little-poverty-stricken-disadvantaged-me act, he'd be all over it."

How many times is it possible to insult somebody in one conversation? Because I think Megan may be approaching a world record. My 'poor-little-poverty-stricken-disadvantaged-me act'? What is she talking about? It's not like I go around slipping judges copies of my parents' income tax statement. (Well, my mom's income tax statement; I'm not sure if my dad has ever actually filed any income taxes.)

Again, though, I don't pursue it. "Well, I'm sorry you went to so much trouble," I say, jeering at her. "It looks like it was all a big fat waste of time, huh?" Now I stand so that we're eye level with each other. "Because I'm still here. And Thomas Benfield does have a thing for me." (Yeah, yeah. I totally made that up. For all I know, Thomas Benfield hates my guts. It's called bluffing, people.) "So you're right back where you started."

Wow. That sounded totally awesome! I am so totally tough. Who knew?

I wait for Megan to say something like, *Wow, you're so totally tough, I don't know what made me think I could screw you over,* but instead, she merely turns and goes over to the closet.

Right. Well, the important thing is that she *knows* I'm tough. Thinking our little showdown is finished, I go over to my luggage and start rummaging for the zip-up sweatshirt and matching yoga pants I'm going to wear to the auditorium.

I've located the top and am just starting to paw through a different suitcase in search of the bottoms when Megan's voice comes from behind me. "Actually, as it turns out, you're not going to be here much longer."

I turn, surprised. She's standing by the door, waving a piece of red material. "What are you talking about?" I say irritably. "I just told you I'm not going anywhere. Your evil plan backfired, okay? Build a bridge and get over it."

She stops waving the red thing and holds it up in front of her. It's her swimsuit, I realize, startled. The red one-piece halter with a gorgeous purple-and-turquoise rhinestone accent at the bust—the one everybody always oohs and aahs over on the message boards. Except I don't think anybody is going to be oohing and aahing over it anymore, because it looks like it was mauled by a lion.

"Ohmigosh, what happened?" I gasp, momentarily forgetting that I hate her guts.

"I cut it up with a pair of pinking shears," she replies.

I stare at her in disbelief. "What? Why would you do something like that? You've ruined your gorgeous swimsuit."

"No, *you've* ruined my gorgeous swimsuit," she laughs. "At least, that's what I'm going to tell Yvonne. And then it'll be bye-bye, Presley." She reaches for the door, tucking the ruined suit under her arm. "You can go ahead and start packing. This won't take long."

With that promise/threat, she pushes down on the door handle and slips out of the room.

For a moment I just stand there, rooted to the spot. Megan is going to take her swimsuit to Yvonne and tell her I'm the one who shredded it. And Yvonne will believe her. And then Yvonne will tell Suzette. Who probably came up with the whole idea in the first place.

In other words, I am completely and totally screwed.

At this point a normal person would probably cut her losses and move on, but unfortunately for Megan, the normalcy gene pretty much passed my family by. Which is why instead of packing up my stuff or crying into my pillow or simply waiting around to get thrown out of the pageant, I fling the sweatshirt in my hand aside and tear out of the room after her.

Over my dead body is she going to accuse me of mutilating her swimsuit.

I sprint down the hall at roughly the speed of light and round the corner just in time to see Megan smiling triumphantly at me from inside an empty elevator. The doors start to slide closed, but never fear! I can fly!

I launch myself at the quickly shrinking opening, making it through by the skin of my teeth. Or rather, the cotton fibers of my hotel towel. OMG, I'm wearing my hotel towel.

Oh, well. I guess it's a little late to worry about that now.

Surprise and (is that fear?) registers in Megan's eyes when she realizes her escape isn't going quite the way she planned. I immediately lunge for the swimsuit, but when I grab hold of it, Megan only clutches it tighter.

Fine. She asked for it.

I let go of the stretchy material, then reach up and yank her hair. Hard.

"You bitch!" Megan shrieks. "No one messes up my hair." She swings her hand around and rakes her acrylic nails down the side of my face. Hard.

"*Ow!*" The pain in my cheek brings tears to my eyes, but I distract myself from the discomfort by pulling Megan's hair even harder. So hard, in fact, that one of her extensions ends up in my hand. Ooopsie!

She responds by grabbing clumps of my hair in both her hands and basically trying to rip them out at the roots. Needless to say, this is not a pleasant sensation. Not to mention—curse her—she's ruining all of Sadie's and Eve's hard work.

We struggle like this for several more seconds, but then

the elevator suddenly jolts to a stop and we're both sent top-pling off balance into opposite walls.

Breathing hard, we right ourselves and look at the doors, waiting for them to open. Except they don't. They remain firmly shut.

Megan looks at me. "What's going on?"

"I don't know." I step toward the number pad and push the OPEN DOOR button.

Nothing happens.

I push it again. The door doesn't budge.

"Move," Megan snaps. She shoves me out of the way and starts jabbing the button over and over again as fast as she can.

"That's not going to help anything," I tell her.

"Shut up."

Rolling my eyes, I try to wedge my hand inside the crack in the middle of the doors. Maybe I can pry them apart. Except it only takes a second to realize that I can't even get my finger-tips in the crack.

Megan is still jabbing the button. "Why don't we just call for help?" I say, gesturing toward the little door that houses the emergency phone.

"Fine." She abandons the button and reaches down to yank open the little door.

We both stare at the empty space in disbelief.

"There's no phone," I blurt out.

"Thanks for pointing that out. I might not have noticed the giant black hole," Megan says sarcastically. She slams the door and holds out her hand. "Fine. Just give me your cell phone and I'll call the fire department."

"I'm wearing a towel, Megan."

"I don't care what you're wearing, just give me your phone," she shoots back.

"I don't have my phone, you moron! If I ran out of the room without any clothes on, do you really think I stopped to grab my cell phone?"

"What are we supposed to do, then?" she demands. "They take roll backstage in an hour."

"One of the chaperones will notice we're gone before that. And the hotel people will notice that the elevator hasn't come down. Somebody will come." I try to sound optimistic, even though the chances of either of those things happening are basically nil. After four p.m. the hotel staff consists of a cranky desk clerk and a porter who looks like he crawled out of his coffin at the cemetery to come to work.

Sure, the chaperones will look for us when we don't show up for roll call, but will they think to search the elevators? More to the point, will they think to search the elevators before it's too late?

Megan and I exchange looks. I can tell from her expression that she's thinking the same thing I am: We may miss the pageant.

We turn in unison and start pounding on the door.

"Help!"

"We're trapped!"

"Please! Somebody! We're stuck in the elevator!"

I don't know how long I beat on the door, but by the time I finally collapse on the floor, my throat feels like sandpaper and my hands are throbbing.

Megan is still yelling. Wearily, I reach up and tug on the hem of her shirt. "Give it up. There's nobody out there."

She continues pummeling the door. "Help me, pleeeeeease. Somebody. Anybody. Help!"

"There's nobody out there." I yank on her shirt again, except I guess I pull too hard, because she stumbles and ends up on the floor beside me.

I half expect her to jump back up and keep yelling, but the fire seems to have gone out of her. She slumps against the wall. "This sucks."

"Yeah, it does."

We sit in silence for a few moments. Then Megan lolls her head toward me. "This is all your fault, you know."

"My fault?" I say incredulously. "How do you figure that?"

"You jumped into the elevator and started attacking me."

"If you hadn't threatened me, I wouldn't have had to jump in the elevator and attack you! Besides, it's not like me being in here caused the elevator malfunction."

"Whatever." There's more silence. Then Megan says, "I have to pee."

I stare at her. "You're kidding, right?"

She shakes her head, squirming. "No, I really do. It's my diuretic."

"Yeah, well, good luck with that."

"What am I going to do?" she whines, shifting her legs.

"I don't know. I guess you're going to hold it," I say irritably. What does she think I'm supposed to do, wave my hands and magically produce a porta-potty or something?

"I don't think I can."

I heave out a sigh. The only thing worse than being trapped in an elevator with Megan is being trapped in an elevator with Megan when she needs to pee.

"You don't have a choice," I say unsympathetically.

She finally shuts up and we sit in silence for what seems like an eternity. "Maybe we should try to climb out the trapdoor," I finally suggest.

Megan looks up at the square in the ceiling. "How would we get up there?" she says dubiously.

"I could stand on your shoulders. Or you could stand on mine," I amend, thinking of my clothing situation. The situation being that I'm not wearing any clothing, except this stupid towel.

"And then what?"

"Well," I begin slowly. This is the tricky part. "I think we're in between floors. If we're not very far from one, maybe you could pull yourself up, climb out, and go get help."

Except you'll probably just climb out and go to the pageant, I think cynically. *And if anybody asks where I am, you'll tell them I joined the Mexican army or something.*

"No way," Megan scoffs. "I'm not Spider-Man."

"Then I'll do it."

"No way. You'll leave me here."

Ha. So she *would* leave me here. Otherwise she wouldn't have come up with that scenario.

"No, I wouldn't."

"We're not doing that. Think of something—" The rest of her sentence is drowned out by a horrible grinding sound as the elevator suddenly comes to life.

Overjoyed, we both gaze around the elevator alertly waiting for it to resume its descent. And it does . . . for about two seconds.

Then it comes to a jerky stop; a beat later the lights flicker and go out completely.

Chapter Twenty-four

What has been the most difficult thing about being in this pageant?

"*Y*ou've *got* to be kidding me." Megan's voice cuts through the inky blackness, echoing exactly what's going through my mind.

Well, actually, what's going through my mind is *You've got to be FREAKING kidding me,* but, you know, same thing.

"The power is out," she informs me.

"Really? I hadn't noticed," I say sarcastically.

"Shut up."

"You shut up," I retort.

"Make me."

"Aaargh!" I clap my hands to the sides of my head and shriek in frustration. This is torture. If I get out of this alive, I am *so* suing the hotel for emotional distress.

I'd like to tell you that after we sit in the dark for a while we get over our differences and have some sort of deep bonding experience as a result of our forced captivity, but yeah . . . I'm pretty sure that only happens in movies. All we do is sit in the dark and listen to each other breathe.

We've been sitting for so long that I'm actually starting

to nod off when the faint sound of thumping footsteps and unintelligible voices comes from above us.

I jerk awake. Megan and I both shoot to our feet and start screaming.

"Hey! We're in here!"

"Help us!"

"Help! Help! Get us out!"

We're still screaming when the elevator suddenly rises a few feet and halts. And then finally, FINALLY, the doors slide open to reveal lots and lots of bright light and two grinning firemen.

We've officially been rescued.

"I'm sorry. When you girls weren't here, we moved the two next-highest-scoring girls into the Top Ten. It's pageant policy." Claire regards Megan and me coolly, as if daring one of us to challenge what she's just said.

First, the good news: (a) I'm out of the elevator (but you already knew that); (b) I was able to snatch the swimsuit off the floor as we were getting out, so now Megan can't blackmail me; (c) The scratch on my face doesn't look nearly as bad as I expected; and (d) I made the Top Ten! And so did Eve!

Now, the bad news: (a) Megan is also out of the elevator (but again, you already knew that); (b) Megan made the Top Ten too, and unfortunately, Sadie didn't (c) Thanks to the elevator fiasco, we missed the first fifteen minutes of the pageant and now Claire says we're disqualified.

"But that's not fair," I protest. "We were stuck in an elevator. It wasn't our fault." I blink at her. Surely the pageant can't hold us responsible for malfunctioning machinery, can they?

"Well, it's not my fault either," she snaps. "What do you want me to do?"

"Actually, it *is* your fault," Megan informs her. "You and your mom are the ones who put us up in a substandard hotel."

"The Majestic is not a substandard hotel," Claire says indignantly.

"Really? Then why was the inspection certificate in the elevator over ten years old?" Megan shoots back. She steps forward; now she's right in Claire's face. "I'm sure my dad's lawyer would be very interested in seeing that certificate, she says softly. "And hearing all about you and your mom's reckless disregard for the safety of your contestants."

I have to hand it to Megan: she does Threatening Bitch like nobody else. I mean, *I'm* scared, and she's not even talking to me. And to make it even more impressive—she's totally bluffing! There isn't any inspection certificate in that elevator. Megan is just trying to psych her out.

Still, though, even with the threat of litigation, Claire doesn't look like she's going to budge. It's only when Megan adds, "I know—why don't we just go run all this by your mom and see what she thinks?" that Claire throws up her red-tipped hands.

"Fine," she says disgustedly. "You can proceed with the competition. But I'm not going to yank those poor girls out of the semi-finals now that their names have been announced onstage. We'll just have to have a Top Twelve instead of a Top Ten."

"Fine," Megan and I say together.

"Fine," Claire repeats. Then, "Well, if you're going to compete, you better go get ready. Swimsuit starts in four minutes."

8:05 p.m.

I strut sassily around the stage in my orange-and-white-striped, rhinestone-accented two-piece bathing suit, smiling as if I'm having the time of my life. Hey, judges! Hey, audience! I *love* being up here in front of you in six-inch heels and a tiny bikini that has been glued to my butt with so much adhesive that it's going to rip off the top layer of my skin when I take it off! It's great! I'm not secretly wishing I was two inches taller and wondering how bad the cellulite on the backs of my thighs looks under the stage lights! Not me. La, la, la.

8:45 p.m.

Wow. Eve is really an awesome violin player.

9:30 p.m.

I'm on top of my chair, tapping my little butt off. Okay, my *medium-ish* butt off. The audience is applauding even louder than last night. This chair thing is definitely the best idea Miss Violet ever had. Although, maybe they're just excited because the girl before me did a dramatic reading from *A Midsummer Night's Dream*, I don't know. *Anybody* would seem entertaining after that, even that chick who plays the tuba.

I execute a perfect toe touch and stick the landing, but

then instead of ending with an Elvis like last night, I slide into the splits.

The audience goes wild and gives me a standing ovation.

Okay, so I made that up. But they *are* clapping really enthusiastically.

I bask in the praise, ignoring my legs, which feel like they're on fire. I'm going to be paying for my impromptu splits tomorrow, I can already tell.

My eyes travel over the faces of the people in the first few rows, trying to spot my mom and Jed. Last night the audience just looked like a big black blob, but tonight I can actually see a little, probably because I sort of didn't do the greatest job of staying in my dance space and now I'm, like, an inch away from the edge of the stage.

Not my mom, not my mom, not my mom, definitely *not my mom* . . . I'm about to give up when my gaze suddenly snags on a familiar-looking figure at the end of the second row. A figure with dark hair and a chiseled jaw wearing a striped button up shirt with the cuffs rolled up so every girl within a ten-mile radius can drool over his tanned, sexy forearms. A figure who is grinning at me like a Cheshire cat and giving me a cute wave.

The sight is so startling that for a moment I actually forget to keep the corners of my mouth turned up into a mega-watt smile. Instead, I just sit there, frozen, in the splits, wearing my sequined jumpsuit, gaping like an idiot.

Ohmigosh, I'm wearing a SEQUINED JUMPSUIT! Mortified, I swing my back leg around and leap to my feet. Chuck is giving me a dirty look; he wants me to get the hell off the stage. *That makes two of us, Chuck.* Remembering my smile, I bow, wave, and jazz-run off the stage at roughly thirty miles per hour.

9:36 p.m.

I am standing in a corner of the holding room for semi-finalists, babbling breathlessly to Eve about what just happened. She has absolutely no idea what I'm talking about, mostly due to the fact that I sound like a raving lunatic.

"Somebody has a cat in the audience?" she says amazedly.

"No, no, he's not a real cat, he just *looked* like a cat. Because of the way he was smiling."

"The way who was smiling?"

"Robbie. The guy who sent me the roses."

"Oh!" she exclaims, finally understanding now that I've come out with something semi-coherent. "The guy who sent you the roses is here," she says happily, reaching up to adjust the strap on her canary yellow evening gown, which would make 99.9 percent of the rest of the female population look completely hideous (can you say "Big Bird in heels"?) but somehow looks fabulous on her. "How sweet! That's so nice that he came to see you."

"Do you think that's why he's here? Really? To see me?"

Eve gives me a weird look. "Why else would he be here? Does he know another girl in the pageant?"

9:48 p.m.

All of the semi-finalists are gathered around the closed circuit TV watching Megan do her talent. Well, everybody except

Paige Graham, who had an unfortunate mishap onstage with her fire baton and is currently on her way to the local emergency room. Don't worry. She's okay. Her eyebrows took the brunt of it, but she also kind of singed her hand, and her parents just wanted to be on the safe side.

I wish *Megan* would accidentally catch on fire during talent, but so far she's isn't cooperating. She's just bent over the piano, pounding out notes like she's freaking Mozart or something.

"She's really good," Eve whispers.

"Yeah, I know," I say grimly.

I scowl at the TV. It's so unfair. Evil people shouldn't be allowed to be good at stuff like playing the piano. They should be ugly and talentless and have a big flashing sign over their head that says BEWARE. EVIL WITHIN.

9:49 p.m.

OMG, forget everything I just said! The world *isn't* totally unfair after all! Because MEGAN JUST PLAYED, LIKE, FIVE WRONG NOTES, AND NOW SHE'S JUST SITTING THERE WITH HER HANDS HOVERING OVER THE PIANO KEYS.

I am so not even kidding.

All of our jaws drop in unison. None of us can believe what we're seeing. This is unprecedented. Megan has never made any kind of a mistake during a pageant. EVER.

Still 9:49 p.m.

Okay, now she's playing (perfectly) again. Her screwup probably only lasted about three seconds, but it doesn't matter.

Three seconds is an *eternity* when you're sitting on a stage *not* playing a piano in front of four hundred people. There's no way the judges can give her a high score.

And *Robbie* is in the audience! He saw the whole thing! Megan will die of shame when she finds out he saw her.

This may be the best night of my entire life.

9:52 p.m.

This is *definitely* the best night of my entire life. Megan just walked into the room and now she is throwing the *biggest* hissy fit you have ever seen.

"Those morons shined the lights right in my eyes!" she screams at a weary-looking pageant volunteer wearing a headset. "They blinded me! I couldn't see anything!"

"I understand that you're upset," the volunteer tells her in a calm voice, "but I need you to try and get control of yourself, okay? Acting out isn't the way to express your frustrations."

Megan's face goes from red to purple. "I'm not 'acting out.' I'm telling you that the incompetent stage crew ruined my talent! They shined the lights so that I couldn't see the piano keys! AND I WANT TO KNOW WHAT YOU'RE GOING TO DO ABOUT IT!"

Un-friggin'-believable. She's trying to blame her talent screwup on the stagehands. She messed up because the *lights* were in her eyes? What kind of an excuse is that? I mean, even if she was telling the truth (which she's not) and the light guy really did flash her in the eyes . . . since when do you need to be able to see to play the piano? BLIND PEOPLE play the piano, for heaven's sake. Hello—hasn't she ever heard of

Stevie Wonder? Ray Charles? It's not like she had sheet music she was looking at. She was playing from memory.

"What is she talking about?" Eve whispers. "I didn't see anybody shining lights on her."

"She's just trying to put the blame on somebody else because she can't handle that she messed up," I whisper back.

The volunteer is either a saint or heavily medicated, because she doesn't offer so much as a blink in reaction to Megan's roared demand. She just continues looking at her blandly and repeats that Megan needs to get control of herself.

10:01 p.m.

I'm standing onstage with the other semi-finalists, including—I'm sorry to report—Megan. I was hoping that she might go completely berserk and start, like, slapping people and throwing things and get disqualified, but no such luck. She just told the volunteer that she was going to make her sorry and stormed off. It was kind of anticlimatic, actually.

"Ladies and gentlemen, please welcome our twelve semi-finalists back to the stage," Chuck booms into the microphone. "They've all done a great job, but only five can go on. And those five are, in no particular order . . ." He pauses to pull a card out of the envelope in his hand.

Presley Ashbury, Presley Ashbury, Presley Ashbury, I chant silently. I can feel Robbie's eyes on me—at least, I think I can—but once again the space beyond the stage is just a yawning black hole. *Presley Ashbury, Presley Ashbury, Presley Ashbury . . .*

"Contestant number thirty-two, Megan Leighton!"

Okay, Chuck, that is so not what you were supposed to say. And how did Megan make—

"Contestant number nine, Tate Thompson!" Chuck plows on, not even waiting for Megan to finish walking to her spot. I think the fun of the evening has worn off for him.

No biggie, I tell myself as I watch Tate hurry forward after Megan. There are still three spots left. No reason to panic.

"Contestant number fourteen, Eve Samuels!"

OMG! Eve is a finalist! I beam at her, clapping enthusiastically. She looks totally stunned.

I squeeze my eyes shut as Chuck glances down at the card to read the next name. *Presley Ashbury, Presley Ashbury, Presley Ashbury* . . .

"Contestant number seventeen, Caroline Walsh!"

My eyes fly open. Okay. *Now* there's a reason to panic.

"And the last finalist of the night isssssssssss . . ." Chuck pauses dramatically, and I seriously think about taking off one of my shoes and throwing it at him. Just say it, already! Can't you see I'm dying here?

I'm comforting myself with the thought that at least maybe Eve might beat Megan, when Chuck finally gives it up and says, "Contestant number thirty-one, Presley Ashbury!"

For a second I'm not sure if he really said my name or if I just imagined it, but then the girl next to me gives me a hug and tells me congratulations, and I realize I'm not hallucinating.

I made it to the Top Five. I'm still in the running.

In other words . . . *game on, Megan.*

Chapter Twenty-five

Do you think you are going to win this pageant?

nd that's why our senior citizens are so important to society," I conclude. I step daintily back from the microphone Chuck is holding up to my mouth and smile at the audience. I answered my onstage question pretty well, if I do say so myself.

Unfortunately, though, so did everybody else. Ugh.

While the scores are being tallied, the rest of the contestants are paraded out to stand on the stage behind us, and then we're all treated to a vocal solo by Blaine—Céline Dion's "My Heart Will Go On." Yeah. Let's just say that Céline's version is a *teeny-tiny* bit better and leave it at that. Blaine needs to stick to dancing.

By the time Chuck brandishes the envelope with the final scores, I feel so light-headed that I'm actually worried I might faint.

"And now the moment you've all been waiting for," Chuck announces dramatically. "I have in my hand the results of the competition."

This is our cue to move together and hold hands.

Chuck tears open the envelope, pulls out the card, and begins to read. "The fourth runner-up and winner of a twenty-five-hundred-dollar scholarship is . . . Tate Thompson!"

Whew. The end of a pageant is the only time when you're hoping *not* to hear your name called out before everybody else's.

Tate smiles and moves forward to collect her bouquet and plaque as the audience applauds politely.

"The third runner-up and winner of a three-thousand-dollar scholarship is . . . Eve Samuels!"

Oh, rats. Although I'd be lying if I said I'm not relieved he didn't call my name, I *am* honestly bummed for Eve. I was hoping that if I didn't win, she would.

"Okay, ladies and gentlemen, we're getting closer," Chuck says once Eve has gone to take her place beside Tate. "Tonight's second runner-up and winner of a five-thousand-dollar scholarship is . . . Caroline Walsh!"

My head swims as I watch Caroline go forward. Megan and I are the last people standing.

We clasp hands and turn to face each other. This is the part where we gaze adoringly into each other's eyes and pledge that we'll always be friends and support each other, no matter whose name Chuck calls out next.

"Bitch," Megan whispers, her smile not moving a millimeter.

"Slut," I hiss back, keeping my smile just as high.

Beside us Chuck is going through the whole "if the winner cannot fulfill her duties, the first runner-up, blah, blah, blah."

Everybody knows the deal, Chuck. Just get on with it.

Megan squeezes my hand so hard I think I feel one of my bones crack.

"Stop it," I grind out through my teeth. I give her other hand a violent squeeze.

"And now, our first runner-up, and the winner of a seven-thousand-dollar scholarship is . . ." The music swells as Chuck opens a second envelope.

It has to be Megan, I think. *There's no way the judges can give her the crown after the way she screwed up in talent. Megan has to be the first runner-up. I'm the winner. I'm the new Miss Teen State. I'm going to be on MTV!*

"Presley Ashbury!" Chuck booms. "Which means your new Miss Teen State is Miss Diamond Hills, Megan Leighton!"

Or . . . I could just be watching Megan on MTV.

After that it's all over. For me, anyway. Somebody thrusts a damp bouquet and a plaque into my arms, and then I'm shoved aside. I'm a nobody, just like the other thirty girls behind me. Now it's all about Megan.

Bile rises in my throat as I watch Katy, the departing queen, pin the glittering Miss Teen State tiara to Megan's head. In stories and fairy tales, the bad guy always loses in the end, but that's *so* not the way it is in real life.

I shake my head, trying to clear my mind of the negative thoughts pressing down on me. I will *not* be a sore loser. I will put on my happy face and concentrate on the fact that I just won SEVEN THOUSAND DOLLARS for college.

With her crown now in place, Megan takes her "walk,"

smiling and slow-motion pageant-waving to the audience. She even manages to conjure up some fake tears.

After that I have to endure roughly twenty million flash-bulbs going off in my face as we all have our pictures taken. And as first runner-up, I have to stand next to Megan in *all* of them. It's awful. And to make things even worse, while I'm stuck in Kodak Moments from Hell, I see Sadie being bundled out of the auditorium by her mom. Who, even from a distance, I can see is crying. That's right. Sadie's *mom* is crying. (See? I told you she was a psycho stage mother.) And now she's whisking Sadie away, and I haven't even gotten a chance to talk to her. I make a mental note to call her later.

"Hey." The voice comes from behind me as I'm threading my way through the mob of people who have taken over the stage, searching for my mom.

A delicious shiver snakes up the back of my spine. *Robbie.*

I want to whirl around and jump into his arms, but I force myself to turn around normally and maintain appropriate personal space. "Hey." I smile up at him shyly. And what I'm about to say is going to sound totally cheesy, but . . . well, when my eyes lock with his, it's kind of like all the people around us just suddenly fade away and disappear. It's like we're the only people in the whole auditorium—maybe even the only people in the whole world.

Shut up! I told you it was cheesy. I can't help it.

He reaches up and strokes the back of his hand across

my hair. "You look beautiful. I like you with dark hair."

I make a silent vow to keep my hair brown for the rest of my natural life.

"Of course, I like you blond, too," he adds, dropping his hand.

Okay, maybe for just *part* of my natural life. I'll switch off. Every other year.

"I got the roses," I blurt out.

I know. It's like I have Tourette's or something.

He gives me a hesitant look. "And the card? Did you get that, too?"

I nod.

"So . . . what did you think about it?"

That maybe you want me to marry you and bear your children? "Er, I thought it was very nice."

"Nice?" he echoes. He sounds disappointed; apparently, he was hoping for a different adjective.

I try again. "It was sweet of you to think of me."

"Sweet?" This seems to disturb him even more.

"Thoughtful?" I offer. What the heck does he want me to say?

"But what did you *think*?" he presses. "About what I said about starting over?"

My pulse speeds up. Ohmigosh. He's talking about the whole second-chance thing. My magic rose petal must really and truly be magic. Because unless I'm seriously misinterpreting the vibe between us, he's not asking me if I want to start over and be buddies. He's asking me if I want to start over and be . . . boyfriend and girlfriend? Romantically involved? Hang out, go on a few dates, and see what happens?

Right. Number three, definitely.

Instead of answering, I do something completely and totally out of character. I take a deep breath and step toward him. Then I close my eyes, lift up on tiptoes, and brush my lips against his.

And—I'm about to be totally cheesy again, so you might want to skip this part—he kisses me back, and I feel like somebody lit a firecracker inside my body. And above my head. And all around us. It's the best kiss of my entire life (sorry Gabe), even though I can't put my arms around his neck because I'm still holding my stupid flowers and plaque.

Luckily for me, though, Robbie's hands are free. He slides his arms around my waist and pulls me closer to him, deepening the kiss. My flowers are getting smashed against his chest, but I don't care because *I'm* getting smashed against his chest too. And he's warm, and he smells like yummy boy skin and cologne, and his lips are so soft and—

"That's a hell of a consolation prize." My mom's voice pierces through my haze of sensual bliss. I jerk away from Robbie, startled. At least, I *try* to jerk away from Robbie. Although he stops kissing me, he keeps one hand draped around my waist.

My mom and Jed are grinning at us. "Does he come with the scholarship?" my mom asks, gesturing to Robbie. I feel my cheeks coloring in embarrassment, but Robbie throws his head back and laughs like my mom is Sarah Silverman or something.

I'm about to do the whole "Mom, Robbie; Robbie, Mom" introduction thing, but then a flash of sparkle in my peripheral vision catches my attention and I instinctively turn to look at it.

Which causes me to lock eyes with Megan, who is literally staring at me and Robbie with her mouth hanging open. Seriously. I think I can see her tonsils.

The sight of her dumbfounded face sends a surge of satisfaction through me. Mostly because it reminds me of the way I felt (and I'm sure looked) the day I walked up on her and Gabe kissing outside the cafeteria.

Oh, well. You know what they say about karma being a _____ (rhymes with "witch"). . . . Megan's getting a taste of it right now, and I'm POSITIVE she's going to have even more coming her way in the future.

As for me, well, I didn't get the crown (this time), but like my mom said, I managed to snag one heck of a consolation prize.

And now, if you'll excuse me, I'm going to go out with my mom, Jed, and Robbie and eat pizza. And cheeseburgers. And ice cream. And quesadillas. And chocolate cake. And one of those big fat cinnamon rolls with gooey icing on top. Ooooh, and maybe a 3 Musketeers and some Reese's Pieces. . . .

Nine Months Later
Bahamas, Spring Break

Have you seen this?" Robbie drops the latest issue of *People* magazine onto my lounger as he leans down to brush a kiss across my forehead.

I glance up from my laptop and peer at him over the top of my sunglasses. "No, why?"

His grin is startlingly white against his bronzed skin. It's so unfair. I swear, he turned into a Hawaiian Tropic guy, like, five minutes after we got off the plane. And I've been lying out for THREE DAYS and all I've got to show for it is a sunburned nose. "Read the page I marked," he instructs.

"O-kay." I obediently lean forward and pick up the mag, then turn to the page he has dog-eared and peer at the words.

Queen Scene
Reviewed by: Laurel McBride

According to its creators, *Queen Scene* is "a reality series that profiles six beauty queens as they prepare for their national pageants," but a more accurate tagline would be "a reality series that profiles six beauty queens as they make complete fools out of themselves on national television." Crying, tantrums, backbiting, gossip, eating disorders, cheating boyfriends—all the elements of good reality are there, but the starring queens are so lacking in anything even remotely resembling charisma that you just can't muster up the energy to care. By the end of the first episode I found myself wondering if it really was possible to die from boredom.

Teen Queen Megan Leighton is the one exception to the noncharismatic cast, although her over-the-top antics and perpetually bitchy attitude are wearing to the point of homicide.

Do yourself a favor and leave the queens to their tiaras. Life's too short to waste time on bad TV. Besides, rumor has it the network is going to pull the plug because of low ratings. *There she goes . . . Miss Ill-Conceived Reality Show . . .*

"Ouch. That was harsh." I hand the magazine back to Robbie.

He tosses it aside, then settles himself on the sun lounger next to me. As has become our habit ever since we arrived on the island at the beginning of the week, we're spending the afternoon by our private pool, the one that's just steps away from the back door of our private villa.

I know. Can you believe it? Me in the Bahamas at a private villa? I keep pinching myself to make sure it's real. Of course, it's not *quite* as romantic as it sounds; Robbie's mom and sister are in the Bahamas with us. (What—you didn't think my mom would let me leave the country without parental supervision, did you? She's not *that* lenient.)

"Harsh, but true," Robbie says. "The show blows. The sooner they pull it, the better."

"Mmmm," I murmur absently.

Robbie pushes his mirrored aviators up on his forehead and props himself up on his side. "What is it you're so preoccupied with, anyway?" he asks, gesturing to my laptop.

I glance over at him. "Can you keep a secret?" I ask solemnly.

He mimes zipping his lips and tossing a key over his shoulder.

I smile. "Okay, then." I scramble off my lounger and crawl into his, snuggling up beside him. He smells like coconuts. I do too, I guess, since we're using the same bottle of sunscreen. I settle the computer on his thighs and position it so we can both see the screen.

Then I aim the mouse and click on the latest video to premiere on YouTube, courtesy of yours truly.

Well, I can't take all the credit. I was just the brains of the operation. Gabe is actually the one who did the dirty work.

Poor Gabe. Megan dumped him, like, two hours after she got the Miss Teen State crown on her evil little head. Although, honestly, I'm surprised she even waited that long. I figured it would be more like two seconds. And in keeping with her soulless self, she didn't even *try* to spare his feelings. I mean, she could have totally given him some generic line like *You're a really great guy, but I think we're moving too fast,* or *I like you so much, but now that I'm Miss Teen State I don't have time for a boyfriend,* but no. She just matter-of-factly told him all the awful stuff she revealed to me that day in our hotel room—that he was an "oopsie" and that their relationship was a sham.

At first Gabe didn't believe her, but after she called him a dumb jock buffoon twenty or so times, he got the message. I know all this because guess who was the first person he called after she finished stomping his heart into a million little pieces?

That's right. Me.

And I'd be lying if I said I didn't enjoy it. I totally gloated . . . for about five minutes. But then I realized how hurt he was, and my glee turned to major sympathy.

I know. I'm a softie. But I did—I do—still care about Gabe, just not exactly in the same way I did before. Besides, it's not all that hard to be charitable to your ex-boyfriend when you've got a smokin' hot new boyfriend who worships the ground you walk on.

Oh, all right. So "worship" is probably a bit of an exaggeration. Robbie doesn't, like, bow before me or offer up animal sacrifices in my name or anything. Let's just say that he's very, very ~~good at kissing~~ sweet.

But I'm getting off topic. Back to the glorious YouTube video.

So, like I said, Gabe was pretty devastated when Megan dumped him, right? And even though I won money for college and ended up with Robbie, I was still ticked at her. I mean, she *dyed my hair*, people (which, by the way, I ended up having to cut up to my shoulders because the peroxide fried it to the texture of straw when I tried to go back to blond.) I'm sorry, but there's no turning the other cheek about something like that. There is, however, sweet, sweet revenge.

The plan I came up with was simple: Gabe would wait a couple of weeks, then call Megan up and invite her to a fancy restaurant to "celebrate" her upcoming television fame (as friends, natch). And during dinner he'd try to get her drunk as a skunk to see if she'd do anything worthy of recording on video.

To tell you the truth, I didn't really think it would work. I mean, there were so many things that could go wrong—not to mention that I had no idea if Megan would even agree to go anywhere with Gabe. But the gods of justice must have been smiling on us.

Because thanks to Gabe (and me), plus a few too many chocolate martinis, you can now go to YouTube and watch a surprisingly clear video of Megan Leighton performing an impromptu striptease while singing Madonna's "Like a Virgin," at a karaoke bar. And when I say "striptease," I mean "STRIPtease." As in, she gets down to her underwear and nothing else.

I can't *wait* until it hits the news outlets tomorrow.

Queen Scene may get canceled, but something tells me Megan's YouTube debut will be around for a long, long, long time.

Love what you just read?
Here's a peek at another novel
by Julie Linker:

Disenchanted Princess

I'm never going to see you again!" I cry, clutching Maria's arm in a death grip. I'm making a scene in the middle of LAX, but I don't care. My whole life is falling apart, and this is my last chance to salvage some of the pieces.

"That's not true," Maria says firmly, trying unsuccessfully to disengage herself from my clutches. "Your father will fix this. You have to be strong."

Be strong? I'm being shipped off to the middle of nowhere and all she can say is "Be strong"? Next she'll be comforting me with something really helpful, like "When life hands you lemons, make lemonade."

I let go of her arm and grab a big handful of her shirt. "Please let me stay, please, please, pleeeeease."

Unfortunately, Maria expected something like this, which is why she brought José, our gardener, along. Even though he devotes most of his life to growing flowers, José is the type of guy you wouldn't want to meet in a dark alley. He's massively built, and you can tell he probably got the hideous scar on his left cheek from a knife fight or some other equally scary thing. I'd love to know the whole story, but nobody in their right mind would dare ask him about it. He's THAT scary.

José steps forward, his face as hard as granite. *"No más,"* he says forcefully, removing my hands as if they were twigs. *"Vas a perder tu vuelo."* José always speaks Spanish, even though Maria says he can speak English fluently. That's probably true too, because the time I accidentally got the gas and brake pedals mixed up and drove Daddy's new Mercedes into the wall of the garage, José said "fuck" perfectly, without an accent or anything.

"Last call for Flight 1725 to Little Rock," a woman's voice says over the loudspeaker.

José pushes my candy-colored Louis V into my hands and steers me toward the security checkpoint. I look back pitifully at Maria, the only mother I've ever known. My biological mother died in a plane crash when I was a baby. She was a really famous fashion model, and her plane went down on the way to a photo shoot in the Bahamas.

That sounds like a made-up story, I know, but it's totally not. Really. There's an *E! True Hollywood Story* about her and everything—"Crystal Kendall: Tragic Beauty."

Maria says it's good I was so little when she died because that way I don't remember her. Maria's mother died when she was twelve, and it still really bothers her. Sometimes she even wakes up at night calling out for her and saying things in Spanish I can't understand.

Except the weird thing is that I DO remember my mother. I mean, intellectually, I know that I don't *really* remember her, but I've spent so much time reading articles about her and looking at her pictures that sometimes it seems like I do. It's like I've constructed this whole imaginary person in my head. Crazy, huh?

"I love you," I tell Maria, holding back the sobs that are threatening to overtake my body.

"Vamos," she says, shooing me toward the gate. Tears are rolling down her face, ruining the MAC foundation and blush I picked out for her last week at Saks. I try to go back to her, but José steps in front of me, an impenetrable fortress. I have no choice but to go through the gate.

I hoist my Louis V higher on my shoulder. All right, if I'm going to have to go through with this nightmare, I'm going to do it with dignity. Like the time I had to go to an Orlando Bloom premiere with green hair because I had gone swimming too soon after my highlights. A lot of people would have bailed, but I just put my hair in a messy topknot, threw on a cute little Galliano and some funky earrings, and went with it. It was a risk, but it paid off. Joan Rivers pronounced it "the most fashion-forward look she'd seen all year," and I even got a tiny pic in *Teen Vogue*. I mean, surely if I can pull off green hair, I can pull this off.

Lifting my chin, I walk forward through the gate like I own it. Arkansas, here I come. *Yee-haw.*

About the Author

Julie Linker was born and raised in Arkansas, where she still lives with her husband and little girl. She is also the author of *Disenchanted Princess*. To find out more about Julie, visit her website, www.julielinker.com.